GEMMA IVERSEN

The Galven Border

Copyright © 2021 by Gemma Iversen

All rights reserved. No part of this publication may be reproduced, stored or transmitted in any form or by any means, electronic, mechanical, photocopying, recording, scanning, or otherwise without written permission from the publisher. It is illegal to copy this book, post it to a website, or distribute it by any other means without permission.

First edition

ISBN: 978-1-80049-675-0

*This book was professionally typeset on Reedsy.
Find out more at reedsy.com*

All that time,
yet you were the greatest storyteller of all.
For what more is the truth,
than a malleable tool.

~

Everything I write is for my dad.

~

Prologue

On the small screen of the television, perched atop the microwave in the darkest corner of the kitchen, a reporter spoke in a dulcet address to the nation. In this household, on a suburban street, off the preferable side of Shaw Road, there was no human audience. A large cat lay sprawled on the floor, its distended belly spread onto the linoleum by the fridge. Somewhere between sleep and consciousness, the cat's ear twitched as it took in the faint noises in the room—the simmering pan on the stove, the stream of words from somewhere up above.

"In response to recent threats, the commander warned there would be a heavy military response, and that Merredin's defence was firmly in place. Couldry issued a statement with regards to likely attacks, saying"—meaningless sounds, stresses and reverberations without form. The cat's eyelids drooped and held still for a second before rising again partway. Steam condensed onto the slip of the windowpane below the paisley netting.

The sound of shuffling, slipper-clad feet drew closer and the cat tensed, his ears flattening as softly encased toes struck him in the broad of his back, forcing him to jump up in alarm with a yowl and a hiss. Fiona walked to the stove and turned off the television. The front door opened and shut with a slam. Stuart trudged into the kitchen much the same way she had, flat feet and a stooped neck like an ox under a yoke. She didn't turn to face him or relax her jaw, despite the way it ached.

"It doesn't look good," he said as he began to prepare his customary mug of tea.

Fiona busied herself with cooking. She could tell by the way he tapped his spoon against the rim of his cup that his tea was made.

"No, no. It doesn't look good at all," he said in one long exhale.

"Did you have to say it twice?"

Stuart glanced at her, gauging her mood as he brought the cup to his lips. He paused before taking a sip, holding the cup inches from his mouth, the hot ceramic slightly grazing the grizzle of hair.

"It was confirmed by the Big Cheese. They're relocating to Galven, everyone is. We've been told to expect redundancies."

Fiona hated it when he said "big cheese"; it was always accompanied with a raise of the mono-brow, the baring of teeth like bent wickets.

"It's not just me that's scared either, oh no, lots reckon they're getting the chop. Of course, we won't know anything else 'til Friday now, when the boss has got it all settled."

Fiona set three plates on the side without looking up once. Her silence made Stuart nervous. He watched her long fingers, like bird claws as they nudged the plates equidistant, picking at any specks she saw and moving deftly around the bulk of him as if he didn't exist. She came to a stop in front of him.

PROLOGUE

"You're in the way," she said, pushing into his space with sharp elbows and raised chin. Stuart felt a low mood settle on him like a weighted cloak, heavy from wanting her reassurance. He reached out to touch her arm.

"Fiona?"

She went still, the serving spoon in her grip. He moved off the counter where he'd been leaning and raised his arms to her like a weary child. "I've had such an awful day. Please." She turned and dismissed him in favour of the plates.

"If it happens, and you lose your job, I expect you to find another one straight away. If we're left here to die, it'll be all your fault."

"Of course, I'll try, but there'll be a lot of others going for the same jobs, people with more experience than me. You know I'll do my best."

"And when has that ever been good enough." She served the sausages, her face concealed.

"Dinner looks good."

"Enjoy it while we still have the money to eat," she said with a hollow laugh, a clink of teeth upon glass.

They lay side by side that night, each occupying their side of the bed. The space was warm, uncomfortably so, in the way that close proximity can be sometimes on a June night in a double bed when the duvet is light but the sheet is polyester, and you don't want to move for fear of taking up too much space. There was no contact in this bed, no merge in this divide.

Fiona lay on her side facing the window, her upper body bare and free from the covers. Stuart lay on his back, held there by his own weight and hating every singular part of his body that was accountable for his shameful mass. He longed as much as he ever had in his forty years to touch, hold and be held by another person. He turned his head towards her to observe her figure in the dark. She formed a bleak shadow that smelled of shampoo and detergent; he was wide awake to his senses and desire. With some caution he touched the hump of her shoulder, first his fingertips and then, with no rebuttal yet, he eased his whole arm onto her shoulder in one smooth movement.

Fiona was near sleep, at peace. When she felt Stuart's touch, her pupils widened and her body tensed, too slight for him to feel beneath his oversized and clumsy hands. Stuart, encouraged by the lack of resistance, shifted his weight so that his body pressed against the curve of hers. He realised that his hand had come to rest just on the swell of her breast, which he could feel under her nightshirt. He shuffled his legs, trying to stem the physical consequence of his arousal, but he was no more able to do so than he was able to blot his excitement at the prospect of intimacy.

She felt him against her upper thigh and reacted with instinctive antipathy. He was so predictable, unable to stimulate her. The weight of his arm crushed her ribs as he fumbled and felt at her like a blind man at a piano. His breath became hot and shallow, irritating her neck. His hands moved lower, fumbling for the elasticated waistband of her pyjamas. She moved so quickly that Stuart heard the snap of her hand against his before he felt the stinging pain. He pulled away, rolling onto his back again and settling into the large indentation on the mattress.

Fiona closed her eyes and sought once again the sleep she'd been chasing. Behind her, she felt the bed shift and heard

PROLOGUE

Stuart's heavy breathing; he was still not able to lay at peace. She clutched her pillow, deep resentment breeding in her gut for the two long minutes that followed. When he finished, reaching a brief and muted climax, she knew that she hated him; black hate that had no bounds. A man whose prowess extended as far as his general attributes—underwhelming, disappointing. She cleared her throat, willing him to fade away.

The long, impromptu walk through the woods had finally cleared his head. The water stilled, the sediment settled, and likewise, his thoughts attained a level of clarity he'd not had for weeks. In this, he had been so consumed that when the path reached a clearing and the space opened out into an expanse of mud and foliage, he did not deviate from the straight and steady trudging he'd maintained for twenty minutes. He came to a stop when the broad trunk of an oak blocked his way. He kept his eyes facing forward; only the scoring and coarse surface of the bark occupied his vision. Dark wanderings ensnared his mind.

The day had been fruitless. He'd left the house at his usual time, as though nothing had changed. At the employment centre, he'd stood beneath the air-con, enjoying the cool breeze in his suit and tie. The polite man that had taken his ID card, returned, presenting him with a bundle of forms and new identification. Stu looked down at the card in his palm. It was the same photo of him as before, but instead of the red border, the background was now a dull brown, portending a terminal unemployment status. He turned and left, not wishing to join the morose hoard of those scouring the machines for contracts.

He'd visited his old HR department as the next destination of the day. Walking into the familiar building that had been his working home for nine years, now invoked a feeling of trespass. Security treated him with scrutiny and suspicion, an outsider to the world of professionals. It was Lorna at the front desk, who despite being a source of comfortable social interaction a mere week ago, now seemed to seek escape. Her shoulders tensed up and her fingers clacked the keys as she made a show of checking her computer. Stu was already memorising the place, taking it all in for the last time. Her parting words fell on inoperative ears, his active legs seeking a destination not tainted with failure.

He looked up at the tree in his drab, ill-fitting suit and smartest shoes. Toes to trunk, his head tipped so far back that he felt the titillation of light headedness. He closed his eyes, breathing fresh air into old lungs. He placed a weathered hand against the rough surface of the bark, the last of the filtering sun glinted off the smooth surface of his wedding ring. He stepped back, making a careful appraisal of the lower branches.

But who would Darren play with when he needed a doubles partner for badminton?

Darren hasn't contacted you in three weeks, and what about that new face you saw in the court last time, far younger and more enthusiastic than yourself.

What of the people who ask you to do photo edits every Christmas? No one else, locally, offers to do something like that for free.

Well, that's a once-a-year seasonal need. Is that a worthwhile payoff?

And your son.

His son; he owed him at least something. With a peek at his watch, he commenced the walk home. Fiona would be waiting.

Stu drew the car to a stop at the lights, the empty intersection of the town laid out before him. His favourite song played again as he pushed the repeat button for the fifth time, the smooth vocals going a little way to ease his turbulent mind.

Good God, it was coming closer.

He shifted into neutral and eased off the pedal, the lights still red. He detected a distant thud, the thrum of a bassline deep enough to move a heady crowd. To his left, the road led into town and he could see the periphery clubs, small groups of drunken people accumulating by their doors. His hand tapped the steering wheel, trying to focus on the music. The light was still red.

He glanced at the rear-view mirror, making out the odd shapes of forgotten items in the boot. Draped in the picnic blanket Fiona had bought last summer, the stiff silhouette of the step ladder reminded him of a body, beset by rigour mortis, draped and shrouded from the world; his own body, shaped by the comforts of an office job and a plentiful fridge, would not be sharp edges and straight lines. His blanket would fall like rolling hills, portly mounds.

The sound of shouting and high-pitched calls came from the direction of the nightclubs—people of Galven either not affected by the restructuring of the city or rather wishing to spend the last of their wages forgetting it. His eyes lingered on the women, their glasses raised, spirits high. He scanned the street's dark and empty buildings, narrow spaces steeped in shadow. There was movement on the far side of the road. Between the library and the metal railings of a small park, an awkward scuffle was taking place between two figures. In the low light, one seemed to be consumed by the dark blot that was the other, as he tried to escape. They moved between the gap, disappearing from sight. Stu paused for a moment, his brain not quite in cognitive gear. The lights changed in front of him but his grip slackened on the handbrake. The road still devoid of other drivers, he stepped out of the car.

The bright lights and intoxicating music seemed to barely reach him on this cold and desolate side of the street, where the landscape was varying bleak shades of grey and the sound of the fervent, hushed discussion became clear. He saw the men; he could make out details now. One was against the wall, his palms raised. Dressed like the other revellers, his skin glistened in the faint luminescence from the street light. Neither had spotted him.

"You ruined my life; do you realise that? You, who had the nerve to make jokes, while taking everything from me. You're ok though, you don't care about any of us as long as you're ok." The black figure with the knife seemed to grow in stature, his victim shrinking in fear.

"I was forced to do it. It was out of my control," the one against the wall pleaded. "It wasn't my decision, but I was the one who had to do it, you know how it is, I'm just the messenger. I wouldn't have if it was up to me, if it was economically viable." At that, the attacker's demeanour cracked.

"You could have done something!" His voice took on a strangled, constricted quality. "My wife left me; I can't make payments on my house. My whole life is ruined. I've lost my friends, my car, I'm nothing now."

"Take what you want, my wallet is in my pocket, my watch-" He moved his wrist as if to showcase the watch, but the knifeman pushed closer to him, blocking the man's hand with his body and pressing the knife to his throat.

"I don't want your watch!" He took in deep, heavy breaths. "I want you to understand how it feels to have no control; to lose everything at the doing of someone else." Spittle flew from his mouth, such was his rage. "You think you're better than us."

"Martin?" a woman's voice called. The knifeman clutched Martin tighter and jerked his hand so that the blade kissed his jugular.

"I'm sorry," Martin said, struggling for air. The woman called again, her voice louder now, closer. The knifeman was stalling and Stuart made his move, his mind ready to leave the scene undetected, but his body surprised him as he entered the alleyway. The knifeman's head whipped around and Stuart was met with the wild, manic eyes of someone who has lost all sense of reason.

"Stay where you are," he shouted. Stu paused, but he could hear the clack of high heeled shoes and knew the fragile state of quiet stalling was about to be interrupted, likely driving the knife to its target.

When the man's attention once again reverted to his victim, Stu took a breath. As the footsteps behind him reached a crescendo and in front of him the men's eyes were locked, he surged forwards with a speed not known to him in twenty years. He kept going until he felt the bulk of the attacker against his upper body, groping for his arms. There was a scream from behind them as he felt the piston of the knifeman's elbow against his stomach.

"Don't you ruddy hurt him. You'll regret it. Don't you ruddy well do it," Stu repeated, managing to get a firm hold of the knifeman as he pressed him tightly to his broad chest, his hand around the wrist that held the knife. Martin, his expression a distortion of panic and pain, managed to slip away and run to his hysterical partner. Stu's grasp slackened. The knifeman freed himself from Stu's hold with a twist of his body, shoving him square in the stomach as he pushed away from him. He cast a glance over Stu by way of brief appraisal, observing his clean but well-worn shoes, the slight fade of his trousers, and the dishevelled quality of his untucked, off-white shirt.

"I don't know what you're protecting them for. They'll shift us all in the end."

He stumbled sideward before catching his breath and picking up a jog. Stu was left alone, his mouth an arid cave. He returned to his car, besieged by a barrage of abuse and honking from a driver busy berating him for where his car had been left.

The work shoes freshly polished that morning with a sense of hope, slowly descended into a muddy, leaf-strewn state. Under what little light the night sky provided, filtering through the overtop canopy of leaves, Stu struggled to navigate the foot worn path that he headed down. He stumbled on a protruding tree root, but pressed on without pause, leaving the ladder trailing behind him to bump over the root, jarring his shoulder in the process.

It didn't take long for him to reach the tree, set in the stage of the night, size and depth magnified. It looked back at him.

PROLOGUE

It knew why he was here, and the audience waited with silent expectation. He placed the ladder on the ground and dropped the length of rope. His heaving breath and heavy footfall had been the only noise filling his ears, but once he caught his breath, the nightlife began to make themselves known with their curious chirrups and calls.

He wasn't in the woods though, standing within the black fingered reach of the oak tree that waited so patiently. Eyes closed. He was in Sandy Park, under one of the many blossoming trees that shivered in the unseasonal breeze. His son rode his shoulders, laughing with joy when his dad shook a branch and the blossoms rained a pink shower on their head.

He was at the Guildridge hospital back in 2002, heading into the maternity ward laden with gifts and Fiona's favourite shortbread. He looked into the crib and saw his son, his boy. The baby's sleeping face resembled that of a small angel gifted to them both. Whatever Fiona or his parents said to him that day, , it could not come close to the high he rode.

He was sitting in the old VW he had bought as a young twenty-year-old, wanting to impress his new girlfriend. He had driven her to Norfolk in the late of a warm September. The rain had stranded them inside the cramped space of his first car, but Fiona had laughed as he'd tried to impress her with jokes over fish and chips. They watched the waves break to and fro beneath a tempestuous, murky sky.

He studied his mother's warm hands as she covered his own to help him guide a plastic racket and hit the swing ball. In the garden of his childhood home, where the air was scented with sweet peonies, and the sound of the mini rock pool soothed in the background, he had laughed without end as they played their first clumsy game.

Those same hands grasped both wrists tight, sending shooting burning pain up his arms and fuelling his cries.

He put the first foot on the ladder. He'd already practised the knot, and the rope swung with ease, up and over the reaching arm.

He looked up from his empty plate. In the white, windowed gazebo sat all his family and friends. Only his parents were absent... finally under the ground. He'd hung his head in mock shame as his best pal Rodge recited stories. Old Rodge always knew how to get him. He looked over at Dodger Rodger, and with a squint of the eye and a twitch of his lip, Rodge had Stu in uncontrollable stitches. Fiona watched him with a speculative expression, but her eyes were twinkling and her hair flounced about as her head spun between the two of them, wanting in on the joke.

The same hair bobbed in front of his eyes like a russet curtain as she held onto his neck with one hand, pushing, punishing. Her new highlights caught the dipping sun, and a teary film covered his eyes.

Stu reached to take a firm hold of the noose he'd constructed. His surroundings were quite absent of any noise now, leaving him captivated. The hand that sported his wedding band fumbled with the rope as he fitted it around his neck. It felt thick and cumbersome, cutting into the thick roll of his tender skin. He took one look at the ground.

Eyes closed, for the last time. Below him was freshly mown grass, interspersed with fallen blossoms like rose confetti. His son's tiny, weightless arms grasped tight around his neck and he turned to try and get a look at his face. He could just make out a beaming smile and flushed cheeks. *Do it again*

PROLOGUE

Daddy! Stu shook the branch, and a myriad of white and pink sprinkled all around them in a cascade of colour, twirling and spinning through the air. His son's laughter tinkled in his ears like the sweetest music he had ever heard, and his hands gripped oh so tightly, ever tighter around his neck, around his wretched neck. All around him, fluttering and floating and floundering through endless air. He did it again, and again, until both their heads were blanketed in tree blossom and their vision was filled with pinks and whites and reds and pinks and scarlet, claret, burgundy red. They tumbled through the sky. Weightless.

Chapter 1

"Come on, Jack. Everyone's gone in." Emily applied gentle pressure to the back of his shoulder, trying to make him move.

"I don't want to go," he said, planting his feet. The door to the Aid Centre remained open, yet the car park had almost cleared. She checked her phone. There were no new messages, but she'd be late if she didn't leave soon.

"Hello? Are you Jack's mum?" One of the female carers approached them. Jack hugged her legs, prodding the back of her thigh with his finger for attention.

"Yes, I am, he's just a bit reluctant to go in today," Emily said, clearing stray hairs from her face.

"I'm Miss Cooper. I wanted to speak to you for a minute; are you still intending to continue his one-to-one support?" The woman smiled down at Jack, her neat hair and immaculate make-up adding to Emily's feelings of inadequacy.

"Well, yes. I think he needs it. He's been coping a lot better since he's had the extra help." She moved her hands behind her to try and release his grip, but his fingers were hidden in the twists of her trouser fabric, and he'd dug in for the fight.

Miss Cooper's face fell.

"Of course. I have to tell you though, the Council is cutting down on funding for extra staff members, and if you want to continue that support, it's something we'll need monetary contribution for."

"I see. I didn't know. How much is it?" She could feel her forehead beading with sweat. The thought of making him wait, of incurring more messages, was one that made her heart rate quicken. She watched Miss Cooper's gaze cast over her.

"We can email you an estimate of the cost. There's still some outstanding lunch money due, too," she trailed off. Emily nodded.

"Oh, I'm sorry. I'll get that paid." She looked at her son who was unwilling to leave his hideout. She used both arms to try to free herself.

"Are you going to come with me, Jack?" Miss Cooper said, but he'd squeezed his eyes shut.

"Now please, Jack. I need to go."

"Are you heading to work?" Miss Cooper reached for Jack's arms, ignoring his resistance.

Emily's breath came out in a small huff. She was too afraid to check the time now.

"Job hunting, still," she said. Miss Cooper managed to pull Jack from her, encasing him gently in her arms as he twisted and turned, refusing to look at her.

"No, no I don't want to," he repeated.

"You're with me now. Your mum needs to go." She looked up at Emily. "He'll be fine," she said with a smile. But Emily hated to walk away from Jack's distress. The image of him being forced through the doors would stay with her until she picked him up.

Jack's cries became louder, but she needed to go.

"I don't have time," she said, reaching for her phone. "I'm sorry."

When you came from Shaw Hill and crossed into the town, the point at which you left what was known locally as the brown zone. Beyond the brown zone, the area was populated by the prosperous, with bright shops and opportunities, and was not in the least bit subtle. A single signpost and a traffic junction parted the classes. Being late morning, the quaint marketplace was almost deserted. Many were at work or busy packing, and the ladies of leisure who, only a few years ago, filled these streets with shopping and top of the range pushchairs were now sparser than ever. Whether a result of ever tightening purse strings or collective concerns about the war, the quiet suited her today.

As was habit, once crossing onto the smart paving of the town she made a quick evaluation of her dress and appearance. Her only smart outfit showed signs of its owner's deception. She knew why; these black trousers and uncomfortable chiffon shirt had been purchased in a clearance sale the previous year. Since then, she had worn them for countless job searches and the occasional interview, and thanks to the rigours of raising a toddler and her nervous perspiration, they had been through copious washes. In the last fortnight, the shirt had also incurred a small but noticeable stain on the lower hem, and the bottom of her trousers was increasingly frayed as well as sprouting errant threads. It looked ok from a distance. She had no intention of getting close to Ronan.

He wasn't yet in the café when she arrived. Her thoughts turned to stalling time in some way, her fingers touching against the loose coins in her pocket. She had counted them three times, but still worried she might be left short. A young waitress with a bright smile greeted her as she slid into the seat closest to the door. She handed Emily a leather-bound menu in one sleek motion and sashayed back to her duties behind the counter. She felt uneasy, disconcerted by the polished appearance and steadfast confidence of the other customers. She had chosen this café because of its proximity to her side of town. There weren't exactly many coffee shops in Shaw Hill, not nice ones by any measure.

The door swung open and Ronan entered. He still had the close cut, red hue hair and stubble that had won him countless admirers in college. She didn't rise to greet him, instead, she shrunk a little in her seat as he leant over the table in his slim-fit suit to clasp her arm and kiss her cheek. He placed the small fob of his ignition key and his black identification card on the table.

"It's good to finally see you. You've done well to avoid me all these years." He took a second to examine her, appraising her body. "You've not lost your looks, it seems."

"It's been a long time," she replied with a thin smile, her hands gripped together in her lap. The waitress reappeared and Ronan ordered a black Americano. When Emily ordered her latte, the waitress seemed pained to look at her.

"Pardon?" she asked in a curt voice. Emily repeated her order, drawing a glance from the waitress before she turned back to Ronan.

"Anything else?" the waitress asked, her pen hovering above the paper.

"Fancy anything to eat?" he asked Emily.

"I'm not hungry."

Ronan leant forward in his seat.

"Obviously, I'm covering the cost. You don't need to worry about that when you're with me."

"Thank you, but I'm fine. I ate before I came out."

He looked up at the waitress.

"We'll have two pastries, any kind." She jotted it down and left them. Emily's pocket seemed weighed down by her change. She had been set on paying for herself, despite the indignity of a four quid coffee. It was now her limitation, not independence. There better be a good reason.

"Why did you want to speak to me so urgently?"

"I'll get to that in a moment. First, I want to know how you are, what life's been like for you since we last spoke. And nothing vague, I want you to be honest on the details with me."

"How long's it been, four years? I'm ok. Things have been no harder for me than they've been for everyone. Looking after my son, Jack, keeps me busy every day; it's been harder to find work because of his needs." Ronan nodded. "He has autism, so I don't like to leave him for too long."

"But he's at the Aid Centre right now, correct?"

"Yes," she paused. "I usually use this time to look for work."

"And your previous partner, Noel, was it? He was conscripted, correct?"

"He's still my partner; we just haven't been able to speak to each other in a while." Ronan sighed, moving his hand towards the table's centre. His gold wristwatch looked like it could pay her rent for two months.

"You know you're unlikely to ever see him again. I haven't checked, but it's possible he's not even alive. The communication department can be a little lax with their letters sometimes. You can't keep struggling on in the slim hope that he might come back. You're barely keeping afloat and you can hardly provide a good life for you and Jack. Anyone can see it."

Before Emily had the chance to reply, the waitress brought their drinks and pastries, setting them on the table with various clinks. Ronan continued.

"From my position in the council as it is now, I can tell you for a fact that we've hardly met the middle of the war, let alone the end. The conscripts are going to be required for at least five more years, and that's being optimistic. Throughout that time, losses are expected. We are at war, as you know. It's a crucial time, and yes, the conscripts play an important role. But people like me, who are at the top making difficult decisions, we're essential. We're the ones with the responsibility of the nation; it's a job like no other."

Emily dropped her eyes, reaching for her cup for comfort, taking a small sip of the sweet, scorching hot liquid. Ronan picked up his pastry without averting his gaze. He took a large, enthusiastic bite before returning it to the plate, his mouth chomping as he watched her. He swallowed.

"My feelings for you haven't changed a bit, you know. I gave you time and space as you asked. You made the decisions you made, which has landed you here. My career meanwhile has taken off and I'm in an extremely good position; I have influence now."

"I didn't ask you for space, I asked you not to contact me again."

"And yet here you are." He opened his palms and leant closer to her.

"Is that why you wanted to meet? To tell me that?"

"It's relevant to the issue at hand."

Emily said nothing. A large vein had risen to prominence

on his forehead. He continued.

"What if you could be in a position where you didn't have to work, you didn't have to leave your son, but you could be safe and provided for?"

"I don't understand."

"You would want that, right? Support? Care? I bet that's something you're hardly getting now. I can't see you mixing and getting on with the other..." He twitched his nose, "... people, if you can call them that, living in that hell-hole of an estate. I bet you've been doing things on your own all this time, haven't you?"

Emily looked down at the flaky pastry on her plate.

"It's just Jack and me, we don't need anyone else. Can you just explain what's going on?"

"Listen, in an ideal world, we'd have more time to get to know each other again, but something big is about to happen, or rather, be enforced upon us, and we don't have the luxury of time. I'm worried that you could end up on the wrong side."

"The wrong side of what?"

Emily's voice had risen, but Ronan spoke so quietly that she had to strain to listen.

"I can't give you details in public. We've had to take measures to protect the council and Galven from every possible threat. These measures will impact you in the position you're in now. Some might say they're extreme, but honestly, they're necessary. The reason I asked you to meet me is that I want you and your son to come with me today, now, and live with me in Galven where I can offer you protection as my family. I can give you a nice home, everything you need and want. I can keep you safe and you won't have to worry about what's to come."

"But what's going to happen?"

"You have to trust me. If you come with me, I can tell you. If you don't, you stand to lose everything."

"The only thing I care about losing is my son. Please, Ronan."

She watched as he reached across the cluttered surface of the table, his watch scraping against the wood.

"Give me your hand," he said. With some reluctance, Emily drew out one of her fists she'd been keeping curled in her lap. She rested it on the table and he took it in his palm.

"Come with me, and you will not lose your son, I promise."

Her mask of calm began to melt away like a thin veneer of ice beneath a match. Her mind scrambled for clarity. She pushed back from the table, her chair dragging across the floor with a high-pitched squeal.

"Don't make the wrong choice for the second time," Ronan said. "I let you get away last time, even though I knew you were making the biggest mistake of your life, one you're still paying for. Come with me now. We can discuss the details and everything else later, once you're both safe. I know it's a lot to take in, but you have to trust me."

She let her weight drop back into the chair, her fingers loosening their grip on the table's edge. She thought of the past year, since Noel had been conscripted. A year of constant financial worry, and bitter isolation. She'd felt guilty since Jack's birth; she couldn't give him the world, buy him expensive things and provide a nice home where he could feel safe and happy. Recently, that guilt had become even more pressing, as she watched him outgrow clothes that she couldn't afford to replace while job prospects grew sparser by the day. She studied Ronan's face. Was being with him really worse than spending another lonely night with all her anxieties?

"Ok, we'll come with you. But that's not to say I want a relationship, not while Noel might still be out there. And even if he's not, Jack is my priority; I'm not jumping into another relationship right now."

He raised his hand to silence her. "You don't have to explain. I know what you want and need." He finished his pastry, chasing it down with a swill of his coffee.

"We're leaving straight away?"

"Yes, the sooner we get to Galven the better. I'm just going to pay. Finish your food."

He got up and went to the counter. Emily gazed with disinterest at the cinnamon swirl in front of her. Her coffee had ceased steaming. She picked up the pastry, feeling its sugary, oily surface crumble at the press of her fingertips. She took one bite but it was so sweet that it sapped the moisture from her mouth and stuck in her throat. She returned what was left of it to the plate. Ronan re-joined her, placing his wallet and identification back into his pockets.

"Do you still like taking photos?" he asked.

"I don't have my camera any more, I had to sell it."

Her voice was airy and distant. She stood up, catching the table with the front of her thigh. She felt Ronan's hand press lightly against her back as if to steady her, but it lingered a few seconds longer than was necessary or comfortable.

"Any camera you want, I'll get it for you. You can have a look later; the new shopping plaza is meant to be good. I haven't been there yet myself."

He held open the door, touching her hip as she passed.

CHAPTER 1

She stepped into glaring sunlight and strong wind. A black Mercedes saloon was parked on the yellow line, just a few metres away. She stopped to fix her hair as Ronan passed her and opened the passenger door. He walked around to the driver's side to get in, but Emily stood still, eyeing the interior in the same way a flighty bird might inspect a gilded cage. She looked up the empty street towards Shaw Hill, hearing Ronan tell her to get inside the car, his voice muffled in the wind.

"Emily?" His door still open, his fingers hovered at the seat belt latch, ready to undo it.

She willed her feet to move; slow steps turning to quick, light ones. The air felt fresher and easier to breathe the further she walked from the car. Ronan called her again, not a question this time, but a command. She fell into a run, morphing from easy, loping strides to a sprint. She cut right down the footpath that would bring her back to Shaw Road. Far behind her, she heard slamming doors and the roar of an engine. Rubber tires squealed in rapid motion against the blacktop, but he would not catch her now.

The Aid Centre came into view, a relief to her painful feet and labouring breath. A crowd of people had gathered around the locked gates, spilling onto the road. Emily slowed to a walk and met with a solid wall of people, backs facing her, all pushing forwards in an effort to gain some knowledge on what was happening. There was a cacophony of shouts, protests and confusion that mingled in her ears, but through all of that, she could just make out that somewhere near the front, an irate man was attempting to address the group. She squeezed through the perspiring mass of parents, some trying to listen to what the suited man had to say, while many stood on tiptoes trying to see their child through the closed gates.

"Listen!" the man shouted, trying to make his voice heard, but gave up on the second syllable as a duffel coated lady, built like an ox, pushed towards him and ordered him to speak with such venom that he felt every inch of him flinch. Kyle had warned him it was like a cattle market out here and he wasn't wrong. The herd had been split, the corral gates slammed shut and now they were restless. A young intern came to his aid, passing him a handheld loudspeaker to wield. With a hasty wipe of his brow and a repositioning onto the small incline of the grass verge, he was able to at last address the crowd with a semblance of authority. Barely into his twenties, still afflicted with the acne of his teenage years, he spoke to the gathered people.

"Listen up everybody. Please quieten down and all will be explained."

The oxen lady placed her sizeable crossed arms atop the descending slope of her equally considerable chest.

"By decree of the council, it's been decided that under emergency temporary measures, your children are safest placed within the newly erected Galven boundary, where there are resources to both take care of them and protect them from attack."

A collective shout of anger came from the crowd.

"Listen!" Terry was starting to lose his cool. He never lost his cool, but then again, he never usually worked in the field. He took a deep breath and the intern gave him the thumbs up that they were ready to leave. He'd soon be able to return to his quiet, detached home, away from this pit. "You should all receive a printed notice explaining what's going on. There'll also be one pinned on the community board. In short, we are taking the children as evacuees seeing that an attack is deemed imminent. They'll be placed with families in Galven where each child will be assessed by a health professional and kept safe until they can be returned to you. Details of how you can contact your child will be released in due course, but for now, our primary concern is the threat of attack. Please submit any questions in writing to the council or better still await further information. Thank you."

Terry stepped off his temporary soapbox and made for his getaway vehicle that was parked a short distance away. Before he could get there, the formidable woman stepped into his path using her body as a block.

"Let us see our kids, who do you think you are?" Terry put his head down and shoved past the small space by her side, his intern holding out his arm as a barrier for extra assistance. "You can't do this!" shouts came as he cut a fast-moving figure, sluicing through the crowd and into the car. The driver did not need to be told to step on it.

Whilst he'd been speaking, Emily worked her way to the fence. She'd been watching two coaches, parked in the playground that was now locked shut. Professional looking people had been busy shuttling back and forth between the coaches and the Aid Centre like ants sent to forage. As the man's speech culminated and others moved to try and get to him, she walked the length of the steel bars that secured the Aid Centre, approaching the tall gates that allowed vehicles in and out. Two Council Law Enforcement officers were guarding them. Ignoring their vigilant gaze, she scanned the playground for a familiar car. She saw it almost straight away, Ronan's sleek, black Mercedes.

"Ronan?" she called. The guards stepped towards her. She

shouted for Ronan again, louder still; desperation making a high-pitched notch at the end of her call as she tried to look for every closed space from which he could appear.

"Move along please miss," one of the guards said, blocking her view. She tried to step around him but was stopped by the other guard, who put out his arm.

"It's ok guys," Ronan's voice sounded, casual and bright. "I can deal with this."

The guards moved away, one ducking forward to release the lock on the gate and draw it open slightly. Ronan walked towards her with an easy stride, one hand resting in his pocket and a boyish smirk on his face. He stopped at the gate, blocking the narrow opening.

"Can I help?"

"This is happening right now?" She could feel her throat closing up, panic swelling in her chest.

"Honestly Emily, all that effort to meet me, you could at least have paid some attention."

"I'm sorry, I panicked. I didn't know. There wasn't time."

"If you had just done as I'd asked, we could have been halfway to Galven by now, your son by your side. I would have told you everything; I just couldn't do it then."

"Please, we'll come with you. It was nothing personal against you, it was a moment of indecision, a stupid mistake. I have a few things to pick up from the house and we'll be ready, it can work."

"Can it?"

"Yes," she pleaded.

Ronan folded his arms and looked at the ground. He breathed out a part laugh, part sigh. When he met her eyes again, all mock ambivalence was gone.

"I don't think that can happen. Not after you've left me like that for the second time."

"Please, Ronan."

"You're a very silly girl, Emily."

He turned away from her. She grabbed hold of his arm.

"Let me see my son." She was crying now. He pulled the gates closed.

"Please!" she shouted. "Let me see my son."

"Lock these gates," he said to the guards with a dismissive wave of the hand. "Don't let her through."

She watched him disappear into the building as more parents joined her, pressing against the metal bars. Children started to file out of the Aid Centre in lines, directed by council officials, into the waiting coaches. The sound of their distress fuelled the hysterics of the crowd as Emily's composure broke and she felt her world fall apart.

Chapter 2

Fiona strode towards the department store feeling a shallow elation that coloured only her smile. Tottering along on her reliable Givenchy heels, she was fronting a wide toothy smile that she aimed at anyone who might look her way. She was confident; she belonged here and damned to anyone who challenged that. Under duress, she would show them her red ID, even though it was not the blue she aspired to. Any observer with a particular interest in her may have noticed that her eyes betrayed her true state of mind. Like the strongman's test at a funfair, the smile hit hard but the eyes atop the scale were insurmountable. They twitched above bags held tight with brows that were trying to meet, but she held them apart. She was the queen of self-control.

The main thing that was bothering her— there never failed to be something to spark her ire—was the way she was forced to make a conscious effort to pin her left arm to her side, so as to conceal the split seam under the armpit of her designer floral dress.

She graced the various aisles with measured steps. She hadn't picked up a basket; why, she must just be breezing through to pick up a forgotten odd or two items, anyone would assume. But she picked up nothing without returning it, giving every precious item a glance of her straight, white teeth before it was placed with care back on its shelf. She looked through the candles, the ornaments, the fine thread sheets and the silver cutlery, all in fine spirits until she sensed watching eyes and noticed one of the store's security guards scrutinizing her from the opposite end of the kitchen-item aisle. Fiona pinned her left arm against her ribcage and headed in no particular haste to the restrooms.

She pushed open the door to the ladies and was pleased to see it was empty. The white and chrome surfaces laid out in front of wide framed mirrors seemed to sparkle under the abundant bright lighting up above. She entered the furthest cubicle and seated herself behind the closed door. Even in the confined space, Fiona still made the customary checks around her before she let herself relax. She brought one hand up to rub the back of her neck and with the other began rooting around in her bag. All she found amongst her old hairbrush, sanitary towels and some dirty makeup was her purse—empty and destitute. The store cards were left there only for display purpose now. She closed her eyes and caught a strangled sob that tried to escape through her throat. She had to keep a lid on her emotions. She had to remain in control.

But wasn't she entitled to be upset? She had no money coming in, debt letters were claiming residency on her kitchen table, she was struggling to keep the mortgage and she knew that Margaret across the road suspected something. She saw it dancing in her pity ridden, mascara laden eyes every time they spoke. Didn't Margaret ever stop to think that she'd just lost her husband for Christ's sake! If things hadn't been bad enough, they'd only got worse when Stuart had decided to go and top himself and leave her to deal with all of it alone, without money; typical, selfish man.

Fiona wiped the overflow of tears from beneath her eyes with one finger. It took great precision to ensure she didn't disturb her makeup. She composed herself, taking a few seconds to listen with complete focus to ensure she was still unaccompanied. She took a piece of tissue paper to blow her nose in, then paused to look at the dispenser. An idea came to her. Acting on it, she carefully removed five handfuls of tissue paper and folded them neatly into her handbag. She had remembered they were running low, and this was softer than the coarse substitute she had been forced to use from the discount shop. The toilet paper tube rattled in the plastic casing, and after another short pause to make sure nobody was outside, she zipped up her bag and exited the cubicle. Her make up intact, she was feeling better.

Upon leaving, Fiona found herself assaulted by the bright sunlight that had reared its unwanted head from beyond a cloud. It made her squint and squinting made her face look haggard so she made a beeline to her car, which she'd parked in a remote corner of the extensive car park. She opened the passenger door and without getting in the car, retrieved her favourite sunglasses from the glovebox; they had the darkest tint and the biggest rims she could find. When she donned them, she felt confident, safe. Without looking up, she headed towards the westerly side of the retail park for the real reason she'd made the journey in the first place. Her heels clicked and clacked in loud objection to her quickening steps, and her gaze darted to every person within viewing distance. Though it cost her in fuel, she hoped that by travelling this close to Galven, she'd avoid being seen, but she could never be too sure.

She reached the discount shop and darted through the doors as though a sudden snatching wind had whisked her off course. She was met with garish pop music from two decades ago, tacky displays in harsh primary colours in every direction and price signs everywhere, big and bold. You couldn't escape money, and this shop, for those with little of the stuff, was all about it. She had twice counted the change in her purse. She had thirteen pounds and eighty-five pence with which to get as many supplies as possible. In desperate times, desperate measures had to be endured, and this was about as low as Fiona could imagine.

Somebody watching a well-dressed woman seemingly snatched into a ghastly discount store may have continued in their suspicion that she had lost her way, owing to her grim expression and her apparent hurry to find her way out. But Fiona was now armed with a bright yellow, plastic shopping basket. She held it out in front of her at waist height, as if a shield, whilst keeping her left elbow still pinned to conceal the hole in her clothing. The store was dotted with the types of people she was used to seeing from inside a locked vehicle. They reminded her of feral dogs wandering a barren land, shuffling in a lacklustre fashion, stopping now and then to inspect something they'd found. Except rather than inspecting a bug or a patch of grass, they picked up a bottle of shower gel or a pair of novelty socks and spun them in their hands before placing them back and hunching on.

These were not Fiona's type of people. She clutched her shopping basket tighter and walked on. She cut an efficient route through the shop aisles, grabbing items on her way and avoiding eye contact with anyone who came near. She started towards the till and then had a moment of panic. She checked the items in her basket doing a mental calculation of their sum. She was thirty pence over her budget, so she placed the shower gel she could go without on the dog food display next to her. She got through the checkout with the least disdain she could muster. The checkout girl kept giving her sideways glances, which she returned with a concealed glare.

"Thank you for shopping at NC Discount, have a nice day."

Fiona said nothing, handling the thin plastic carrier bags, emblazoned with the store's logo in bright, bold text as if they were evidence of a dirty protest.

She couldn't wait to get out of the place. She would have paused once outside to appreciate the space and fresh whip of air, but ladened with the bags, she scrunched them up into bundles and, in this manner, carried them back to the boot of her car. She placed each item into department store bags she had saved and kept carefully without a crease, stuffing the discount store bags with little regard into the far corner, under the bottle of windscreen wash where they were no longer visible. Satisfied, she drove home.

Fiona pulled into her driveway in a sour mood. A black cloud had stalked her the whole way home and now hung above her like a bad omen. The car shook as she pulled up; she'd now driven over sixty miles since last buying petrol. She stepped out of the car with mild relief at having made the journey, but any positive thoughts disappeared as she opened the boot to retrieve the bags and the sight of Margaret's breasts clouded her peripheral vision, signalling an imminent cheery greeting.

"Hi Fiona," Margaret called at an intense volume, drawing out the "a" in Fiona's name. Fiona plastered on her greatest battle worthy smile before turning around to face her neighbour.

"Hi Margaret, just bringing the shopping in, it's been a busy day." She nodded slowly as she spoke.

"Oh I'm sure, what with everything you have to sort out." Margaret's face dropped from a beaming grin to an exaggerated frown at the obvious inference to Fiona's recent loss. That bitch, thought Fiona.

"Yes, it's non-stop really." Her eye was caught by the erected for sale sign that was now posted amidst Margaret's manicured lawn. Margaret nodded in theatrical concern.

"You've probably noticed the sign," Margaret said without turning her head. "We're moving to Galven, along with half the neighbourhood it seems. It's quite a lot of money, but with the rate these houses are dropping value at the moment, it doesn't feel like we have much choice." She lowered her voice, putting her hand to her mouth. "Who knows what will be left behind."

Fiona put on her most cynical smile that she reserved for situations such as this.

"I haven't had a chance to look into it yet. How much does it cost to move there?"

"Well, there's a residency permit, which is around five thousand. Then you have to provide evidence of earnings and savings of at least forty thousand, so it's a reasonable amount. The houses are lovely though, and the town is all newly built. No worries about crime or a great big eyesore like Shaw Hill."

"I don't know if I could leave this house, no matter how big the risk. Sometimes the sentimental value is more important than money. That's if Stuart going and ending it all hasn't left me destitute in any case." Her voice was erratic in its pitch and volume, her hands flailed of their own accord. Margaret stood perfectly calm, her stance one of funeral appropriate demeanour.

"That's true; your house must hold so many precious memories." She paused. "However, Brian has been telling me that those who stay are going to be in for a very hard time."

"Is that right?" Fiona replied breezily. Margaret nodded then made a sharp intake of breath.

"Well, if you want any help with anything then Brian and I are just across the road."

Sure, thought Fiona, Margaret's placid oaf of a husband Brian; a man with no redeeming qualities other than his monthly pay-check and yearly bonus. She wondered how Margaret managed to endure him making love to her, with his considerable waistline and numerous chins, although she would be dishonest if she were to deny envying her. She picked up her shopping bags with one hand, ensuring the department store branding was on display on Margaret's side.

"I'm managing, really. Thank you so much." Fiona noticed her gaze twitch to her arm and she remembered the split seam in the underarm of her dress. She dropped her arm so fast that for one mortifying moment she thought that the discount items would tear through the bags and spill with ghastly, discounted celebration all over her drive. The bag held and Margaret lingered, her eyes averted and her mind grasping at some thread of small talk that would spare them both some awkwardness. Fiona felt a rush of blood to her cheeks, prickly heat at her neck.

"I was pruning the mulberry tree in my garden the other day. I think it snagged my dress a bit."

"Oh, how unfortunate," Margaret replied.

"I best go and check on my son, he's not been well." They bid a curt goodbye and Fiona took every bag in one trip to the house. Inside, she unpacked the bags without a word to her son upstairs, who unbeknownst to her was filling his head with the prospect of conscription and military training; pushing out the dark domain in which thoughts of his dead father dwelled.

Chapter 3

After the coach's departure, Emily had been swept up in the crowd of parents that followed them by foot, gaining in number as the news spread through Shaw Hill. The few cars in the estate were filled within minutes by friends of those who drove them, but Emily had no friends.

When she had lived with her mother before moving out, trips into the old Galven had been frequent. A spacious, developing town, Emily had even gone to school there, which welcomed Merredin's students of repute. Living in the gated estate just outside it, the old Galven had become familiar to her. That once thriving town was now falling into disuse and the Galven Road that used to lead into sparse woodland, travelled only by dog walkers and couples, was now the only route into the new Galven, the length of which she now walked alongside a vast number of other women. At its end, they met something beyond anyone's imagination. A formidable barrier, formed of great concrete blocks, extended without end in both directions; a wall of such magnitude that nothing could be seen beyond. The only break in the span of dark grey was the high-rise security gates made of cast iron, glossed in black, the likes of which might be expected at a military compound rather than a town entrance. This served as the sole entrance and exit into Galven, marking both checkpoint and perimeter with booths at either side to house the Council Law Enforcement.

There was a queue of cars that had not been permitted access. Cars from the estate with mismatched bumpers, dents and sun-bleached paint, spluttering engines. Their entrance had been denied at first sight. The guards were waiting for them, protected by the booths. They addressed the crowd as one entity, their faces expressionless, unsympathetic. Emily tried to force her way to the left side booth, retrieving her identification from her pocket.

"Red cards only. People with red identification cards only," the guard was repeating.

At the front, a handful of rambunctious young men that had avoided conscription, feeling the ineptitude of their position and their own virility, began to press the guards with the same demands and questions albeit now with squared shoulders and bared teeth.

The burliest of the guards responded to this affront by asking to see their ID. The frontrunner and nominal leader of the Shaw Hill group produced his card with the kind of flourish usually reserved for the indignant eighteen-year-old upon ordering their first pint. But this soon turned to anger when the guard asked why he'd breached the laws of enlistment at the age of nineteen. This sparked yet further aggression, more armed guards watching on from behind the iron bars, facing off with the diverse and animated group.

Emily could see nothing of the coaches that Jack and the other children had left in. Aside from those who surrounded her, all she could make out beyond the border was the same continual road and a green landscape that gave no indication as to where he might now be. A door was opened to their right and from the small cabin stepped out a junior council member, dressed in a shirt and tie. He held a scrap of paper in one hand and was led towards the gates by a grey-haired guard whose unflappable nature was in contrast to the anxious posture of the younger man. He came to a stop in front of the gates, avoiding direct eye contact with those who watched him.

"I bring word from the council who are aware of the situation here and have expressed strongly that you must disperse." He unfurled the paper and squinted at it. Around Emily, others strained to listen to what he had to say. "The Council wish to reiterate that this action has been taken with the best interests of the children in mind, and to remind parents that in Galven, their children will benefit not only from greater protection in event of a strike, but will also be able to access better nutrition and medical care."

"This is bullshit," a purple haired, pallid armed woman said next to her. "You think you can take whatever you want. They're our kids!"

"I urge you all, please disperse. Further communication will be made within the next few days. Return to your houses, your children are safe. If you do not do so then we will take further action against those loitering and acting aggressively."

He re-crumpled his paper and raised his eyes expectantly. He ignored the few indistinct shouts and some heckling at the front. Around her, the crowd began to fall away, finding friends and family, the subject of their conversation turning to home.

"Well, they can't keep us locked out forever. There'll be trouble after this," the woman who had spoken earlier said to

CHAPTER 3

no one in particular.

The low sound of an approaching car caused Emily to lift her head. Sharp pain flared in her back. All was muted grey and darkening beneath the looming evening sky. She was somewhere west of the hospital, having passed behind it as she'd tracked the length of the wall without aim. Her hands were marred with dirt from where they'd been resting on the dusty ground.

An old Ford Fiesta drew to a stop on the road a few feet away. In the low light, it appeared a dusky pink. It emitted a knocking sound like a jackhammer running out of power. Two women watched her from the lowered windows.

"There a reason you're sitting on the ground?" the driver asked, her right arm hanging jauntily on the outside of the car. She found a hold in the scrub and stood, mumbling to herself. How had rest been possible when Jack was still lost? Loose grit fell from the wall at the lightest touch yet the blocks were cool and impassable. She had to carry on and find the border's end, whether sea or cliff or something else.

"Do you have somewhere to go? You look done in," the driver called after her, followed by a grinding sound as the car was put in gear. It rolled alongside her.

"I need to find my son, he needs me."

The woman questioning her had corn coloured hair, which hung limply around her shoulders and ended in split ends. She made no effort to conceal her scrutiny.

"You from the estate?" she asked with a slight raise of her chin.

"I live on Cheshunt Avenue," Emily replied. "I need to go. My son has autism, he'll be scared." She started walking again but heard the car door open. The passenger caught up with her; a tall, lanky woman wearing ripped jeans and a vest top, which accentuated the sharp ridge of her clavicle and the smooth musculature of her shoulders. Her hair had been combed back, tight against her skull into a lank ponytail and her face was almost masculine in its absence of anywhere smooth, anywhere rounded or full.

"Get in the car, we'll give you a lift back. No point wandering 'round 'ere by yourself."

"I can't go back until I know where my son is. He's autistic; he needs me."

"All the same, we can't do anything abou' it today. Most of us 'ave lost kids, but there ain't nothing we can do today. Not till we come up with a plan."

"I don't want to go back. I can't face the house without him."

"Well," the woman turned away and went back to the waiting car, calling over her shoulder as she walked. "We got hot food, Linda's puttin' people up. You won't be by you'self." She pulled out a cigarette and lit it, leaning against the car as she smoked. "You want to make yourself ill and be no use to anyone, that's your problem."

The barren path stretched before her, just as empty as her own house would be. The bleak vista of the wall was rivalled in its absence of colour and hope only by the abstract wilderness of the side of it that she was stuck in. Denuded trees shivered in the breeze. A lone bird passed mutely overhead, free from brick boundaries but not from the absence of company, comfort. There was nothing to be amongst but resilient weeds, grown from the dust since the footfalls of construction, and an empty home, waiting like a mausoleum of all the dark things from her past, waiting to eat at her without the solace of Jack's bright presence.

"Ok, I'll come."

Gina gestured towards the interior with her open hand, as if bidding entry to a limousine.

"Put the seat down Stacey, will ya?" The driver, Stacey, leant across and pulled the lever to fold the passenger seat, allowing just enough space for Emily to squeeze into the back seats. The smell of dust and stale smoke enveloped her. It pervaded both the hot air and the fabric interior in equal measure. Outside, the woman finished her cigarette and crushed it with her foot. She exhaled out one great puff as she got in the car and closed the door with a slam.

"Good job an' all. Linda would only 'ave gone on at me for it if I'd left ya."

The car came to life again, and after making a five-point turn in the road they headed back to Shaw Hill. Emily sat in the back corner, her shoulders hunched and her fists on her lap, wishing she could rest her head. The one named Stacey navigated the quiet road south, where the rugged countryside morphed into sparse civilisation. The one who had coerced Emily into the car sat sideways with her back against the door, not hindered by a seatbelt. Her legs apart, she switched her gaze from the road to Stacey, then Emily.

"Thought I knew near everyone in Shaw Hill, but I don't recognise you."

"I've lived there for about four years now," Emily replied.

"What's your name?"

"Emily."

"Second name?" Another flash of those razor thin brows appeared in the rear-view mirror.

Emily paused, of the two names she'd used, neither was

suitable now.

"Bird," she replied, watching out the window as they passed disused buildings with shops that had been closed; the empty shell of a town that had once been the country's hub for those with money to spend.

"Haven't heard of that one; I know most of 'em."

They reached Shaw Road. From there it was a few right turns before they were in Shaw Hill. Living on its northern outskirt, Emily had never been further into the estate than the extent of her road, always turning right whenever she left the house, seeking a middle ground between them and us. It was a maze of similar streets; rows of terraced houses bearing little difference to one another, barring the state of the front garden or the peeling paint colour of the door.

She was thrown forward as Stacey hit the brakes and turned into the downwards slope of Burbank Close. A concentration of residents milled about in small groups at its end. Due to the conscription and now the evacuated children, the crowd was mostly women, interspersed with a handful of men who were older or impaired in some way.

They parked on the curb, killing the ignition and leaving the windows wound down.

Emily struggled through the narrow gap of the seats, relishing the fresh air as she stepped on to the pavement. Stacey melted into the crowd without a goodbye, yet the other one, the passenger, came to her side, a fresh cigarette between her thin lips.

"That's Linda's house, might as well meet her now." Stacey pointed to one of the terraced houses, this one with mown grass and a weathered stone fairy by the step leading up to the small porch. The sound of laughter and the loud conversation came from beyond the open door.

"I think I'll just head to my house. I need to pack some stuff up for my son," Emily replied.

"Gina? Who's this new person you've brought?" A great, booming voice came from beyond the threshold of Linda's house. A striking woman, whose bright clothes and even brighter demeanour was overshadowed by the size of her chest, presumably Linda herself, stood waiting for them, the great mound of her yellow top rising and falling with her breath.

"Who's this? Is this one you've picked up? Come in, come in darling."

Emily felt obliged to accept the invitation. Linda's large hand, embezzled in sparkly rings, cupped her shoulder as she passed. A narrow hallway opened into an antechamber of a kitchen. The smell of perspiration and cooking food filled the air. Linda cut a path to the cooker like an ice breaker, forcing those in her way to move this way and that to accommodate her body, which was as big in breadth and stature as the hearty tones it produced. She had the bustling gait of someone with much to do and not enough time to do it in and the discerning eye of one who had dealt with many a fool in that precious time.

At the stove, she checked each of the pans in turn, all bubbling on full heat. Wiping her hands on the grubby thighs of her trousers, she turned to Emily.

"I've got plenty of hot food here, casserole, veg. Plenty for everyone." Emily politely declined, her voice like a small bird trapped inside her. "What's wrong darl? I s'pose you're all shook up with what's happened. They won't be able to keep 'em, don't you think different. We won't let 'em for starters.

Don't think we will."

Emily nodded, still looking for an escape.

"Well, if you change your mind and want some food, come find me. We're gonna get everyone together and look out for each other, work out what we can do." She turned back to her cooking, her crudely coloured lips pursed.

"Thank you," Emily said. "I don't know if I'll be of much use though. I don't know anyone."

Linda stopped her stirring and set her blue lined eyes back on Emily's.

"How've you been living here and not got to know anyone? I guess not every street is like ours. Must be lonely though." She paused, thinking of probing further, but what she saw in Emily's face was enough for her to put it off for a later date.

"There're others in the living room that 've lost kids. You want me to show you there?"

"Thanks, it's ok; I'll find my own way."

She excused herself, her chest tight as the humid air of the kitchen cloyed her throat. She manoeuvred to the open front door, pressing against the cluttered edge of the kitchen just to avoid coming close to other people that had crowded in. Once outside, she turned right towards home, keeping her head down.

She'd not spotted the woman sitting atop the low wall across the road, who watched her leaving Linda's and carried on watching until she reached the crest of the hill and disappeared from view. The woman's gaze remained fixed on that point for a few minutes. A coiled strand of hair from the uncropped side of her head was blown by the will of the wind across her freckled, downy cheek.

Her keys hit the table with a brief clatter, then silence. Her only greeting was stale air and the quiet space of a vacant house. The living room was still strewn with Jack's toys, that he'd scattered just this morning. The sight served as a reminder of everything she had lost in a span of a few hours and Emily lost all tenuous control of her emotions. Finding the floor, she cried until she slept. A dull, unbearable ache in her chest would stay with her until he was back.

On waking, she gathered some essentials in a rucksack, with the last photographs she'd managed to find and Jack's favourite items: His eye mask, his weighted blanket, his soft toy dog, his earphones and his toy aeroplane.

Loud noises from outside interrupted her preparations. She went to the kitchen window that faced the street, hanging to the side so as not to be seen. A group of teenage girls were walking down the street, emitting high pitched shrieks and in evident high spirits. They laughed and jostled, one carrying a refuse bag, heavy with its contents, another wielding what looked like a piece of fencing, swinging it as if envisaging a hefty target. They passed Emily's house. Once their voices had died down and Emily's heart rate had slowed, she left the house and locked the door.

Chapter 4

Black asphalt seemed to melt away before the bonnet of Ronan's Mercedes. Galven road was straight for miles, offering little variation in surface or scenery until entry into the heart of the new Galven, set a sufficient distance away as if to mark its status as home to only the prosperous and well-bred of Merredin. A vista of various buildings, maintained parks and busy people started to appear.

He was glad to be alone, aside from the convoy of coaches behind him. At the Aid Centre, he'd dropped into the driver's seat and locked the door before any council delegate could get in. He needed solitude and quiet. His fingers drummed the steering wheel to a tune without melody. The image of Emily recurred in his thoughts with irrepressible persistence, his last vision of her haunting him like an overlay on his sight. She'd merely stood there, her eyes fixed upon his, with an intensity that he'd found thrilling, stirring. She'd held her hands by her sides in tightly clenched fists, and though her pale and slightly chapped lips had been parted as if on the verge of an outburst, she had maintained her civility, begged, yes, pleaded briefly, but not without some restraint.

He had turned away and not looked back, though he wanted

to. At the border, he'd kept his eyes fixed on the road whilst passing through the growing mass of people that were not permitted to enter, people who once the gates were shut again might lapse into a posture and expression similar to Emily's own, one of resigned desolation. Something had shifted; his resolve perhaps. She had often frequented his thoughts over the years but now he'd seen her again and she had been within his grasp, the thought of her, memory, fantasy and possibility became all consuming.

There was so much about her that set her apart from her environment and the people she'd ended up surrounded by. In that last depleted look, she possessed a kind of stoic vulnerability. She didn't belong in that crude, deprived wasteland of an estate; she knew it but would not admit it. Her decision had cost him in humiliation. Now it was she who would feel the consequences. The thought was a cheap plaster on his wounded pride.

He pulled up outside the tall, grey council building where signs stated "no parking". A small crowd of councillors were waiting by the tall double doors. Inside, as part of the recent work undertaken on the building, the old conference hall had been given a new lease of life as a space for public use, as an influx of residents now required.

Ronan stepped out of the car and signalled to the slow-moving coaches to pull in around the back of the building. The councillors watched him, expectant; he considered them little more than circus monkeys in cheap suits; yes-men in polyester.

"Is everything set up?" he asked without making eye contact. He heard a hasty "yes" from somewhere to confirm it was.

The sound of his footsteps reverberated through the large space, set out with adjacent columns of chairs that faced two tables by the platform, covered in forms and with ample room in front for queueing. What looked like a young recruit was carefully organising the papers into piles. At Ronan's approach, the man straightened and turned to face him.

"I've set them out as instructed." He added a "sir" as a precautionary afterthought. Ronan cast a glance over the forms—one to take a register of applicants and their basic details, one extensive application form and one to be completed upon receipt by those manning the operation.

His peace was brought to an abrupt end as a small television crew hauled their equipment in from outside and started to set up a base by the platform steps. The reporter was ushered in by a couple of councillor ladies. He instructed the recruit without once looking his way.

"Fix your tie and stay on the side-line." The man looked down, blinking rapidly. His slender fingers fumbled over the messy knot of his tie that had loosened and slipped down his shirt.

"Yes, of course, sir."

Ronan had settled his glare on the busy news crew. He checked his own suit and adjusted his cufflinks before taking a deep breath, plastering on his showman smile and turning around in one smooth sweep like someone about to introduce the crowd to a treat of a performance.

"Are you the lieutenant?" the female reporter asked.

"Indeed I am. Ronan. pleased to meet you."

"Rachel, likewise. Well, we're going to get set up and ready for me to do the report. It'll be shown on the evening news. There's already a crowd waiting outside."

CHAPTER 4

"That doesn't surprise me. My proposal was taken up with quite some vigour by residents as well as the Commander himself." He put that winning smile into fifth gear. "I always know I can rely on those within the Border to pull together and help in fractious times like this, no matter what's required."

The reporter nodded, her flicky brunette hair bobbing in double-time.

"Excellent, better save that for the cameras. Well, I'll leave you to it." She turned and began motioning to her cameraman. Ronan's smile took instant leave of his face as he whirled a compact three-sixty on the spot, taking in the increased level of activity in the room.

A voice called his name from the entrance.

"Shall we start letting them in?"

"Yeah, bring them all in here," he replied. From the doorway, the first wide-eyed residents began spilling into the hall.

"Make your way to the head desk please to collect your forms," he called, leaning against the stage. "Then you may start taking seats on the left-hand side."

He stepped aside, smiling at all who filed past him. There were plenty of uptakes as he expected. Nothing less would do. The television crew were panning the room for the best background shot whilst the reporter preened her hair for ultimate volume. A familiar buzzing grew in his chest. This was the atmosphere that favoured him most; when he ran the show.

Most had taken their seats and were mulling over the forms they'd been handed. He reckoned a good proportion of Galven was before him, and considering the demographics of the town, that was pretty good going.

The side door was being propped open by a woman's foot as she conversed with someone beyond his line of sight. He went to her, quietly enough that she didn't notice him.

"Caroline?"

The woman flinched and faced him, one hand flying to her chest.

"Ronan, you gave me a start."

"Do you have the evacuees ready?"

"Yes, they're all here and accounted for. We've just taken a quick register and have been having a hard time trying to settle some of the younger ones."

"What's wrong with them?"

"The evacuation has distressed them a bit. They've been crying, you know."

"Well, make sure they're cleaned up and fresh-faced for the cameras. We're going live in a few minutes.

"They'll be ready."

"Good." Then, lowering his voice, he said, "I need you to locate one in particular and set him aside. His name is Jack Blake. Keep him next to you when we take them in. I'm going to need him during my speech."

"Ok." Caroline's brow was furrowed but Ronan cut her off before she could act on her curiosity.

"Get organised and bring them in."

As the children entered the room to take the vacant seats at the front, Ronan stood on the stage and watched as everything came together. Many of the children came in simpering and blubbering, but quietened when they saw the multitude of sympathetic eyes on them. He waited for them all to be seated and for the volume to drop, then just paused for a fraction longer so that people would begin to watch him in anticipation. The cameras were ready.

"Hello everyone." His hands clapped together with a loud smack. He surveyed his audience. "Thank you all for coming. You once again show us how generous the residents of New Galven are when called upon. In just a short amount of time, we will be selecting a group of you at a time to find your allocated evacuee. It means a great deal to the Galven council, and I'm sure, the families of these children that you are willing to offer safety and care as a break from their deprived upbringing in the most destitute area of our Island. Once you have your evacuee, you will just need to complete one final short form and collect your personal information documents. Your evacuee will come with a new yellow identification card that will temporarily replace their brown one, courtesy of the council. If you have any questions, please direct them to the lovely Caroline." He gestured to where Caroline sat, her cheeks flushing.

A collective murmur sprung from the crowd, assuming he had concluded. He raised his eyebrows at Caroline who jabbed her finger towards the small boy hunched in the adjacent seat.

"Before we begin," his voice boomed across the hall, silencing the crowd, before he finished softly and paused, garnering their focus. "I'd like to christen the proceedings as it were, being a product of my own initiative, by doing my bit to help. I'm going to take in young evacuee Jack." He spread his palms and the crowd craned their necks to see Caroline ushering the timid boy from his seat and into the aisle. There was applause as he stumbled up the steps to the stage and walked to Ronan's side with his hands bunched on either side and his knees knocking into each other, Caroline's gentle encouragement becoming a pushing hand in the small of his back. Ronan rested his left hand lightly across the boy's slight shoulders, which tensed at his touch.

"This boy's mother is an acquaintance of mine, and I know she'll be extremely grateful to find out I'm ready to offer young Jack the safety she cannot provide due to her disadvantageous circumstances at this time. Now, please begin." He turned towards the camera crew, holding his position and exposing his white teeth for the photos. In front of him, the officers began to organise the residents and take on the challenge of assigning every child a new home. Ronan looked down at Jack.

"Hello Jack, I expect you'd like a chance to rest after all this excitement. I should think we can find a little space for you to relax while I oversee what's happening here, then we can get you to my house, yes?"

Jack didn't reply. He was not even looking at Ronan, instead just shifting from one foot to another and fiddling with his hands. Ronan led him, still smiling, to the back of the stage where a small room sat unlocked. Inside was a stack of chairs against the wall and one solitary chair next to it.

"Here we are. You have a little quiet time in here and I'll come and collect you as soon as I'm ready to go." Jack watched the strange man's mouth.. His fingers stroked the dimpled plastic of the chair. Ronan left and closed the door, leaving Jack to study the manila paint and wait for his return.

When the door finally reopened, Jack took his hands away from his eyes and got to his feet. In the car, he hid his face within his folded arms and began to cry. The radio was off, and in the absence of any other noise, the muffled simpering of the boy was a distraction. Ronan glanced at the forlorn figure of the child in his rear-view mirror.

"I take it you're missing your mother?" There were only some abject sniffs in reply. His grip flexed tighter against the steering wheel.

"Don't want to talk?" He took his eyes off the road again, surveying Emily's only son, swamped in the black leather of the back seats. Jack quietened, hiding his face. Once again, Ronan could settle into the steady rumble of the road, the passing greens and greys.

"Suits me."

He parked outside his house; double oak doors were flanked with hanging baskets and some stone rabbit ornaments that Grace had bought on a whim. He opened the passenger door and crossed the neat paving to the door, assuming the child trailed behind him. Jack came to a stop on the threshold, his dishevelled hair and sodden eyes owing him a certain pitiful quality. This was the largest house he'd ever been to.

"Grace?" Ronan shouted, making Jack flinch. "Grace, come here, it's important." The sound of hurried footsteps came from the far end of the house. Within a few moments, Grace reached them, appearing to Jack like a vision, adorning a paisley dress and an apron bearing cartoon animals across its front. She stopped a few metres away in the bright hallway, taking in the sight of Jack with an expression of shocked and cautious delight. Ronan was making a snapping noise with his fingers against the keys in his palm.

"Sort him out will you please? Give him some food or something."

Grace went straight to him, wiping her hands across her apron to dry them and smiling as she crouched to his level.

"Is he here to stay?" she asked.

"Yes, for a while anyway. He's one of the evacuees."

"Evacuees? From where?"

"Turn on the news Grace. There's a world outside the house you know."

Grace dropped her eyes back to the boy's face. She raised a hand to touch him but he pulled away, staring into the space around her. She resisted the urge to take him in her arms, press his hair to her face.

"What's his name?"

Ronan was shuffling through the mail left on the oak side table.

"Jack. I expect you'll be able to handle him."

"Absolutely," she replied in a soft voice. "Would you like to help me in the kitchen, Jack? We can find you something nice to eat." She went to wipe one of his tear-grubbed cheeks but stopped herself, sensing his discomfort at her closeness. She stood, ready to lead him, but was stopped by the rough press of Ronan's hand on her shoulder.

"I've got to attend a meeting but I should be back sometime this evening."

Grace nodded; her mind was preoccupied with the thought of small fingers clutching her own. He leant in and kissed her, one hand turning her face to his, the other against her back, preventing her from pulling away. He let her go.

Ronan adjusted his tie and knocked on the dark wood of Marsh's office door, beneath the plaque that read Commander in gold lettering. It was meant to be Marsh's private space for work and rumination but had recently begun serving as the meeting room for council members; whether due to some misallocation or Marsh's reluctance to move from his chair. A gruff voice called for him to enter and he stepped inside, noting that he was the last to arrive.

Marsh sat at his broad, cherry oak desk, reclined deep in his leather seat, moulded around his backside from years of use. Behind him, the closed blinds blocked all the natural light from the dark green panelled room. He looked on impassively as Ronan perched on a quilted barstool to his right.

"Good for you to join us, Ronan," Marsh said, crossing his hands across his stomach in contentment. His cheeks were flushed redder than their usual scarlet, given by the roadmap of burst capillaries scattering his nose and cheeks. The scotch cabinet door had been left ajar. "Had to make a diversion?"

"Yes, I had to drop the boy off at the house. Grace took him in."

"Playing your part as it were, I saw," Marsh spoke with a smile. Ronan squinted, looking away. Terry and Gaz sat on Marsh's left, looking disinterested. Kyle was propped forwards in his seat.

"That did take me by surprise. You don't strike me as the paternal type," Kyle said with some amusement.

"Grace will take care of the kid, probably made her day," Marsh said.

"True."

"Moving on, we need to discuss our next actions," Ronan said. Marsh let out a long, weary sigh and reached to sift through the notes atop his desk. He thumbed through them at his own pace.

"Well," he began, "the initial stage of the evacuee operation has been seen through successfully, many thanks to your innovation and input on that Ronan. I'm told there was some disturbance from the Shaw side today at the gates, but the new border is secure and should be sufficient enough to keep out any wayward…" He gesticulated with his hands… "wayward undesirables, shall we say? So, with that taken care of, Kyle tells me the uptake in houses is good, that just leaves the threat of Nemico to contend with. I'm happy with the newly implemented defence structure. It means we can finally offer the level of protection advertised to our residents; that's what they're paying for." Ronan caught his eye with a stern expression. "Well, I need to take in the most recent reports but being optimistic I think we can sleep fairly soundly for the time being, ensure this transition period goes smoothly and form a plan of action that puts Galven's interests at the forefront," he finished, looking pleased with himself. All except Ronan made noises of approval.

"I'm just putting together the full report now," Kyle said. "All the new properties have been taken, with the last few going to the highest bidder, some for as much as almost a million. I can tell you already that the revenue has been significant."

"Excellent, Kyle. Good job on that."

"Sir, are you forgetting there is a war on?" Ronan's voice cut through the jovial atmosphere with his deep, no-nonsense tone.

"That's a strange question to ask. Of course, what of it?"

"Well, I would think it inadvisable to opt for complacency in such circumstances. There's a good reason I've just spent the day evacuating children into New Galven."

Marsh looked sincere. Terry discreetly checked his phone.

"Yes, I'm aware. It's not that I'm being complacent, more so that when I consider the sum of funding, which has been put into our new defence system, I expect it to be up to scratch."

"I've only had a chance to skim read the update that Couldry sent today, but just from that, I know that we remain under significant threat. It's not something we can just leave to chance."

"It will be handled; I assure you all." Marsh made a movement akin to a leg slap, but his hand merely flip-flopped limply against his ample thigh like the last exertion of a fish on land.

"I'd like to discuss it further with you, make sure every option has been considered."

"Yes, yes," his hand stayed on his thigh. "I want to ensure we maintain the prosperity of our new town. The morale of our citizens is in many ways as important as high walls and big guns, and with all the recent upheaval, I think a period of calm would do us all some good."

For the next twenty minutes, Ronan waited whilst the others engaged in a flaccid discussion about community spirit that wasn't in the least stimulating. Essentially it boiled down to distraction; nothing like the guise of a party and some mindless frivolity to make people forget there were a growing number of outsiders baying for their privileged blood.

His thoughts ran amok, turning to Emily against his will like a petulant child. He might manage to dispel them with momentary distractions but she would return on replay; the dewy pallor of her skin, her broken nails and dreamy artistic eye.

The meeting came to an end in a typical self-congratulatory fashion. Terry and Gaz were at the door before Kyle had finished speaking. Ronan hung back as they left, his eyes boring into Marsh as the Commander sank back into the musty leather and let his fingertips trail, unseen, over the brass knob of his liquor draw. He was unsurprised to see Ronan remain. He often encroached on his personal time.

"You've not got that report on you now, have you? I'd like to call it a night."

"No sir."

"What's the issue then?" Marsh spoke like a parent with a forever minor ailing child. Ronan began to pace.

"It may seem like I keep pressing you on this, but I don't do it for my own interests. If we don't address this now and get it under hand, then by next year the chance will be gone and we'll be facing a problem far greater than one we can solve at present."

"Are you still referring to the war? I thought we addressed that. It's a discussion for council meetings in any case."

"I'm referring to those in Shaw Hill, of which a growing number are now wishing to challenge the council and potentially bring us harm, even overthrow us. You might laugh at that but it's a potential menace if things get out of hand. There's an undeniable threat there that we'd be foolish to overlook." Marsh raised an untidy eyebrow as Ronan took a breath. "If you had seen it over there today at the border... These people are angry, violent, beyond any means of civilised reasoning. If an attack were to happen in the coming weeks, it would be a tragedy of course, but an expected one. People are anticipating it. The children are safe. If there was a hit on Shaw Hill then our citizens would be reassured that no children had been harmed and feel relief that they have moved to an area of safety, that the cost was justified. It would be a flash in the pan that would not only eliminate the threat but also reinforce our position amongst New Galven citizens."

"But we can't control when and where Nemico hits, even if

we wanted to," Marsh said.

He thumbed through a cluster of papers as Ronan watched and waited. He settled on the one he wanted, skimming over a summary of a previous emergency council meeting.

"The last actual, legitimate attack was over a year ago now and that was off the coast."

"But we're expecting—"

"I know that we're expecting a hit, but as I said, we don't know when or where that may happen," he stated gravely, settling his calm and heavy-lidded eyes on Ronan.

"Sir, it is possible that a hit does not have to be left to chance and out of our control. It can be orchestrated if the threat is great enough; if the result is worth the personal price that on every other account is the cost of war. I am willing to take the burden on myself if you agree."

"Surely you can't be serious about what you're inferring?"

"I just want to lay every option on the table. From the things being said, and what I have seen, I can assure you that a group of them, mobilised, might challenge our right to exist and I don't want to see that happen."

"Rumours Ronan, you shouldn't pay credence to them."

Ronan leant back against the oak sideboard, one hand in his pocket.

"And when they infiltrate our new town? Take families hostage? They speak only in a language of fists and blood," he said, dropping his shoulders even though his jaw remained clenched. "Is that the kind of settled calm and high morale you want?"

Marsh poured himself some bourbon, studying the golden stream as it decanted into the used glass.

"Listen. I know I may make a comment or two when the

drink is flowing." He frowned. "I vaguely recall a conversation we had, and I might have said something offhand about those people but I don't wish them death." He tried to laugh but it came out as a chesty cough on the first inhale. "When under the influence, it's easy to find simple, if nihilistic solutions. You're overworked, Ronan. You've done a great job today, but you need to shut off your creative mind and take the proper channels." Ronan saw the marbled underside of the glass as Marsh took in a hearty sip of its contents. "Lucky for you, I understand your thought process; you're just very overzealous at times."

"Your understanding is the reason I thought we might be on the same page."

"Not tonight Ronan. Not on this one." He finished speaking and let his eyes close, savouring the trace of alcohol on his tongue. He heard the door click shut.

Chapter 5

The pervasive wail of three-year-old Kaden cut through the house with desperate need. "Mum. Mu-um. Mum!" The target of his plea was sat at the kitchen table, her face turned away from him and held within her hands. He approached her and placed his hand on her knee, trying to see her face. "Mummy, I'm hungry. Breakfast please."

His big sister Sarah descended the stairs.

"Come over here Kaden, mummy's not feeling well." She led him away and opened one of the cupboards.

"There's not enough to do breakfast," Helen croaked through her fingertips. "I was relying on the next lot of vouchers, and now they've stopped." A spatter of dry sobs broke free from her throat like choked gasps before she stopped herself, clutching at her neck with brittle fingernails.

"It's ok mum, I didn't want breakfast today anyway. I'm not hungry," Sarah lied. She took the light packet of cereal that Kaden was reaching for, mostly air, and prepared a small bowl for him, sitting him down with a spoon. Her hands knotted against her stomach as she watched him. "We should go out today," she said to her mother. "There might be some news at the Aid Centre or someone who can help us."

"Oh I doubt it, there's so many in need of help." Helen's mind tarnished all hopeful thoughts. To her, help was something that happened to others; it wasn't something she could rely on. She looked at her daughter's seeking eyes. On her other side, Kaden tipped the bowl in search of milk.

"We'll go for a walk. Maybe there's something."

The Aid Centre offered only previously circulated bulletins and long-standing public notices, showing signs of age. She had spent more time in the playground watching Sarah and Kaden play than trying to find a solution to their problem. Kaden was now restrained in his buggy after exerting himself on the slide, his head lolling drowsily as they approached Ise Hill. Ahead of them, a trio of teenage girls appeared from the footpath leading to the private estate. Helen's heart rate rose as they came closer. Although they showed no interest, they were loud and boisterous, passing round items from a carrier bag to inspect. Sarah nudged her arm.

"Mum, they've got food," she whispered. Helen stopped as they passed, feigning interest in the basket of the pushchair. The girls were giggling together in bursts. Helen looked from her bent over position to see what they were holding and saw the gleam of a tin, the clear wrapping of cellophane. She straightened, steering the pushchair towards the kerb. "Did you see it? Do you think they got it from the posh houses?"

"I don't know Sarah. Who knows?"

"Shouldn't we go and see for ourselves?"

"I doubt it's just out for free and we won't steal."

"But there are lots of empty ones now. It's not really stealing if it's going to waste."

Helen's mouth tightened in a grimace. It was far from her

comfort zone, going anywhere new. "Let's go, please, quickly," Sarah persisted. "Kaden's going to need food again soon."

"We can have a look," Helen said, repositioning the buggy with a sigh

They walked the remainder of Shaw Road and turned left onto Ise hill, where the low terraces came to an end and tall houses with pointed roofs sprung up, with lush green areas of their own. A lot of them were empty; curtains drawn and for sale boards, some still standing or marooned on garden lawns. There were signs of looting too; open doors, the innards jumbled up and stripped of their valuables.

Kaden had quit his mewling and was quiet in his buggy, studying the new landscape. Sarah slipped ahead and walked with purposeful strides, taking a measured view of each property in turn. She darted across a garden and ran towards the door of a large detached house.

"Sarah wait!" Helen called. Sarah was pressing the doorbell, peeking through the frosted glass pane.

"I'm just having a look," she replied. Helen struggled to get the buggy across the gravel of the driveway, the small wheels wishing to avoid the paving and instead twisting and jamming in the loose stones. When she looked up, Sarah had disappeared through the side gate.

"Sarah?" she called as she hurried to follow.

"There's a backdoor into the kitchen, and it's unlocked," Sarah called.

She caught a glance of Sarah's triumphant expression, not able to stop her in time.

"We shouldn't go inside. Sarah, it's not our house." But her daughter was already inside. Within three cautious steps, she entered a stranger's kitchen with Kaden scooped up onto her hip.

Upstairs, Fiona lay in a deep sleep. She was fully dressed, spread across the crumpled sheets. She stirred for the first time in four hours, as yet unaware of the intruders downstairs. The night had been long, and she'd not had any restful sleep. She'd spent the late evening and early hours pressed against the upstairs windows, her body on high alert after hearing a raucous group of young people prowling the street. They'd broken into her neighbour's houses, leaving with a variety of bulging refuse sacks.

If it came to having to defend herself, she was both unprepared and unarmed. That power and strength she had exerted over Stuart was a distant memory, anger replaced by a rational fear. A quick root through Stu's stuff yielded one of his old golf clubs. He'd purchased a set years ago when some of his colleagues had taken up golf and it had been catching on, invites passing freely. Mistaking his wife's nonchalance for approval he had splurged on a mid-range set of clubs to use; but when his incessant talk of plans came to any sign of fruition, Fiona made her disapproval clear. It would be selfish of him. What chance would she have to do the same? What reckless spending on some far-fetched fantasy. The clubs were retired to Stu's tat cupboard, and after a couple of declined offers to join them, the invites ceased.

The club was a weapon, a fraction of reassurance. After waiting for what seemed like hours, she succumbed to the sleep her body craved, and only now did she twitch. Her easy breathing stalled at the sound of strange voices from the stairwell. The intruders were here.

CHAPTER 5

In the stairwell, Helen paused, unwilling to go further. Her moral compass was awry and it burdened her. Downstairs, Sarah had rushed ahead to explore. She had looked into every room on the ground floor before Helen had even crossed the conservatory. They'd filled up a plastic bag with food from the cupboards, Helen picking over items with a fretful expression, Sarah bundling in everything she saw and adding to the haul with a coat, two scarves and a book. Helen had caught her daughter admiring a pair of beautiful, soft stitched cushions, her fingers tracing delicately along their surface.

"For my bedroom?" she asked. Helen answered with a slight shake of her head and Sarah turned away, leaving them. You could have nought to show in this world, but if you had your values and more than a scrap of virtue then it was something to be proud of. That said, where the end justifies the means then needs must.

It was Sarah who'd suggested they pop upstairs and get toiletries and toothpaste. Helen's forehead had further creased but she couldn't deny that they needed them. She looked down and underwent an internal panic at the sight of her grubby shoes on the plush, cream carpet. Realising there was no host to apologise to, she continued her ascent, Kaden still resting on her generous hip. Sarah slipped past and began thundering up the steps.

"Sarah, stop," she hissed. "Let me go in front."

"Why?"

"I want to go first, just in case there's anyone up there." Sarah pressed herself flat against the wall to let her mum pass.

"We would have seen them by now."

Helen shushed her. Upstairs, they faced a number of closed doors. A cute, vintage sign indicated the bathroom. Keeping

Sarah close to her, she entered the bathroom and started picking up an assortment of shampoos, soap and toothpaste before feeling a small hand tug the back of her top.

"Can you help me hold the bag please?" she asked.

There was no reply. When she turned around, a tall, red haired woman in a state of disarray was filling the doorway. She held a golf club, slightly raised, watching them with a tremulous lower lip.

"You're in my house," the woman said, raising the club higher as she spoke. Helen put Kaden down on the floor behind her, next to Sarah, to a chorus of indignant cries. Now her hands were free, she offered them palms forward, part defence, part surrender.

"We thought all the houses were empty, we wouldn't have come if we'd known you were here. We're just trying to get supplies," she paused, gauging the woman's reaction. "They've stopped the vouchers. We were desperate."

Fiona's eyes flickered to Kaden and Sarah, who looked back at her with forlorn faces. She lowered the club, but her grip remained tight.

"I'll show you out," Fiona said, stepping clear of the door so they could exit. The four of them made a solemn procession across the hallway and down the stairs. The bag with their ill-gotten gains lay on the bathroom tiles where Helen had dropped it. She thought of all those items she so lacked and so desired. Every step took them further away. In the hall, Fiona made an abrupt halt by the door. Helen dipped her head in thanks and ushered her children towards it.

"Would you be interested in staying for a meal? I need to cook anyway, and I'd appreciate some company," Fiona said with a particular terseness. Having said it out loud, she was suddenly desperate for them to stay. Helen glanced down at her children.

"If you're sure you don't mind then that would be very kind, thank you."

The bag was retrieved from the bathroom floor and the kitchen cupboards hastily replenished. Fiona put together some tinned meatballs and pasta, topping it with the remainder of some grated cheese. It was the first meal she'd had in days, unwilling to deplete her staling stock. They ate at the dining table in the corner of the kitchen, exchanging stilted conversation between tepid mouthfuls. Fiona's voice turned curt at the mention of Shaw Hill when Helen answered an inquiry into where she lived.

"I don't know it," Fiona said, studying her food. When gentle probing turned to her own situation, she was more engaging. "If it wasn't for my husband's tragic accident, you would almost certainly have been free to clear the house without interruption. There's no way we'd have still been here. I used to have my only son here, living with me. But they insisted he offer his skills to the military campaign. I told him not to fret. I can cope fine by myself. I just miss some human interaction on occasion."

Time slipped by and when the table was cleared, the day was drawing to its eve. On an impulse of generosity, Fiona had packed a small bag for Helen to take, adding a few extras from the bathroom. Helen placed it by the door and told the kids to put their shoes on whilst she nipped to use the bathroom.

She was drying her hands when a violent bang punctured the previous quiet of the house. She flung open the door and raced down the stairs, cursing herself for having left the children. Fiona stood in the hallway, Sarah and Kaden umbrella'd under her fanning arms. She hissed at Helen, her face pale.

"They're here, they've got in!"

Helen didn't understand. She was about to speak when a clatter came from the kitchen. Incoherent voices followed. The four of them stood frozen in the hallway with indecision. Kaden had discarded the club in the living room. He began making a slight mewling noise, picking up on the tension. In reply, the heavy tread of feet approached them and from the kitchen appeared a group of three teenagers, one male and two girls with an excitable countenance.

Fiona sprung forward to pick up an empty shoe rack, waving it in their vague direction.

"All of you, out! As you can see, this house is not vacant. This is my property and if you try to harm me, my very well built and well-connected son will ensure there are severe repercussions."

Distracted by the erratic movements of the woman, it was a minute before the boy's gaze had a chance to settle on Helen, who was watching Fiona with a kind of startled rapture. His face relaxed in recognition and he lowered the arm holding his sack.

"Hey Helen, you know this woman?"

"She gave us dinner, me and the kids."

Fiona stepped back and a kind of shadow darkened her eyes. There was a new defensiveness in her posture.

"Should've just come and knocked if you're short on food. Linda's cooking enough for everyone that needs it every day, and we're all puttin' in to help each other. We got a set up down Burbank."

CHAPTER 5

"Can you all get out of my house, and stay out," Fiona interjected, her voice low and threatening. "I don't know who you people think you are, but I expect to be able to live here in my home without vandals breaking in and disrespecting my property and me."

Sarah gathered her children close and backed up towards the door. Jordy and the girls shuffled their feet in the same direction with some reluctance.

"Sorry," Helen said. "If you're worried about safety or want some food then I'm sure Linda would help you too."

"There's a few that came from round here," Jordy said.

"You think I have no money?" Fiona said, her voice verging on hysterical. Helen was reaching for the door handle with one hand. "You think I belong with you people? Do I look like I do? I'm only here to honour the memories of my husband and I'm keeping my son's home ready for his return. I don't need your charity." She laughed, her eyes remaining wide and alarmed, the result was unerring. "People like me don't belong in Shaw Hill."

Helen let herself out, her eyes downcast, mumbling an apology. Jordy rolled his eyes. The girls were more occupied with rolling their cigarettes than listening to what the woman had to say.

"What a bitch," he muttered, scuffing the gravel with his trainers.

Chapter 6

The evening stretched ahead like the spread of a grey gull's wing. Not long ago, it had been her favourite time of day to take her camera outside and experiment. Now, without her camera or a reason to be home, and unable to bear Jack's absence, Emily was left to wander the maze of quiet streets. The disparity between areas, with only a road in between, was like a divide of sedimentary layers. Large, fancy houses with their big driveways and swanky adornments were a stark contrast to the sprawl of monotonous dwellings of the Shaw estate, where people's lives spilled out of their houses and aesthetics were a mere idea. It wasn't home. When Noel had lived with them, she might have touched upon the sentiment, but she was not rooted anymore, a flower tossed into weeds.

The newly named base, a word perhaps of aspiration rather than function, was alive with activity and the hum of conversing people. It was inevitable that she was drawn there again, as if she had any other option. Ronan still would not respond to her messages and calls.

The slope of Burbank close ended in a turning circle of patchy tarmac and unkempt grass. She saw the rise of smoke from a crude pyre set up in its centre, assembled with tossed wood and rubbish. Gathered around it on a jumble of mismatched kitchen chairs and upturned boxes, sat small huddles of people. She wandered towards them, careful not to lock eyes with anyone until she was at the outer edge of the assembled residents, close enough to catch drifts of the conversation that was passing around the fire. She'd hoped to remain on the fringe, but a man departing middle age, sporting a sparse sprouting of hair and sitting squat like on a low plastic crate, noticed her shadow and motioned to the vacant chair at his side, shifting away from it as he did so. Unable to decline his eager gesturing, Emily took a seat. She tried to tune in to the speaker.

"Surely, it's just a matter of sitting tight, getting by with what we have until we get a better idea of what's going to happen long term?" spoke an antiquated woman, grey hair, grey clothes, even greyish skin, from the right end of the group.

"I'm sure that's what they'd want us to do," said a cynical voice from one of the multitudes of shadowed faces. "Not sure I can handle sitting around, hoping we don't get bombed and that the council might stick to their promises for the first time in our lifetime."

"And say we cause a nuisance, make some noise, what good would it do? They're providing us with rations to live on. We need to be smart about this and make the best of a bad, hopefully, temporary situation without giving them a reason to cut us off entirely," said a man astride a mobility scooter. People around him made thoughtful, concurring noises.

"Looked like they were clearing out the place, last I saw. I wouldn't be so hopeful about the ration packs being delivered for much longer," said a young woman with her hair cropped on one side. She was kneading her knuckles, leant forward in her chair.

"I reckon Raine's right; they've got us by the neck. Without those ration packs or vouchers, we're screwed, and they know that," Linda said, standing near the centre. Thoughtful silence followed her words except for the dissent of a muffled snigger that emerged from beside her. Emily looked to her left and saw a tense looking woman with flame red, rather bedraggled looking hair and oversized sunglasses. Linda continued undeterred.

"They've lied to us in the past. Who's to say they won't do us over again? I reckon, smart thing to do would be to take 'em on or at least be ready to. Let 'em know we're willing to. I'm not talking guns blazin', riotin' and what have you," her gaze lingered on an animated bunch of teenage girls, "but sod waiting 'round to let them decide what happens to us, like they'd care if we starve or suffer."

"Goodness, it's almost like a terrible nightmare, isn't it," the red-haired woman on her left muttered to the man who had offered a seat. Her accent was clipped and indicated attendance at a better school than anyone here had been within a mile of. She addressed the man's jacket rather than his face, but he lit up with a keen smile, his jowls moving alarmingly in the waning yellow light as he replied.

"Oh, I'm not so sure. I mean, I've lost my car and my house is barely habitable, but I don't have to worry about clocking in to work and dealing with accounts. Plus I reckon a bit of rationing will be of benefit to my waistline." He took a breath. "It's all a bit of an adventure isn't it, that's the way I look at it. A chance to reinvent yourself and see what you're made of."

The woman raised her chin and looked upon him with a

humourless, thin lipped smile.

"It will certainly be an adventure when there's not enough food for us all and civilisation is a mere memory." Her entire manner was aloof, but she leaned a fraction closer to her new acquaintance.

"There's already a group of us," Raine spoke again. "If we could get some more people together and start to get organised, it may well open up more options. At the very least it may mean that the council will take us seriously."

"Well let's get the basics sorted first," Linda said. "The ration packs we received this morning, in addition to the existing stocks and what's being offered and gathered, are enough to keep us going for now. I think we're all in agreement that we're safest sticking together and it's the easiest way to make sure everyone is getting by. I'll be serving communal meals twice a day from my house. Sleeping arrangements are down to preference, but if anyone's wantin' a bed or anythin' then you come to me and I'll get it sorted for you. Hopefully, we'll get some news soon; I know a lot of you are missing young'uns," she trailed off, looking unsure how to conclude. "We'll pull through," she surmised, looking on the verge of expanding on the sentiment but the moment passed and people looked inwards to their own quiet reflection.

Subdued conversation sprung up from the small huddles of friends and family. Emily was startled by the sight of the bulky man shifting towards her in his chair, but he was just fumbling for a tissue, angling his body to gain access to his back pocket and handing the retrieved tissue to the well-bred woman, who had dissolved into ungainly tears. By accident, she locked eyes with the one named Raine and quickly looked away. She stood and left the heat of the fire and the commotion of converged people behind, walking a wavering line to one of the wilting patches of grass that lined the pavements.

Where was he now? Jack. Needing her, wanting her? As much as she needed him or more? Nobody else had shared the same history that they had, learning painful lessons that had forged each's understanding of the other. They wouldn't understand.

It was going to be a long night.

Chapter 7

He watched with wide, curious eyes. The pencil meeting paper, its soft lead tip touching the fine white surface of the sheet; a line, marking the shape of a long, slender ear. She could hear the whisper of his breath by her side and smiled as the rabbit came to form on the page.

"Do you like rabbits?" Grace asked. Jack didn't reply. They were sitting in the dining room at the table next to the plush ivory curtains. Grace never sat in there without reason, preferring the close familiarity of her room to the cold, open space of the downstairs, where Ronan prowled the recesses; but today she was more than comfortable here, happy even. She had brought down her artist's pad and her finest drawing pencils. Jack had crushed and stubbed them on the paper with his clumsy grip but she didn't mind. She drew the rabbit's surroundings, the tree it sought shelter beneath and the soft grass around its paws. She smiled at Jack. "Maybe his name is Jack too?" Jack jumped off his chair and went to stand behind the curtains. There had been no tears since the morning. Hopefully, the worst was over now.

Footsteps approached, echoing off the white, characterless walls.

"There you are," Ronan said. Grace kept her eyes on the paper. "There's not much time. We need to leave in twenty minutes."

"Where are we going?"

Ronan huffed in exasperation. "I told you yesterday. The council is putting on a celebration for the evacuee kids, making it positive, you know. There's going to be rides and games and stuff." He smoothed down his shirt and patted the pockets of his grey slim fit suit trousers before adjusting his cufflinks.

"I'd rather stay here. Jack's still settling in, he needs time."

"He needs to actually get some sleep tonight, that's what. I'm not suffering another night of his crying," he said as he went to the kitchen. She could hear him fumbling around the countertop looking for something. He returned, checking his phone.

"Think about how it would reflect on me if you don't show up. The boy will be fine; there'll be other kids for him to play with and your father will be there as well." His gaze switched to her face.

"Well, that's not exactly a surprise."

"Get changed into something nice. That blue dress you've got would look good if you put your hair down. You've got fifteen minutes before we're getting into the car."

Upstairs, in an act of small rebellion, Grace pulled on one of her favourite paisley dresses that Ronan had dismissed as an unflattering smock. She was pulling a brush through her hair when Jack edged in through the bedroom door.

"Are you ok?" she asked. "We have to go in the car and see some people. There'll be fun stuff there." Jack covered his ears with both hands. His expression threatened another meltdown. She went to him, reaching for his shoulder, but he turned away.

"Car!" Ronan shouted from downstairs.

The market square was busy with the sound of late summer entertainment. Well-dressed residents were gathered on the white flagstones lined with upmarket cafes and boutiques. A selection of children's rides and stalls had been put on by the volunteer committee. The rides were enjoying busy queues. The whole town had come out for the proceedings and was milling around soaking up the sun. Ronan parked on the double yellow lines, council privileges and headed off at a brisk walk to meet his colleagues. Grace kept Jack close to her, leading him to the bright, noisy environment of the market.

"Do you want to look at the rides?" His mouth remained shut, but his eyes were wide and staring. Was it fear or wonder? She wished she had a way to look inside his mind, understand what he would not say and wrap herself around his unspoken pain. They dawdled past the various amusements. Jack refrained from the excited squeals and screams that the other kids were full of. Perhaps, catching his sadness, Grace couldn't help but feel detached from the happy people around her enjoying their day. But still, Jack's small warmth at her side kept her going.

They came to the carousel. Its bright, fairground music and glossy horses with ornate gold trim had drawn a host of families to enjoy its loud and colourful entertainment. Amongst the crowd, Grace could pick out a handful of children she guessed were also evacuees—they possessed a kind of lost and found dejection, unable to clear the clouds from their countenance.

"Do you want to go on the carousel, Jack? Ride a horse with me?" Jack turned away; his body bunched like a coil. "Jack?" He put his hands over his ears, twisting his body and squeezing his eyes shut.

She moved him away. They stopped by a small hook-a-duck game where stuffed toys hung above the floating yellow ducks.

"Jack, look. They have rabbits, fluffy ones."

He peeked through his fingers and studied the soft rabbits hung up as prizes.

"Do you want to try and win one?"

"Two pounds for three goes," the trader said. She dug out some coins and paid him, taking up one of the sticks with a hook at its end.

"Jack? Take hold of this, look."

He wrapped his fingers around the stick and with her help, aimed it at the floating ducks. But every time he tried to hook one, the duck bobbed away, and after a couple of tries, he let go.

"What's wrong? Try again with me, look," Grace said. But he was covering his ears again and his expression threatened tears. She straightened.

"How much for a rabbit?"

The trader pulled one from the display.

"Ten pounds."

She passed him the money and pressed the rabbit's soft fur against Jack's cheek.

"Here you go," she said. He took it in his arms and let her lead him away from the loud rides, rounding back to the north end of the square where Ronan and the other council members were gathered by the microphones and cameras.

Ronan clocked her from ten yards away and plastered on his public smile. He groped for her with an outstretched hand and placed a rough kiss on her cheek.

"Did Jack enjoy the fair?"

"Not really. Can't I take him home? I don't think he likes the noise." she replied, but Ronan was already looking the other way.

"Commander!" he called. "Here's the boy. Grace has been taking good care of him." The fulsome form of Commander Marsh appeared from behind the other officers, the wide girth of his midsection preceding the rest of his appearance.

"Of course she has. I wouldn't expect anything less." His voice carried across the entire raised space. He took her in a brief but enthusiastic embrace, before turning his focus on Jack, leaning forwards to study him. "He's a fine lad," he exclaimed. "I imagine it's been quite difficult having so much to take in all at once. You're in a safe place now though." He straightened with an audible crick in his knees. "He's not been any trouble for you, I assume?" His eyes flickered to Grace's belly and his mind alighted on the thing they did not speak about.

"None at all. He's a pleasure to have around."

"I should bet you're rather glad for the company," he said, glancing at Ronan's back who was now occupied with adjusting the microphone piece. Grace lowered her voice.

"Is this going to take much longer, dad? I'd rather be at home and give Jack the chance to settle in."

Marsh's brow furrowed. The remaining members of the council and their families convalesced around the newly assembled speaker's platform behind Ronan, who had moved on to directing the cameramen.

"Is everything alright?" he asked, but Ronan interrupted.

"Grace? What's wrong with him?"

Grace looked down and saw Jack was no longer standing next to her but had wandered behind the cameras. He was covering his ears again and twisting his upper body, squeezing his eyes shut like he wished to shut out all light. She went to him and picked up his rabbit from the ground. She started to guide him back, taking his slender hands into hers.

"Sort him out, will you? You need to stand with the others."

"Ronan? We're ready," one of the camera crew said.

"Attention, everyone," Ronan said, leaning towards the mouthpiece. "Could you all gather round please? I'd like to occupy just a few minutes of your time."

The residents began to drift closer, forming an audience. Terry, Gareth and Kyle stood next to Marsh on his left. Grace and Jack shuffled to his right to stand with the wives and their token evacuees in a neat line.

"It's not for long, Jack, ok? Just stay here with me."

Grace was next to Rosie, Kyle's wife. They knew each other from previous appearances as extensions of the council. On Rosie's other side stood Melissa and Dawn. All three had their nominal evacuee child propped in front of them. Grace could feel a nervous energy coming from Jack. His hands were over his ears again, pressing against the side of his head as though he had something he desperately needed to keep in.

Ronan cleared his throat.

"Welcome everyone, and thank you for coming."

Marsh stepped in front of the mic. Ronan dropped back just a fraction behind Marsh's shoulder.

"Firstly, thank you all for turning out today," Marsh began.

"We've been lucky enough to enjoy some sunshine and it's great to see so many people out enjoying themselves despite the circumstances of late. What this really is, ladies and gentleman, it is a celebration—a celebration of our safety, prosperity, and the good fortune to be able to extend that to the most vulnerable in our society."

"Would you believe," Rosie said in lowered tones to Melissa, "when Kyle first brought ours home you could positively *see* the head lice jumping off his scalp. It was quite disgusting."

"I have been overwhelmed, as I always am, by both the willingness and generosity of you all in coming forward and taking in these children," Marsh continued. "And together, helping to offer invaluable security and care for those who have had a difficult start in life."

"I got through two bottles getting rid of them, two! It makes my skin crawl now just remembering it," Rosie said. The slight boy of around seven who stood in front of her, reached a hand to his hair to scratch in sympathy. Rosie's sharp eyes jumped to him with startling speed.

"You should all have received an information pack on the day you collected your evacuee. Please ensure the form inside is completed and returned to us as soon as possible if you haven't done so already."

"The first thing I asked Terry was if we could change their name," Melissa hissed back. "It sounds quite bizarre when I call Theodore and Abigail next to Nevaeh." She laughed under her breath, more of an impassive huff. "Worse, she goes around telling everybody it's heaven spelt backwards, how embarrassing."

"If you have any queries or issues, please direct them to the council during office hours."

"In the end, we settled on giving her a nickname, Hannah. It's an improvement. If I can just get her to answer to it, it will make our social outings more bearable." Rosie laughed in agreement.

Rosie and Melissa turned to acknowledge Grace and looked over Jack.

"How are you finding it?" Rosie asked.

"A pleasure, Jack's a lovely boy." Grace's cheeks flushed. Rosie grinned tightly, her forehead creasing into lines.

"I bet it's strange having someone else to worry about other than yourself."

"Not at all, I love having him." Grace made a noise in her throat and turned away, thinking of home.

"And that about concludes everything I wanted to say. Just continue as you're already doing and let's hope we can return these children to a safer environment soon enough." Marsh stepped back from the microphone to loud applause. Ronan replaced him in two swift steps, brushing past the commander.

"Thanks, everyone, enjoy the amusements!"

The crowd dispersed and Ronan made sure the cameras got a good shot of his smile.

"Ronan, help!" Grace knew better than to shout out to him in public but she had to. He turned to her, his first instinct to quieten her, her inside voice swapped with her outside voice, seen and not heard. But she wasn't standing with the others.

"Grace?" he called.

"Help!" her voice yelled again, somewhere amongst the crowd. "The road!" Now he could see her, a lot further than he'd expected from the volume of her plea. She was running straight towards the traffic of the main road, her unflattering paisley dress flying behind her and around her shapeless ankles. A short distance in front of her, Jack ran blind, selectively deaf to her calls. He hurried through the camera crew, not willing to lose his composure, but once past them, he broke into a jog, craning his neck to try and see her. He caught up with them standing a matter of meters from the curb. Grace's face was a startling scarlet colour, trying to catch her breath. Jack struggled in her arms.

"He just bolted off," she said.

"You were meant to be managing him. He can't be running around like that in public. Get a hold of the kid."

"Can we go back now?"

He tossed her the keys.

"Wait in the car."

"What are you saying?" Ronan asked.

"I just would have expected an attack by now, multiple ones, from what you've been telling me," Marsh said.

"We've had to use our anti-aircraft missiles more than once, and there've been sightings on our satellite."

"Yes, but way up north over the ocean, nowhere near the southern border." Ronan returned his stare. "I spoke to the guard General and he seems to think you hugely inflated both the risk and urgency prior to setting this border operation in motion."

"Was there not a slew of attacks just a couple of weeks ago?"

"Yes, but I understand they were amateur efforts by a faction of our own populace. Hardly sufficient to warrant the kind of action you've taken, let alone are suggesting."

"Look, Commander, with respect," Ronan struggled to pause, feeling heated. "I don't see the problem here. Whether attacks are happening or not, there are no disadvantages to be had by the safeguarding situation we've set out. Morale is high, people feel like they're contributing and in the event something terrible happens, then we've ensured the prevention of further casualties." Marsh frowned. "Let me take care of the situation outside. I'm monitoring Shaw Hill."

"Keep me informed please, on everything that goes on."

"I will sir. You'll be thanking me by the end of summer."

Chapter 8

The midday sun would have glinted off the hoods of low mileage cars and been soaked up by the flowers planted in neat rows last summer, but now the saturated sky only served to brighten the unruly gardens where weeds grew without chemical hindrance and sale signs pricked the soil. There was not a lawnmower to herald the day or a barbecue to scent the air. This was one of the first areas to be squeezed at the pockets, tightened at its life source.

Raine, Gina and Stacey matched each other's stride in an easy saunter. Gina was making careful observations of each affluent house.

"If they're empty, they'll have been picked out already," Raine said.

"I get what you mean. Houses with people still in 'em are probably packed with stuff," Gina replied, stopping to face a large detached house with a white fascia and broad gravel drive.

"Like what?" Raine said. "What are they going to have that we actually need right now?"

"Might be jewellery, stuff to sell or stuff to keep," Gina said. Raine carried on walking, scuffing her shoes on the pavement.

"Imagine living in a place like that," Gina continued.

"Just dead space, away from everyone you know," Rain said.

"Yeah, dead space and a whole lotta comfort. Reckon I'd feel right at home."

"C'mon," Raine said, lingering while she waited for them. "Let's get to the Aid Centre before we get side-tracked."

Gina picked up the dislodged sale sign and broached the driveway. Raine carried on, but the footsteps following her had stopped.

"She's going to the house, might be worth a look," Stacey said, hesitating before she too stepped onto the gravel.

"Gina, can this not wait," Raine called. "We're meant to be doing something important."

Gina looked back at her.

"Yeah, this is important to me, you don't have to stay."

"We told Linda we'd do it, remember?"

But instead of replying, Gina directed Stacey to check round the back for an open door, whilst she got to work examining the front windows. Stacey returned after a minute.

"All locked, but it looks decent inside."

Gina lifted the sign and tested its point against the window. She noticed the pale face of a woman at one of the upstairs windows, peering from around the edge of a curtain.

"Who are you going to sell stuff to? No one has any money," Raine called from the end of the driveway. Stacey looked between the two of them, an inane grin on her face. "There are people inside," Raine shouted behind her as she started walking again.

"Yeah well, we can't help everyone," Gina replied.

Raine heard the smash of glass under blunt force.

CHAPTER 8

The pedestrian gate to the Aid Centre was still chained shut. The double gates for vehicles were partially open and Raine slipped through, seeing two identical black Mercedes parked adjacent to the main door with their boots left open. Raine saw the girl she'd noticed by the fire standing at the door; she recognised her long, auburn hair and freckled cheeks. She had the same lost expression, the same lost and anxious expression. She moved closer.

"Is he here? I need to speak to Ronan," Emily said, blocking the doorway. Raine walked up to the door and stood beside her as a suited man took hold of the door and walked straight into Emily, forcing her out of the way while he held it for the woman who followed, laden with a stack of boxes in her arms and struggling in her heels.

"Where is he? Can you give him a message?"

"This is private property, you need to leave," the man replied.

"Please!" Emily cried, pushing forward to try to stop him from following the woman who was loading the boxes into the boots. She reached for the sleeve of his shirt.

"Get away from me." He shoved her aside with one hand. "Ronan is in Galven."

"Don't you touch her," Raine said.

"Lock up, Anna," he called to the woman. He stood by the cars as Anna hurried back to the centre with the keys, her shoes click-clacking on the tarmac.

"Are you giving out food vouchers here tomorrow?" Raine asked.

"For a short time, if people can behave in a sensible and cooperative manner." He looked at Emily pointedly.

"My son was one of the evacuees, he'll be very distressed," Emily said. "Please, he has a medical condition, he needs me. I just need to know where he is and if he's ok."

"I can't give you any information."

"Tell Ronan then."

"Gareth?" his colleague called as she waited by the car door

"He knows me. Tell him that Emily wants to talk. Please. Tell him I'll do anything."

"Gareth, let's go. It's three pm." The woman got into her car and shut the door.

"Get out of here both of you. We'll bring the guards next time if we have to."

"Bring the guards, it won't make any difference. Come on," Raine said.

"Don't take anything for granted," Gareth called after them, waiting for them to leave before getting in the driver's seat.

Emily stopped by the hawthorn hedge and watched the cars pull away, heading to a place she could not follow. Raine was by her side, her hands deep in her pockets.

"I'm going back, no point waitin' around," she said. "You wanna walk back with me?"

"I don't know if I should."

"Why?"

"I don't really belong anywhere."

They walked without direction, Raine staying next to her.

"I saw you down there last night, by the fire. Have they taken your child?"

Emily nodded, not wanting to incur more pain. She was at her limit. "You don't know anyone around here? Even though you live on the estate, right?"

CHAPTER 8

"Yeah, I do. I just never really went out meeting people. When my fiancé was living with us, I just stayed with him. After the conscription, it was always me and Jack."

Emily stopped, looking towards home.

"Well, I can't leave you on your own," Raine said. "We're puttin' some people up. If you're worried about being on your own, we can sort something out."

"Thank you. I can't though, I don't like to put people out."

"You won't. We're all pulling together," she lit a cigarette, taking a deep inhale before letting out her breath. Emily noticed tattoos on her hand but was too polite to look properly. "It's the only way we'll get through this," Raine breathed out.

"You're really kind, but I can't. I need to get some stuff organised at my house."

"Come for dinner then? I'd like you too."

"Ok then," Emily said, out of plausible excuses. Raine took a deep drag, her mind elsewhere.

"Awesome. Let's check out what Linda's making today."

When they arrived at Linda's front door, they were met by the smell of food. She served them each a plate of casserole, which although consisted of some rather gristly cuts of meat and vague lumps of vegetable, tasted good after the lack of proper food. Emily pushed her plate away after eating what she could manage and looked around the room. She saw the lady from the night before, sat by the fire; the one that spoke in a clipped, airy tone and had a bouffant of flame red hair. She was sat at a fold up table a few metres away, placed there to accommodate the extra guests. She was picking at her food with her fork whilst the man she had struck up small talk with chattered away next to her.

"I said to 'em, I said so long as I've got a soft place to sleep and reasonable peace, that's me off that is. I'll sleep anywhere. So it's not been as bad as I first thought. Probably been irritating hell out my new housemates, just like my Uni days. Just keep on, that's my motto, just keep buggering on, as Churchill said." He laughed heartily, his whole body forced into movement, his eyes creasing into small slits. The hand that held his fork aloft quivered with the rise and fall of his belly and the food stuck on it threatened to fall. "I've been asking about, and there's lots we can keep busy with, you know. I was talking to someone about preparing some sort of bomb drill, in case it's not just talk, you know? I like to think ahead. There was that one scare we had— "

"What was your name again?" the woman interrupted him.

"Paul. Or old motor mouth as they used to call me in my last job." He laughed again. "Fondly, I hope. You're Fiona, am I right?"

"Yes," Fiona replied at a volume barely higher than a whisper. She seemed to give up on eating and put down her cutlery with delicate attention. Paul continued.

"I was mostly known for my reputation as a comedian, would you believe. Nothing, you know, professional or anything, no gigs, but I just liked, well not the past tense, I like to cheer people up. If I can make you laugh, I'm happy."

Next to him, Fiona dissolved rather abruptly into noisy, wet sobs. Paul looked worried for a moment, but then seemed to consolidate himself and reached a hand towards her with the kind of tentativeness seen by one reaching for a stray, sullen dog. She accepted his touch on her shoulder and leaned into it. He held her at the dinner table, amidst those who passed by and continued their conversation without noticing the two of them, huddled on the flimsy foldaway chairs.

The food that remained on Emily's plate was turning cold and growing a faint, luminescent sheen. She went through the motions of eating, putting pieces in her mouth and chewing every lump into tasteless mush before swallowing. She thought of Noel for the first time since her mind had been relentlessly occupied with Jack. She tried to remember the sound of his voice, but could only recall his hoarse goodbye as he had hugged them both by the bus. She tried to remember the parting of his hair, the small explosion of his iris, the lines of his mouth and the concave of his jaw, but she could only summon the bleak oval of his face through the smeared glass of the bus windows as the doors were shut and all around her other women cried. She put her hand to her cheek, imagining it was the coarse touch of him.

"Are you ok?" Raine was behind her.

"I'm fine. I feel better now I've eaten a little bit." Emily breathed through her mouth to clear her throat.

"Our first meeting is scheduled in twenty minutes. Feel free to join us in the sitting room when you're ready."

"What kind of meeting?"

"Come and see. It's just a get together for all of us who want to do something about the situation."

All memories of Noel had been allayed. There was no one but herself to rely on.

They gathered within the dim and cluttered confines of the living room. Emily stationed herself in the corner, in the hold of a worn leather armchair, wide enough to grant her some personal space. They waited until the agreed meeting time, and then onwards until enough time had passed that the clock was an immutable presence that could no longer be ignored.

"No one else is going to come. This is it then," Gina said in her usual acerbic tone. Raine glanced at the clock and then the door. Her hands moved from the pockets of her cargo trousers to between her knees, her chain necklace swinging forward as she moved.

"I was hoping there'd be more of us, but it doesn't matter. The reason I wanted us all to sit together is so we can work out what we're going to do next. I think we all agree that as a group we can challenge the council, ideally get the children back."

"You're leading this are you?" Gina challenged from where she was reclined.

"I'm trying to get things in motion, it's not about who's leading."

"Because we haven't elected anyone." Gina looked around the room at those gathered—Stacey and Kay lounging either side of her, Raine and Sasha by the low chipped mantelpiece, a dark haired willowy young man of about Emily's age by the door and next to him a boy occupied with his phone. She turned her gaze on Emily last.

"Do we need to spend time doing that now? I'd have thought at this stage we need to focus on action rather than politics," Raine said.

"Maybe," Gina shrugged. "I think it's important, personally; before people start assuming that position."

"We've been storing weapons, stuff we had and stuff we've found," said the young man by the door. He was dressed smarter than the rest in a loose-fitting sports top and jeans, but he had a certain tension about him, a shift of the eye, a clench of the jaw.

"That's good, but it'd be better if we don't have to use them. Remember that they have guns, they have the centres. If we simply make an armed attack too soon, they'll wipe us out."

"What can we do then?" Kay asked.

"To start with I want to get some ideas together between us, come up with a plan and then see where it takes us, find out what works. At the very least we can give those bastards a hard time." No one seemed to have an instantaneous reply. The young man left through the doorway without a further word.

"I'm going to get through the border," Emily said. "I don't care how and I don't care who with, but I'm going to get into Galven and find out where my son is."

"We can help you. We all have our reasons."

"You're that girl I picked up off the side of the road," Gina said. "She's with us now, is she?" she turned to Raine.

"Why shouldn't she be?" Raine replied. "Going back to the issue. We need to focus on the Council; they're the ones behind all of this. While the Council still exists, we're not going to be safe. Even if we get the children back or the conscripts freed, they're just going to keep coming after us."

"In an ideal world, we'd get rid of the Council and never have to worry about them again," Emily said, "but it's impossible. When I get my son back, I'll be taking him somewhere they won't find us. I'm not going to risk losing him again."

"And spend your life looking over your shoulder? You still might get put away when they catch you, then what will you do?" Raine turned to the others. "I want us to work as a group on this, as many as we can get."

"Power to the fucking people?" Gina said in one long sigh. "We're letting anyone be part of this then? Even outsiders?" Her gaze fell on Emily.

Raine's eyes flicked between the two of them.

"There're no outsiders here."

The man who'd left reappeared in the doorway. His face was pale and drawn, his hair hanging in untidy, dark strands.

"What's up, Ethan?"

"There's a broadcast, Linda's got it on now. Red alert for airstrikes tonight, there's been sightings on the coast."

"We've had tons of sightings before. It's Galven that Nemico wants, not us," Raine said.

"I need to check on my mum," Sasha said, standing up in her worn trainers.

"Yeah, I guess we better prepare anyway," Raine said. "Blackouts, cover, we all know the drill."

"Sure, I'll get some cans, sit on a wall and wait to see if the fireworks come," Gina said.

People left the room a lot quicker than they'd come in. Emily was the last one in the room with Raine. She could see Ethan lingering in the hallway, listening to the broadcast that Linda watched in the kitchen.

"I don't need to be a part of things if it's going to cause an issue."

"What issue? There isn't any," Raine replied.

"If it's going to affect your plans or upset people, I'm happy to do things alone."

"Is this about what Gina said? She just has to have an opinion on everything, create conflict, don't pay attention to her."

"She was right though; I am an outsider. All I care about is Jack, I don't have time for any drama."

"Give it another day, please. I want you to be a part of this, I know we can help each other."

They headed to the kitchen, but as they entered, Emily felt the touch of Raine's hand on her shoulder, her chipped, black nail varnish catching the ends of her hair.

"Stay with me tonight. I have a spare bed and it'll save you having to walk back on your own if there is a raid," Raine said.

"Are you sure?"

"Of course, we need to stick together."

"Raine? We need to get ready," Linda called from the dining area.

"I'll come and join you in a bit, you can get settled in. Ethan will show you where to go," Raine told Emily as she went to join Linda, who was beginning to pace.

Emily touched the thin fabric of her rucksack, thankful that she'd been carrying it everywhere. Ethan pushed off from the wall where he'd been leaning.

The streets were turning dark, even more so as people shut off the lights and blacked out their windows with thick curtains and cardboard. She followed Ethan to the end of the street, past the charred remains of the fire, cutting left through a short alleyway that took them into an adjacent road.

"In here," he said simply, without turning to look at her. He cut across the front lawns and let himself in one of the terraced houses that lined the left side of the street. There wasn't a lot to set it aside from the other houses; it had the same brick, a patchwork of algae, the same stone path in desperate need of re-levelling. The walls inside were bare and undecorated with all manner of objects pressed up against them.

She paused by a partially open door, which she guessed led to the living room going by the slip of brown carpet and the sound of a television set blaring from within. Had the front windows been blacked out? She didn't think so.

"This way," Ethan said, standing by the stairs, waiting for her. She thought better of saying something, intimidated by his scowl and the hunch of his shoulders.

Her room consisted of a bunk bed, a faded black rug and a single closet. The walls were covered with stickers—some had been removed or partially removed and left grey marks in their outline. The wardrobe had been scrawled upon with a pen and the wash basket was spewing out its overloaded contents. But it was a warm room and the bed was made. She put down her rucksack.

"Thanks," she said to Ethan. He flicked his hair from over his eyes with a toss of his head.

"I live over the road," he replied, "if you need anything."

"How come you haven't been conscripted?" She regretted the question almost as soon as she spoke it, remembering the list of disabilities and conditions that exempted young men from service, but he met her with steady eye contact for the first time since Raine had asked him to show Emily to her house, his chin jutting up with an air of defiance.

"I'm never going to work for those bastards. Let 'em try and catch me." He let go of the door handle and imitated a gun with his fingers. He moved it to his temple, tapping it with his pointed fore and middle finger. "I know things, things about them and what they're really doing out there."

"You haven't got in any trouble?"

"Couple of letters," he shrugged. "They haven't bothered

with anything more yet."

"Well," she bent to open her rucksack, reassuring herself that everything was still there. "Thanks for your help."

"Remember, just shout if you want a hand."

"Ok, thank you."

"Don't forget to do the window." He gestured towards the window where pieces of cardboard and tape had been left on the floor. "Raine usually does both."

"Thanks."

He left the room. She could hear the creaks of the stairs as Ethan left. Once the footsteps receded, she took out her toothbrush and pyjamas, the window could wait. The sky was clear and matte black; it was hard to imagine it could be lit up at any moment, deadly streaks of light that sought brick houses like tinderboxes.

She found the bathroom across the narrow hallway. The ceiling was patchy with black mould, and after washing her face, she dried it with a towel smelling of mildew.

She struggled with the blind, trying to hold the cardboard against the cold glass with one hand, and manoeuvring the tape with the other. When that was done and the window was covered, she closed the curtains gently, hoping the tape would hold.

She got under the covers of the bottom bunk, settling into the scratchy, foreign sheets. The light from the landing cast the bedroom in a dim glow. It should be off. All lights should be off. But to sleep in total darkness was an antidote to peaceful rest. Jack wouldn't like it, but he wasn't here to protest or comfort her. She left it on.

The night seemed endless, scattered with panicked awakenings. Everything was wrong. How could the light be on without a mewling complaint? How could Jack be somewhere she wasn't, behind barriers of brick and paperwork. She woke again, this time plunged into a blackness no less than what lay behind her closed eyes. She reached tentatively for her side, seeking the spot where Jack would usually nestle, now occupied by rough cotton and the cool hardness of the wall that her mattress pushed against. All sense of direction was lost without light

She heard the floorboard give out beneath someone's feet and the soft hushing of someone shedding their clothes.

"Hello?" she asked the dark, stemming memories of large, groping hands and searching lips.

"It's just me," Raine replied. "Did I wake you up?"

"No, I've not been able to sleep much."

She still couldn't discern much more than the suggestion of a shape, the slightest shifting of the room's muted blackness.

"You left the light on in the hall," Raine said. "My dad sleeps in his chair downstairs, I doubt he even noticed."

"Sorry, I must have forgotten."

"Don't worry about it, the sky's been clear all night." Raine pulled down the blackout blinds, ripping the tape from the wall and filling the room with the pale first light of dawn. Emily reached for her bag, pulling out her phone to check for messages. Still no reply from Ronan.

"Is everything ok?" Raine asked.

"Yeah." She rolled to her side, covering her lower face with the duvet. By the window, Raine continued to undress. She pulled her loose black top over her head, tossing it into a corner as she turned away to reach behind her with both hands to the delicate dip of her back. She unclasped the plain fastening of her bra and slipped it off her shoulders. Even in the low light, Emily could make out the small constellation of imperfections that scattered her shoulder, the subtle indentation of her spine and the soft dimpling of her bare hips. She slipped into a plain cami top and looked over her shoulder.

"You really have no family at all other than your son?"

"I had my partner, before he was conscripted. My mum might still be alive, but she lives out of town. I haven't spoken to her in a long time."

"Was your partner from around here?"

"Yeah," Emily said. She rolled to her other side, facing the wall. She heard Raine climb the ladder to the top bunk and settle on the mattress.

"There's a group of us heading out in the morning. I can wake you up if you want to join us."

"I'm sure I'll be awake," Emily replied. In the renewed stillness, the darkness seemed to creep back with insidious reckoning. Her tired mind focused with painful clarity on every dark shadow and corner. She held her phone to her chest and told herself it was a camera. The darkness didn't matter. If she reached out her hand, she would feel the generous warmth of Jack's small body. If she wished to move then, she could move.

The room was dark as pitch, but the tremulous quivering by her side was enough for her to know he was still alert.

"You need to sleep," she said, her voice soft with weariness. "Daddy won't be happy if you're still awake when he comes up here."

Jack kicked his feet from under the cover and covered his

eyes with his hands.

"The curtain," he whined. Though she had already gone through the ritual of securing the door and checking the curtains, she rose out of bed. She pulled the curtain's edge, much the same as before, but in Jack's fraught mind it might be enough to cover the last slip of naked glass. Back in bed, she drew her feet in and turned towards Jack.

"Sleep now." There was no reply other than the shallow exhale of his breath in small huffs. She let the weight of her arm rest over him. Slowly, she felt him become still.

As Jack began to settle, her thoughts turned to the door; that indeterminable black shape that marked the entry to the room. With her free arm, she drew up the duvet to press tight against her back, tight enough to act as a deterrent. She listened for the creak of the stairs, the muting of that indiscernible hum of the television. As Jack's breath tapered to the longer intakes of steady respiration, her own became stilted and short. How she wished for some light.

"Sleep," she soothed. "Sweet dreams," she whispered.

Chapter 9

The next morning seemed slow to break, the sun itself not wishing for the day to dawn. The chill, the dampened grass and the dark cloud, all seemed to linger like a pernicious omen. Regardless of nature's unreadiness, a good portion of the Shaw Hill residents had come together for the walk to the Aid Centre, gathering in one great unit.

Emily had been with Raine since leaving the house. They walked in the centre of the group, pressed together by those close around them. Perspiration and palpable excitement at the prospect of fresh rations permeated the air.

Despite Linda's presence at the front, her voice carried with crisp clarity through the humid air over their heads.

"They wanna be givin' us some decent stuff. They'll get both barrels off of me if they ain't."

"I don't care if it's rations or not. They can afford it and they know it," she said after a pause.

Raine was quiet by her side. Behind them, Gina was having a loud conversation with Kay and a group of teenage girls much like the ones frequently seen wielding bats and sacks in recent days.

"Got me a bloody huge TV, fifty inches or summat for sure.

Got it hauled over on a trailer we got out this garden, we've been using it for all the stuff we find." Gina spat on the ground; her lips pursed like something sour was on her tongue. "Kay found a load of jewellery an' that. Show her what you found, Kay." There were noises of admiration as Kay let a doe-eyed girl look over the spoils adorning her fingers and neck.

"That's real diamond, that one," Kay said. "Can tell by the shine."

"They don't need it no more, do they? They was just glad we didn't beat 'em for it," Gina said.

"You'd have thought stuff like that would have been sold. Some houses are stripped bare like, but maybe that's how they afforded to move and these ones didn't," a girl said, not much more than fifteen from what Emily could see of her.

"Lost its value though din't it. So many people were trying to sell everythin' at the same time," Gina replied.

"Sentimental value, some of it," Kay said absently.

Emily noticed Raine's relaxed tread had become tense and stilted.

"That stuff's worthless now, nothing more than a waste of time and energy," she called behind her.

"Yeah well, I'll take what I can get," Gina shouted back without turning. "Rather be surrounded by some nice stuff while I starve or get shot at from the sky. Let 'em try and take it off me, no-one will."

"Fancy televisions aren't going to help you when we're struggling to survive. Just means you'll see the Council broadcasts on a larger display," Raine said, but Gina ignored her.

They passed the vacant playground next to the Aid Centre where children from the estate would usually convene; the young after day-care, the older after sunset. The grey swings hung from their rusting chains, subject only to the whim of the breeze. The playground was a hive of noise for Jack; a place of great temptation and threat, where sounds and shapes and sight and activity and movement and sensation all existed as a paradox of joy and torture; a careful counterweight needed for its enjoyment. Emily used to look into his soft, compliant eyes every time she placed the headphones over his delicate ears, watching his restive features settle as the environment was dampened, dulled into a world that he could process at his own pace and preference.

She used to take him at dusk, seeking the narrow window of time after the young ones had been pulled by the hand into the cover of their homes and before the older children left their houses to seek the cover of low light. Jack used to break away from her protection at the sight of the empty play equipment, his excitement bubbling over into an incoherent stream of shouts and sounds. The swings had to be both first and last, an object of worship and wonder to his small frame. He would stand beneath it and appraise it, push the swings, rub the chain, watch its motion; like a monument to the senses—its creaking, its cool metal, coarse rubber and the smooth arc of its motion.

"I want to go really high, mum. Mum, I want to go really really high."

She would push him to mid-height, not daring to go higher as she watched him reach peak excitement, his laughter and whooping drowning out the high-pitched protest of the un-oiled joints.

"Higher, Mum. Push me to the sky," he used to shout.

"I am, that's as high as it'll go. You're super high."

And when the shadows had grown long and the sun was no more than a low bulb in a mottled grey sky, fingers of clouds stretching out as if to cast a duvet over the impending night, and Emily's camera strap felt heavy around her neck. That would be the perfect moment when her fingers would find the groove of the shutter button, worn smooth by all her presses. Jack would be in the swing seat still, knowing these were his last few minutes of idle happiness. His feet would hang freely, kicking with every slight impulse of contentment. His fingers would be holding the cold metal knots of the chain in a tight caress, kneading the loops and the holes and the smooth curves that were holding him in suspension.

If only she could capture this moment—her son at rest in a place that made him happy, where the world had melted away into a window of peace and the light behind him touched his cheek like mellow butter. But as soon as she raised the camera, the aperture and shutter speed already set and ready, his focus would snap towards the camera.

"No! No, Mummy. The flash, the flash!"

Despite all her reassurances that there wouldn't be a flash, his physical reaction was always instantaneous. His knees would raise and hit the bar as he struggled to try and get out; his hands would release their grip on the chain, making high, frantic circles in the air as his level of panic rose, knocking his headphones from his ears.

Gina stood in the swing seat, her scuffed, dirty trainers poking through the leg holes. She craned to see over the hedge enclosing the Aid Centre, exposing the sharp angles of her hip bones as her top rose.

"There ain't no one in the car park," she shouted.

CHAPTER 9

Linda came back into view, pushing back through the group that waited by the gates and walking towards them, her face red with exertion.

"All them gates are locked." She stood by the playground gate, hands on her broad hips as she caught her breath. "They gotta be coming. They can't just leave us."

"We'll have to wait for 'em," Gina said, still on the swing.

Emily looked at the low grey building, usually a hub of children and community assistance. Now it was bleak and barren, a dead stump of a building behind a padlocked fence. Raine's face was turned away, but Emily could see the balls of her fists in her pockets, and hear her huffing sighs.

"They have to turn up," Emily said quietly. Raine turned to her.

"And even if they do, you think we can rely on them to come every week? For as long as they decide to keep us shut out of the city?" She kicked the dirt, where litter of all variety interspersed the weeds.

"For now, it's all we've got. They've never let us starve before," Emily said.

"I just hate feeling so fucking helpless. Like they've got us at their mercy no matter what we do. We couldn't get out of here whatever we do, and they know it."

"There's no point talking about it to Miss Privilege there, she wouldn't get it," Gina said, off the swing set now and leaning against the slide. She was facing Emily directly, with her lips upturned in a smirk. "Turns out there is someone who knows who you are. Tegan told me; she remembers. When Noel Carson had a red-card shipped in from out of town to shack up with, it was the talk of the street. Guess it was pretty easy for him to keep you hidden away all this time, after what went down with him an' all."

"I've had this card for years," Emily said, heat rushing to her cheeks. She pulled her ID card from her back pocket, brown around the edging, hanging from the hook of her black, council-issued lanyard. "You don't know anything."

"They're 'ere," Linda called, rushing in the bobbing, lilting walk of hers towards the gate. "Let me in front, I need to take stock of what's goin'."

A familiar convoy of characterless black cars had come to a stop at the padlocked gates. Three officials stepped out from the cars, one to unlock the gate and two to keep the crowd back. Emily was on the periphery of the crowd, having drawn back from Raine after Gina's comment. They moved through the gates, a combined forward push in their eagerness to get at the aid packages.

Gareth, still flustered from the day before, was waving his arms at the front.

"Get back," he shouted, his composure falling further apart with every resident that brushed past him without a look, already crowding the cars that his colleagues were trying to unload. "You all need to get in a line or no one will be getting any packages."

"You'll do your job, now you've bothered to turn up," Linda said, getting a good measure of him. Gareth assessed the broad stance of her shoulders and her raw complexion—the skin of a woman whose only beauty regimen was a vigorous scrub every morning and a touch of rouge twice a year. He turned away with a frustrated sigh and went to help ferry boxes to the Aid Centre. He sprung up an animated conversation with the woman in heels, his comments interspersed with frequent disparaging looks in Linda's direction.

CHAPTER 9

Emily gave Raine a gentle nudge, the skin of her arm felt like cool, downy silk.

"It doesn't look like they're planning to hang around for long. There's not even that many packages."

"I ain't happy with this," Linda said next to them. "Not at all, that wants to be proper food in them boxes."

The crowd waited with anxious faces, palpable tension in the air as the last box was taken from the car and dropped with the rest of the messy pile just inside the doorway. By instinct, they pressed forwards. There was little choice but to move with the group when they pushed at your back, knocked at your sides, eager and empty bellied. They could see the officials in the central corridor, hastily unboxing the provisions onto two foldout tables.

"Form a line for Christ's sake," Gareth said, back outside and gesturing with a pale, flailing hand. "There'll be no handouts at all unless you all form an orderly queue."

Emily looked around, but there was little movement in an effort to line up. The combined noise and bustling of the group was enough to drown out his protest. Something hard hit the back of her leg and she turned to see a young man in a wheelchair pushing past her on his way to the front. He wore a tracksuit and had unkempt, mid-length hair and pockmarked skin. A harried looking woman in black leggings followed close behind.

"Let's have it then," the man was saying loudly, showing little regard for the legs he continued to catch with the wheel of his chair as he got through the doorway.

"Hold on, Liam," the woman said behind him, reaching for the back of the chair.

"No, Kelly, leave it out. You've been after me all day. I'm

fed up of waitin' around now. I just want to take what we need and go. I can't deal with all these people, man. All these monkeys in suits, man, get out the way."

"Liam, wait a minute," Kelly said, making a grab for his chair, but he manoeuvred past Gareth and towards the table, shunting Gareth's leg with the broad spokes of his chair. Linda moved with him, sparking a collective push from the group behind her as they crowded the table and began to examine the rations.

Linda scooped up one of the packets of rice from the heap, examining the plain description on its front.

"How long are we meant to live off rice for then? You giving us anything else? There ain't much I can do with this."

Gareth snatched the packet from her hand.

"You'll get what you're given and be grateful for it," he snapped. "And it will be distributed evenly, in an orderly fashion," he shouted. He placed the packet back on the table, smoothing its surface. Linda's face flushed pink with anger and humiliation.

The suited woman pushed her way to the front of the table, trying to organise the group. One of her waving arms caught Gina on the shoulder, who retaliated with a colourful verbal recourse.

"Don't you dare touch me, who d'you think you are?" She retaliated with a shove. Meanwhile, in front of Emily, the man on the scooter had trapped Gareth in the small space against the wall.

"I need to ask you about my medication," he was saying. "I need to find out whether you're still funding my prescriptions. It's the first one what's worked for me in two years, but the Doctor did say it costs more. Now he's over the border and I can't speak to him."

"You'll have to phone the hospital. I can't answer individual queries," Gareth replied, but his voice was drowned out by the increasing background noise. "Get back," he said, trying to squeeze past the scooter but the man swiftly cut off his escape.

"I tried that you see. I just got passed from one person to another, left on hold, disconnected. I can't afford the call charge, it's extortion. What happens when they turn me away, and I run out of pills, huh?"

Gina had grabbed one of the empty boxes that the rations had come in and started to pack it again with food.

"Hey!" Gareth shouted. "Stop that now!" He tried to get to Gina but was yet again blocked by residents. "Move out of my way, bloody idiots."

"We want answers," Linda shouted. "You represent the Council; we need to know you're not just going to leave us here without any way to survive."

The volume was now at a feverous pitch. Gareth managed to get around the man in the mobility scooter in one swift movement to the side, knocking the scooter's handle as he did, causing the man to cry out in alarm.

He went straight to Gina, who was still harassing his colleague but she saw him coming. She turned to him and pushed him square in the chest with both hands, giving such a forceful shove that he staggered back into the front of the table, groping behind him in a desperate bid for stability.

Whilst his female colleague made a noise like a struck fox and the other went to unlock the car, the crowd took this as their cue to take what was left of the food.

Gareth's shock and anger were soon replaced by fear when

Gina gripped the breast of his shirt, her face close to his.

"We're worth no less than you, you think you're better than us. Well, this is what happens when you try and treat us like crap," Gina snarled, a torrent of such intensity that Gareth was consumed by the overwhelming need to put as much distance as he could from these people.

"When will we hear from our children?" Emily asked, trying to get the attention of the councilwoman as she rushed to the cars. "When will we get some kind of update?"

"I- that's not something I can tell you," she replied.

"Because you don't know or because you're not allowed?" Emily asked. But Gareth had managed to snake his way out of the building and encouraged his colleague to get into the car.

Gareth paused by the second car, fumbling for the keys in his pocket. Kay made a grab for the black ID card hanging from his neck.

"Hey Gina," she called. "Reckon we'd get somewhere with one of these? I reckon we'd get treated right proper."

"Get off me, scum," he spat, swiping her away and getting into the driver's seat as quickly as he could manage.

"Let them go," Raine said. "We've got what we needed, not that they'll be back in a hurry."

"You giving orders again?" Gina said as the cars rolled away.

"Here now, none of that. Let's get this stuff back so I can work out what I'm gonna do with it," Linda said. "They'll be back, no doubt to lock them gates for good this time."

Emily picked up one of the boxes ready to take it back to the estate. As the others set off, she waited, watching as Raine shut the door to the Aid Centre and took out a cigarette.

"You think we'll get anywhere like this?" She exhaled an

CHAPTER 9

acrid plume of smoke, her eyes like slits in the sunlight. "They've already won."

And with that, the faint optimism that Emily had been nurturing began to darken.

Chapter 10

Grace lay curled under the freshly laundered Egyptian cotton sheets. Despite the soft goose-down pillows cradling her head, she rarely found solace or comfort in bed. In fact, she dreaded the approach of night, in the same way a child might dread a pending, interminable bath or exam. Her body resisted sleep like it was something to suffer. Her head swam like a stew pot of pictures and fragments of memory. Her womb ached with a physical pain, an empty yearning, the shadow of loss. And every night her back remained untouched and cold; a host of lonely surfaces in a room that was dark and still.

But this night was different as from down the corridor came a now familiar mewling noise, one of exhaustion marred with distress, piqued with dogged persistence. It rose and fell like an antiquated siren.

"Will that child not sleep?" Ronan asked aloud from his edge of the mattress.

"He wants his mum," Grace replied.

Ronan shifted first onto his back and then to sit up. His agitation was palpable.

"Well? Are you going to get up and sort him out then or what?"

CHAPTER 10

She swung her feet out from under the cover and found the floor.

"There's only so much I can do. You have to be patient," she said.

"Yeah, well I have to sleep. I've got an important meeting with your Dad in the morning."

She was glad to get away from him as she padded down the carpeted hallway with bare feet. She pushed open the door to the spare room, lighting up the small space. Jack flinched in his bed at the great shadowy figure that took up the entire doorway. His face was streaked with tears and his eyes were red from rubbing. He was doing it now, balling his fists against his eyes and twisting them against the delicate skin of his eyelids. His knees were bent to his chest and he rocked between the ruffled bedsheets and his pillow.

His rabbit had been pushed down to his waist, crumpled and face down against the sheets. She moved it back to his shoulder.

"Here's your rabbit. He doesn't want you to be upset, he wants to sleep with you."

"His name's Bunny," Jack whined.

"Bunny," she repeated. "I'm sure he'd like a hug."

She sat next to him and watched him clutch Bunny in his slender arms. It was the fifth time in three hours that she'd had to comfort him. Though she could coax him to lie down, move his fists to his side, the crying wouldn't cease. She sat with him, as she had done every time, her hand cradling him until his breathing slowed and his fingers relaxed, the purple hue of his eyelids softening in their pink irritated surroundings for long enough that she might creep away. Is this what motherhood was? The willingness to tear yourself apart from the inside, and submit to personal torture just for your child to find some form of peace and take from you what they needed.

She was halfway down the hallway when he started again, his tears full of renewed strength and anguish at almost succumbing to sleep's beguiling charm. She heard a loud thump from the bedroom and paused. Ronan appeared, hulking through the door.

"This is an absolute joke," he spat, taking a blanket from the cupboard. "I hope you're getting a taste of what you're missing out on now. Maybe it'll stop you moping so much when he's finally gone."

As he descended the stairs to spend a night on the sofa, Grace returned to Jack. With some gentle encouragement, she was able to get him out of bed and lead him by the hand to her own warm sheets, showing him how to fill the empty chasm in the middle, next to her. She lay on her side facing him, stroking his hand and listening as his abject sniffs faded to a whisper, the wetness on his cheeks slowly drying until he fell into slumber. Only now could she get herself to rest, hoping that his touch might be enough to assuage the distemper of her mind.

Ronan had woken late and with an irksome crick in his neck. Neither his breakfast nor the drive to the council building had done anything to improve his mood. Emily held dominion over his every waking thought. In the first few days, she had messaged him, as he knew she would, begging, pleading. It had been an amuse-bouche to his incessant hunger, his need for her attention. But the messages soon stopped, dropping him like a hot coal, as she'd done too many times before.

CHAPTER 10

So now there was nothing, no piece of her except that which she held dearest, a son she cherished over everything. The same one that probably had kept her from his arms, and living in that cesspit estate. But what use was it without her knowing? He checked his phone as readily as he blinked. Spent every idle minute thinking about her, what she was doing, what she could be made to do.

There was a stir in the building as he entered his workplace. Gareth and Anna had returned from their venture out into the estate to make the last drop. He entered the civil hall and found a small commotion buzzing around their figures.

"What's happened?" Ronan asked. Gareth's lanky form turned to him and he was surprised at his dishevelled appearance. One hand was trying to smarten his tie, the other was busy smoothing his ruffled shirt. Ronan noticed a slight tremble in his fingers.

"Those people, if you can call them that, are unbelievable. Totally out of control," he blustered. "Like a pack of animals. I refuse to go back out there again without proper protection. You need to do something about this before it gets worse."

"Well, are you going to tell me what went on? You're not making sense."

"It was a hit and run," Anna said. "They came in and took the lot out of our hands. Gareth got trapped against the wall by some raving cripple, then we were attacked by these women, some of them hardly out of school, but real rough types, you know?"

"We were lucky to get out of there. It seems all sense of cordiality is non-existent in that place. What's worse is they know they can get away with it now."

"What women?" Ronan asked. "What did they look like?"

"There was a big, broad one. Great big, booming, brash type with a mouth to match. Then this other one with thin hair. Slim but strong, masculine, quite fearsome really," Anna said. Ronan looked to the ground, tapping his foot.

"You don't need to worry about it, it'll get dealt with," he said.

"How though? They—" Ronan silenced him with a raise of the hand.

"I said it'll be taken care of." He checked his watch. "I've got a meeting, just leave it to me, will you?" He left them to their simmering. It was obvious they'd need at least three cups of coffee to settle their nerves.

On his way up the myriad wooden staircases and echoic corridors, his phone began to buzz. Fumbling to retrieve it, his heart raced with anticipation, but it wasn't the name he wanted to see. He pressed it to his ear.

"Rosie? What is it?"

"Hi, I wanted to ask if you could give me a comment for the piece I'm running tomorrow. It's all written, just a finishing touch from you, if you would."

"What piece?" His brusqueness was no more than she expected.

"A two-page spread about how residents are coping with the new evacuees. There have been concerns expressed by teachers about their integration and effect on the schooling system here, and there's criticism of the Council for their delay in making necessary provisions." Ronan's scowl deepened.

"Arrangements are underway as we speak. The evacuees will be educated in the workhouses from next week so they won't intrude on the education of the existing students in any of the schools. Where's the criticism coming from? Because it's not coming straight to my inbox where it should be."

"Some people have questioned the rationale behind the operation. They think Marsh may be acting in haste."

"This is my project," he said.

"Right, well—"

"No, you get that straight. I don't want any of this being levelled at Marsh. He's backed the whole thing from the start, but it's me who's initiated it."

"Anything else?"

"Don't quote me on that, Rosie. You know how this works."

"Ok. Well, I'll leave it out then," she sighed.

"Wait, actually," he thought it over for a moment. "I do have something else. There's been an incident during today's aid delivery. Our own council members were attacked by browns in Shaw Hill. They were described like savages, stealing and looting the donations, using violence to mob council officials and demonstrating absolutely zero gratitude to the members of the Council who were there to deliver rations. It seems the situation there has deteriorated. We will need extra safety considerations before we can enter the area again. Thanks to the border, our safety from any such criminal behaviour is secure."

"Thanks, I'll write something up."

"An anonymous source, right?"

"Sure."

"Thanks, Rosie." He ran his free hand through his hair, checking there was no one else on the staircase. "I'll, um, I'll see when I can get an evening free, alright?"

He snapped the phone shut without bothering to acknowledge her reply.

Marsh's office door was closed. A quick double rap

produced no response. He thought about the events at the Aid Centre, imagined the people, if he was being generous enough to consider them as such; tense, sweating, heaving together as one angry entity. Had she been among them? Pressed arm to arm with the unthinkable, the unfathomable—that from which she couldn't be farther away. She must know, must feel the difference, couldn't she?

He knocked again. An incoherent sound reached him from the other side of the dense wooden door. He eased it open and looked in upon a dim, cramped cave. The floor-length royal green curtains were drawn shut and the shape of the Commander sat at the gold edged desk, his face resting in his hands. A decanted bottle of sherry was by his elbow.

"Sir?" Marsh looked up and hauled himself from his seat.

"Take a seat," he said. Ronan sat, watching Marsh lumber to the window and drag apart the curtains, letting in some of the afternoon sun. He coughed, a tremulous, rattling cough, and it seemed to draw even more red into his eyes, and flush his skin with a darker tinge.

"I can't say I'm in the best of shape to be taking meetings today," he rasped.

"It's nothing formal, sir. But I do need to talk to you about something urgent."

Marsh motioned for him to proceed. He sat back on his leather seat and dropped the empty bottle into the bin meant for waste paper. Ronan described the morning's events with the same dispassionate care he had used to report to Rosie.

"And what do you make of this?" Marsh asked. "I assume that's what you've really come to tell me."

"I think it's further evidence, a further warning sign, of what's to come. We already knew that these people have no respect for the Council's authority. We already knew the rumours of militants getting ready to organise a direct attack. This all points in the same direction, we'd be stupid to ignore it."

"And you're sure these are not just desperate, hungry people, Ronan? It is unfortunate, in my opinion, that it has to be like this. If it were possible, I'd extend our protection to all people of Merredin, no matter what their card."

"Commander, with respect, you need to take a greater perspective on the situation. Now's not the time for philanthropy. If you offer aid to these people, as we have done, they do not accept gratefully, they do not appreciate the generosity of the Council and extend to us due respect. Instead, they grab and take and steal and only look to take more, take everything, even if it means harming the source. These are selfish, short-sighted people. Right here in this city, we have respectful, law abiding people. They power our economy, and in turn, our defence against the outsiders that want to bring us down. We have the workforce to sustain it and the ability to preserve a decent standard of living for those who are able and willing to maintain it. This is all to your credit, of course."

"And then? Where do they, the outsiders as you called them, fit in all of this?"

"Out there we have a group of people living on the fringes of society. Unable to meet any basic expectations. they consist of crude women, lifelong disabled, career layabouts who've never even considered doing a stroke of paid labour in their lives. They've collected and amassed out there like a malignant tumour. They drain our resources with the cost of their upkeep and now seek to bite the hand that feeds them. When word gets out about this, Galven will look to you."

"You come close to speaking out of turn. You're lucky that I understand you, Ronan."

"Forgive me, sir. I just care. I don't want to see you make a mistake. I can't help but think of a very real possibility that these people may be armed, building up their strength and numbers."

Marsh appeared to be deep in thought. Stray, straggly hairs that stuck out, perpendicular from his eyebrows moved as one.

"There have been reported sightings," he said. "Nemico planes," he trailed off, shuffling papers with one hand.

"Yes, off the coast."

"Perhaps that will keep them occupied enough to prevent them from staging a resistance. I can hardly imagine such a ragtag group as you describe having the gall to take us on. It appears I'm still waiting on the reports, Ronan."

"Yes, sir. Perhaps I should conduct some further investigation into this to determine the level of threat, if any?"

"Yes, that might be wise."

Ronan took a step back towards the door. Marsh bent to the drawers of his desk.

"I was just looking for something before you came in."

Ronan left, stepping from a thin beam of diminishing sunlight into a harsh, artificial glare. He had what he needed.

Chapter 11

They walked side by side, the edges of their wide cardboard boxes occasionally glancing off each other as they took up the crumbling, asphalt pavement. The others were almost out of sight, walking at a faster pace than Raine's, who was taking long drags of her cigarette as she struggled to balance her box under one arm. Emily wasn't sure if Raine wanted her company, she was too nervous to ask and lacking the confidence to assume otherwise.

"What if we got a message to those of us on the inside, in the conscript camps? Maybe Ethan or someone like him could get taken in. We could send a message for them to help."

"There's no one else like Ethan," Raine laughed, but there was no humour in her voice. "And he'd never go for that."

"What about Kay's idea? Steal an ID card from north of town, maybe it'd get us through the gates." Raine finished her cigarette with a guttural cough and a flick of the wrist as she tossed its brown stub at the weeds. "Or a hostage," Emily continued. "We need to get inside somehow, get some leverage."

"Yeah, and then what?" Raine replied. Emily noticed the downturn in Raine's mood.

"If nothing else, it would be really helpful just to know what's going on over there, where they've taken the children." They walked in silence for a minute. Whilst Raine was quiet, eyeing the potholes ahead of them with a frown, Emily's mind was racing.

"If I could get a message to Noel, I'm sure he'd have a good idea."

"So, it's true then," Raine said, all at once focused on Emily again. "Did he never introduce you to any of his friends? Family?"

"He cut contact with them before I met him. After I got pregnant and had Jack, we never seemed to have the time or energy for going out much."

"That was his version of events, huh."

"Do you know him?"

"Know of him. Enough to know that he's not someone we should aim to rely on."

Emily stopped, all at once the box she held seemed to have tripled in weight.

"Is there something I should know?" she asked. Every gust of wind seemed to prick her skin with needles, and her arid mouth was a desert of thirst. "Because I'd rather you just tell me." Her eyes squeezed shut as her face crumpled and the tears came. She wished desperately that she was alone. Only Jack had ever been with her during a panic attack and the knowledge that Raine was with her, judging her, only made it harder to breathe, more difficult to settle her thoughts and stifle the raw emotion that had taken the reins of her physical reactions. The box fell to the floor and she hid her face with her hands as she felt Raine move closer to her, telling her to breath, coaxing her to exhale. Every sucking intake of air was not enough.

"I can't do this," she gasped, her voice jarring. Raine's hand moulded to Emily's wrist and with a gentle pull, she took it from her face and held it to her chest where thin, worn cotton met the soft give of skin against bone, the small plane of the hard surface before her chest curved into a place of softness and warmth.

"It's ok," Raine breathed near her ear, a soft rush of air pushing against her lobe. Emily's eyes opened. Looking down as she was, her bleary gaze fixed on the intricate black traces of tattoos that marked the gentle bend of Raine's forearm. Against the delicate structure of her wrist, where gossamer skin guarded a vital network of nerves and ligaments, three words were inked, dark traces over the iridescent pastels of her delicate skin, *Love is love.*

They reached Burbank Close, where the place that had been a roaring fire was now a heap of grey ash and the skeletons of burnt things, they went to Linda's. A handful of residents with nowhere to go or no one else to be with lingered in the kitchen, the unshaded bulb casting a garish glow on their pale, drawn faces. Linda was by the oven, her feet planted wide as she finished unpacking the large boxes of rations, the thin material of her leggings stretched to its utmost capacity with every bend and exertion.

"You two took a while," Linda said.

"What's going on?" Raine asked.

"Well, I'm just about done unpacking all of this. God knows how I'm gonna make it stretch, but we'll 'ave to. Other than that, the broadcasts have been happenin' again. They reckon we might actually get an attack. Well, seems more likely to happen than the last time anyway."

Raine turned to look at Emily.

"Stay with me again," she said. "Is everyone prepared?"

"Spread the warning best I could," Linda said. "I'll 'ave a full house tonight no doubt."

"I don't mind having more people at mine if you have too many. It seems there's more and more that don't want to be on their own and I don't blame them."

Linda put down the cloth she'd been using and looked away with a grim expression.

"I know we keep doing this and we try and stick to the positives, but it'll happen one day, it'll happen." She looked past them with a watery, morose gaze. Across the room, lowered mutterings of a different nature were being exchanged.

"I do find all of this very scary, you know. I've been through some frightening stuff before, but this feels so real all of a sudden," Fiona said. Paul was distracted by the lively movement of her crimson lips.

"Oh yes, quite, that's understandable. You mustn't worry. I'll be right by your side, whether you want me to be or not, bombs regardless. Though I hope you do want me to be," he replied.

"My old husband," Fiona continued, "before he died, he was hopeless at keeping me safe or even making me feel like I was. Could hardly look after himself when it came to it."

Paul registered the subject rather than the content of what she said, looking away as she spoke. In Fiona's mind, a memory resurfaced, one from years ago when during a day off work, Stu had busied himself with re-decorating the spare room, probably humming and singing to himself in that grating way of his, likely with the radio on too loud to boot. Thieves had slipped in through the unlocked door and taken the laptops. It had been afternoon before he'd noticed.

"Stupid man!" she'd shouted. Over and over and over whilst buffing him around the back of his head with a paintbrush. He had cowed to her ferocity in his usual quaking fashion, taking his beating with the browbeaten submission of a struck dog, offering her tea once she'd calmed down and tidied her hair.

"Well, I can assure you fair Madame, that I am quite imperceptible to fear. I can remain calm even in the most stress-inducing situations," Paul lied in a grandiose tone. He felt her soften into his side.

"I would prefer you to stay with me," she said, and inside Paul, a long-neglected emotion stirred and writhed as he exhaled the contented sigh of a happy man, despite the circumstances.

They went back to Raine's with a small group. Most settled downstairs with the blinds shut and all sources of light extinguished. In the pitch black of the bedroom, it seemed to Emily that only Raine was with her. Her eyes and ears strained for a creak on the stair, the easing of a door. She remembered when almost every night used to be like this. When she wasn't allowed her phone and every minute was a torturous exercise in rest resistance. When the night was a cover for pain and fear, but for the squeal of the door hinge, the tip of the mattress beneath the weight of him; only then would her body find a kind of stillness.

Now, her bed offered cold solace to her worries. The dismal lack of sound or surroundings was agonising until finally, the rumbling drone of something flying low could be heard. The unmistakeable sound of a plane coming close. A rustling, a thump. A cold hand groped for hers and pulled at her fingertips. It was Raine.

"Get under here. Come on, lie down."

Emily sunk to the floor on her knees and felt the small gap beneath the lower bunk that Raine was pulling her to. She slid beneath the slats, her belly pressing against the dusty, laminate flooring. Then they waited, the low hum of an aircraft still audible outside. Emily tried to stifle her rising panic, increased by the suffocating blackness and the shuffling bulk of someone next to her, pushing against her body.

"Are you ok?" Raine whispered.

"Yeah," Emily replied.

"Scary isn't it, the plane."

"Yeah, I don't like the dark either."

They were quiet again. Emily's hip began to ache from the hard floor.

"I was thinking, tomorrow we can take a look at the wall, see if there's a way we can get over the top of it."

"Me too?" Emily asked quietly, the reminder of Jack hitting her like a stab to the chest.

"As long as you stay with me."

"If we make it through the night, I will." Her breathing was still fast and the muscles in her neck protested but she did not dare to relax her head. "I wish I still had my camera," she said, trying to divert her thoughts.

"What happened to it?"

"I had to sell it. I needed the money at the time."

"Did you get to keep any of the photos?"

"Not really, I lost most of them. Though I never really had

any of Jack."

Raine was thoughtful for a minute.

"Maybe we can find you one, then you can take all the photos you like."

Emily closed her eyes and tried to remember how the shutter felt beneath her fingers, the whir of the zoom, the click of capture. In the dark, in her bed. A press of the shutter lighting up the room for a fraction of a second, enough to catch a single shot of the room illuminated, cast in a harsh, electronic glare. Still, there'd be no photos of Jack.

"It'll be morning again soon," Raine said, but Emily felt no desire to reply.

A memory struck her of the day she'd moved in with Noel. Her mother had dropped her off with her bags at the edge of the estate; a last gesture of goodwill. Emily had felt like a dog left at the pound.

"Well, this is what you said you wanted. Good luck to you, because you'll need it the way you're heading." Her mother had almost spat the words at her through the half open window of her convertible. Looking back, Emily could have said the same in return. A fitting end to a fraught relationship progressed from strained to volatile within the space of two years. Still, it couldn't have been the end that either of them had anticipated or wished for in the halcyon days of years long gone.

Noel stood waiting on the curb. After her mother had gone, he'd greeted Emily with outstretched arms and an uninhibited grin. He helped her with the bags, both their arms aching by the time they reached the house. Her new home. She'd dreamed of escape for so long; been talking about this day together on a nightly basis since learning of the pregnancy.

The path was rutted and the door in dire need of some paint and varnish, but he'd flashed the keys in front of her with an easy smile.

Whilst she waited for him to unlock the door, conscious of the children circling the empty road behind her on their scooters and bikes, Emily caught the eyes of a small huddle of women that had gathered in one of the neighbouring front gardens. They paused their conversation and waited for her to look away. She felt their frosty glares on her back as she pulled the sleeves of her cashmere sweater down over her wrists. After some swearing from Noel, the key proving sticky, the door swung open.

A combined smell of dust and damp mould hit her as she stepped inside, assaulted by odours that were new to her. But shutting the door and being alone with Noel, in a space that was theirs, gave her a feeling that made all of the stress and the worry worth it.

They'd eaten dinner on the floor, sat on pillows. Their exhaustion from unpacking wiped away any possibility of making love. But she felt safe and loved as she lay on the mattress. It had been placed on the floor and had a sheet slung over it. As she fell asleep, her hands moved by instinct, cradling her expanding stomach, where a new life burgeoned inside her.

The next morning, Noel left at first light to work at the local factory. Left alone, Emily had done her best to make the house more homely but their possessions were sparse. A couple of picture frames, a few ornaments and a candle would not a home make. She looked outside and saw bright flowers in the window of the opposite house. She recalled seeing wildflowers growing in the small green space by the bus stop, so acting on impulse, she went there with some kitchen scissors and a plastic bag.

The kids from the day before were hanging around the tree nearby. They'd parked their bikes and scooters and were busy raking the dirt and hitting the wall with sticks. She gave them a brief smile and began to gather some of the dainty white flowers she'd seen, adding some dandelions for colour.

"What are you doing?" a voice chirped behind her right shoulder. She turned to see one of the older boys of the group; a ruddy looking lad with unkempt hair. He sat astride his bike, studying the scissors with interest.

"I'm getting some flowers for my house," she replied with an airy cheer. Her stomach twisted in her belly and she felt a hit of nausea at the back of her throat. Rather than reply, the boy just looked confused, his mouth parted. He watched her a little longer, scissors to flowers to scissors to bag, and then cycled away to join his friends. What a lovely young neighbour, Emily thought as she stood, her cheer being chipped away by the ever-insistent morning sickness.

As she approached her new house, her next-door neighbour's door opened. From it appeared one of the women from the day before. She wore a garish, pink dressing gown and off-white slippers. She held a bag of rubbish for the bin but noticed Emily by the door. She looked her up and down, making no effort to be subtle. Despite the waves of sickness, Emily put on her warmest smile.

"Hi, I've just moved in. I'm Emily," she said. The woman's reaction was minimal, except her expression suggested Emily may have caused her some affront.

"Oh. 'ave you?" She straightened from her stooped position with a hand pressed to her back.

"Yes, me and my partner, Noel."

"Are you from 'round 'ere?" she asked in a gruff voice, cutting in at the end of Emily's last word. Emily hesitated.

"Er- well no. I used to live on Oak Rise."

The woman leaned against her outer windowsill and looked her over again, a little slower this time. Unsure if the conversation was over or not, Emily reached for her keys. Just as she put them to the lock, the woman spoke again.

"Didn't think you was. Normally, sight of someone like you, all fancy like, means the bailiffs are about."

"Ah." Emily gave an awkward, half laugh. A few, uncomfortable seconds passed. She raised her bag. "I have to get on, it's been lovely to meet you."

The woman blinked and scratched absently at her leg. Emily couldn't close the door behind her quick enough.

When Noel got back, he'd not taken off his boots before she brought up the awkward interaction.

"It was so awkward. Where I used to live, people would at least be polite, friendly."

"She was probably just sussing you out. Don't worry about it."

"But she said 'someone like you'. What's that supposed to mean?"

Noel came towards her and wrapped her in a hug.

"It's just your appearance. You stick out like anything in these parts, but it's not a bad thing. You'll get used to things around here and they'll get used to you. You'll make friends."

She looked up at him, comforted by his warm, familiar smell.

"Do you think so?"

"Of course. It's not often someone new shows up around

here. Almost everyone is either related or has mutual friends. As they get used to seeing you around and trust you a bit more, they'll open up."

It was easy to forget her worries when he held her like this. She could close her eyes and let herself soften into the feel of his strong, calloused hands. Despite her growing calm, her worries fading into some dark recess of her mind, stacked behind a multitude of others, one more question came to her, and she spoke without thinking.

"But what about your friends? You've never let me meet anyone you know here, maybe that would help?"

He stiffened, his body becoming hard and fixed around her.

"Soon," he said. He kissed the top of her head and no further word was said on the subject.

Things hadn't improved. Before Jack's arrival and after, Noel kept himself in the company of only her and she never did manage to move past a half-smile, a brief raise of the hand from her neighbours, before now. As Jack grew, so did her days become filled with his company and laughter. With or without Noel, his chatter and babbling in the day and his silence in slumber, his little arms touching her skin and keeping that connection between them alive, palpable. He'd always been enough. Now she had nothing.

She sighed and rolled over to face the cold wall. At some indeterminate point, she slipped into a restless and uncomfortable sleep.

The next day came and they crossed what used to be the main town, now a rat run of empty streets and boarded shop fronts. They were joined by two others, including Ethan. They carried an extension ladder between them, draped beneath a sheet as if that made it less conspicuous.

"I thought you said we were just looking?" Emily asked.

"We are. Over the top of it, hopefully."

In the brief stretch of open land, situated between the old town and the straight length of Galven Road, Emily caught a view of the distant ocean. Like a distant jewel, glinting between the scraggy scrub and the smattering of clouds. She'd taken Jack once, making the arduous trek to reach the cliff edge, where sixty feet beneath them, turbulent seawater crashed and rallied against the rocks. They'd sat as close as Emily dared, Jack being as wayward as he was. She'd helped him to hold the camera securely, his slim fingers having to clutch tightly around it's smooth edges. His breath hitched with excitement as she tried to coax him into pressing the shutter.

"See all of this? Imagine being able to take it home with you. Then you can look at it whenever you want to."

When they reached the smooth tarmac of Galven Road, they cut right and walked amongst the trees that lined the road, hoping to avoid the detection of any border guards. Walking amongst this sparse narrow woodland, thick clouds gathering overhead in great swathes like a caul to cover the sun while underfoot, wild grasses muffled their step and uneven footing diminished their conversation, the setting took on a murky kind of depth much unlike the bright summer they'd been used to.

"Gina said she'd meet us there," Raine said.

"I'm not waiting for her," Ethan replied.

"She'll probably be waiting for us, knowing her."

The trees began to thin and the wall came into sight, stretching across the horizon. Emily was watching, waiting for the border guards, but on this side of town the street was deserted. The formidable, fifteen feet wall underwent a progressive growth as they neared it, until finally, they were before it—a great tower of stone and mortar, the physical embodiment of all that kept her from Jack.

As predicted, Gina was there waiting. She hardly acknowledged them, rifling through a large bag whilst Kay stood abreast of her, hands on hips. She greeted them in the terse style that Emily had come to expect, casting a shrewd and unfriendly eye over her. But she could do nothing to deter her from being here where Jack's closeness was a palpable pull.

"How high will that thing reach?" Emily said. She reached for the ladder, but Ethan took it in both hands, propping it against the wall and pulling the rope to extend it. Emily reached in.

"Here, I can help," she said.

"It's alright, I got it," he replied, extending it to its full height before propping it against the wall. It had barely settled against the blocks before Emily managed to get in front of Ethan, taking the rails in both hands and setting her foot on the first rung.

"Hey, hold on," Ethan said. "We have to make sure it's stable."

Emily kept her grip on the ladder whilst he adjusted it. No one was going to stop her getting to the top of the wall first. He stepped back, stabilising it with one hand.

"You don't want me to go first? It looks like there's wire on top."

But she was already climbing. All she could see was the peak, an expanse of aquamarine sky; the same sky that Jack would see if he were outside.

"Emily," Raine called. "Slow down." But her shouts seemed far away. She was almost at the top, her fingers stretching to reach above the last rung and get a grip on the flat, ungiving surface, but as she let her right foot sink onto the next rung, the ladder made a sudden creaking sound. She thought she could feel it giving as she lifted, almost willed herself to make a grab for the peak. There was no way she was having Jack pulled from her reach at the last moment again. She pushed up and gripped the wall's edge.

"Be careful!" Someone shouted from below. One last effort. She stretched her other hand to the top, but felt the sharp pain of hooked wire cutting into her skin. There was already blood. She looked back.

"Do you have any cutters?" she called.

Ethan was already holding them.

"My brother found these, they're the best we've got." She climbed down to retrieve them, being careful to retrace her steps without another slip or panic. They were small wire cutters, barely bigger than her hand. They'd have to do. She was back at the top before anyone could stop her. Her left hand was still bleeding from where the wire had caught her, but she used both hands for the cutters, putting her trust in the ladder. The wire was thick and taut from its recent fitting. It was hard to avoid the sharp, needle like barbs lining its length. She cut, managing to make a barb free space, big enough to sit on.

"What's on the other side?" Raine called. The wall backed on to an empty park. Further ahead, an expanse of newly built houses populated either side of the main road. She could hear Ethan coming up the ladder. He squeezed beside her, swinging a leg over the top.

CHAPTER 11

"It's a long drop but I reckon we can do it." She looked at him. "On your right, down there." He pointed to a small area of shrubbery; the soil was still fresh from where it'd been put in. "Guess they have to do something to disguise their open prison, make it look pretty. It'll be better than the hard ground anyway."

Behind them, Raine was on the ladder. Ethan moved to the other side of Emily, pressing briefly against the unforgiving barbs. Before she could pass the cutters, he'd dropped, hitting the shrubs with a hard thud and tumbling to his side. He got to his feet.

"Quick, before anyone sees you. You can make it," he said. "I'll help you, just bend your knees."

Raine clambered next to her, but her focus was fixed on the ground, so close to defeating the physical barrier that kept her from Jack. She didn't give herself too much time to think about it. Broken legs or not, she'd get to the ground, and though the thought of another man's hands on her body filled her peripheral thoughts with horror, it was background noise compared to the excitement of what awaited. She fell rather than jumped, trying to let her legs down before her upper body strength gave out. Ethan met her with his lean, open arms, his crumpling legs taking most of the impact. She got up and brushed the dirt off her clothes as Raine flattened one of the bright green bushes with her landing. Kay and Gina were laughing and shouting as they got atop the wall, but immediately quieted down when they noticed Raine's stern glare.

"Hey, wait up." Raine caught Emily by the arm before she could go too far. "We've got to stick together."

"I'm here for Jack, nothing else. I'm not losing the chance

to get him because of those two." Gina chucked a large duffel bag towards the grass, before jumping down to help Kay.

"Feel free to go, darlin'. Don't let us hold you back."

"Shut up," Raine said with a hiss. "Emily, you're staying with us. We need to keep each other safe." She kept a loose grip on Emily's elbow, making a quick scan of the park with a frown. Gina bent to open the bag. She grinned, revealing crooked teeth like old swayed gravestones on a soil of receded gums.

"I brought some disguises. Might help us fit in an' all." She pulled out some leather loafers and a smart women's jacket. She finished off the look with a large designer handbag that dwarfed her slight midsection. "No prizes for guessin' where I got these." She slipped an expensive looking men's watch to Ethan, while Kay tried to flatten his hair to the side with much amusement. Neither Emily nor Raine were laughing.

"Let's get on with it," Raine said.

"Don't forget to talk posh too," Gina was putting on an accent. "Books on your head, innit."

"Enough! Plan is to walk around, try and find out stuff. Don't draw attention to yourselves though. The guards will be on us in minutes if people get suspicious."

Ethan's face blanched as he thought of the guards.

"Maybe we should have got some fake IDs," Emily said.

"If it gets to the stage where we're asked for IDs, I don't think it'd matter much what was on them," Raine replied. "This way; let's avoid the houses."

They cut across the grass, on constant watch for curious dog walkers or attentive window dwellers. In the far corner of the park, a narrow alley led them to a thin strip of wasteland; a dead area between a spread of low warehouses and tall corporate looking buildings. Looking at the penned-in warehouses, their low grey facades like oversized pigsties, made her think of Noel. Was he in one of those? Put to use with the other brown-carded men? Or was he cast in a heap somewhere, his body lost to a cause he'd never subscribed to. Most of all, for the briefest of moments, she wondered, had she been as absent from his mind as he had been from hers?

They found the main road, bunching together to follow it into town, keeping their eyes to the ground as occasional cars with tinted windows and shining alloys cruised past them.

Looking at Raine, Emily thought she could pass for an older daughter of one of the local affluent families. Her edgy hair and androgynous clothes could be interpreted as the rite of rebellion. Emily was thankful she'd put on her smarter clothes today; you'd have to look pretty close to see the signs of wear, scrapes of dirt, the scuffs and worn heel of her shoes. It was Ethan who looked most out of place and he knew it too. His joggers and plain tee hung off his narrow frame and the flashy watch stuck out like a diamond in the dirt.

Despite the conspicuousness of the group, New Galven's exclusivity worked to their benefit. The quietness had a sterile quality to it. Emily knew that despite the commodities, the cleanliness, all of the good aesthetics that money could provide, misery within the shiny veneer of prosperity was no less suffered than that without. She felt small and Jack felt as far away as he'd ever been.

They came to a junction. After a moment's consideration, Emily started on the right-hand path.

"It looks like the town centre's this way," Emily said.

"Is it a good idea to go straight there?" Raine said. "We might be able to find a back route, keep a low profile." Emily looked to the road that curved right, where the traffic picked up and the bright, unmissable shop signs dominated the skyline.

"I can't afford to take my time. Jack needs me." Ahead of them, Gina and the others sauntered towards town, spread out across the pavement.

"Then we'll go that way," Raine shrugged, but her face was dour and downcast. "I thought we were doing this together, as a team, that's all."

They caught up with the others and within minutes they'd reached the bustle of the centre. Shoppers thronged in the wide streets, an echo of what the Old Galven had once been like, before the war. Groups of women with enormous pushchairs sauntering by shop windows in huddles, men in a muddy hued array of suits in ceaseless conversation and an endless hurry. Was this what success looked like? They were overshadowed by great daunting shop fronts. Their double doors opened onto the street, emanating enticing scents of heady perfume and decadent food; tall posters in the windows showcased perfect flawless people.

"Where d'you wanna look then? I wouldn't mind tryin' one of these fancy shops. How much d'you reckon I can fit in this bag?"

"In there," Emily pointed to a store across the road, advertising a food section alongside its other departments. "They might have newspapers." They crossed the road, Gina too occupied with talking to Kay in her usual animated style to argue. Ethan was pale, keeping his head low and his hands deep in his pockets.

The small supermarket section was towards the back of the store. Emily was so focused on finding the newspapers, it wasn't until she got there that she noticed only Raine and Ethan were still with her. It wasn't important now. Whoever was with her, her goal was the same. She picked up the closest newspaper on the stand. The headline on the front stated: 'Now they take over our schools'. She tried to scan it, the words blurring together in her hurry.

At the end of the aisle, one of the store's security guards was beginning to take an interest in them.

"Hey," Raine whispered, nudging Ethan's elbow. "We shouldn't all look at the same thing. Go over the next aisle or something and look casual."

Ethan wandered off, letting his eyes trace over the various cereal on offer. Raine smiled at the security guard, then went to the aisle's opposite end, approaching a woman browsing the biscuits. Emily flicked through the pages, looking for where the article continued. She could hear Raine's conversation.

"Hi there, I'm conducting a public survey, trying to get some opinions on the recent evacuee situation for my college radio slot. Would you possibly answer some quick questions?" She was polite enough, but the tone of her voice was forced and unnatural. The woman stepped back in alarm.

"Sorry, but I have somewhere to be." She began to usher her children towards the exit, but Raine blocked her way.

"Have you taken in an evacuee? One of these?" Raine persisted, pointing to the three children accompanying the woman.

"No, excuse me." The woman stepped around her and hurried away with a clacking of heeled boots. The security guard passed by again, this time being sure to give Raine a good visual evaluation. Their eyes met. It was enough to make Raine return to Emily.

"We need to get a move on. They're watching us." Emily

glanced at the guard; he was reaching for his walkie talkie. She turned another page and saw what she'd been looking for. The article continued, a double spread of the page, and in the centre, a picture of Ronan. She froze, her eyes fixed on him. He was at a podium, the Council emblem behind him on the wall.

"Come on, let's go."

"I have to read this," Emily said, she looked towards the checkout. "I don't have any money though."

Raine took it from her hands and folded it tightly.

"Don't worry about it."

"Excuse me?" The security guard interrupted them. "I'm going to need to see your ID cards." From the next aisle, there was the sound of boxes falling to the floor, then Ethan came into view.

"Hey, it just slipped out of my hand. Maybe if you weren't breathing down the back of my neck."

Raine reached around to her back pocket.

"I have it, don't get too close." The guard pressed forward though, and with one glance at Raine's expression, Emily knew they'd have to run. They heard a scuffle, then saw Ethan, already running for the door. The security guard made a grab for Raine, but she was quick. They followed Ethan, dodging startled shoppers as they hit the main walkway. Gina and Kay were near the door, browsing the alcohol. At the sight of them running towards them, followed by the guards, Gina scooped the closest bottles into her oversized handbag and darted out of the door, letting it close on them.

Raine hauled it open, letting Emily and Ethan out before she followed. Gina and Kay were already on the opposite side of the street and running at a considerable pace, Gina slightly unbalanced by the weight of the bag over one shoulder.

"They're not taking me," Ethan said, panicking. "Quick!"

They rushed to catch up with Gina, leaving the guards at the door, one of them making a phone call. The whole street, everyone they passed it seemed, stared and watched, screamed and rushed to move away from them. Emily's hope of finding Jack began to crumble.

"They were on the phone," Emily shouted to the others. "CLE will be here any minute!" They took a turn down a side street, leading to a car park. They stopped to catch their breath.

"That was a total mess back there," Ethan said with his hands on his thighs. "I ain't getting caught. I know what they do after they get you in those camps and it's nothing like their fancy adverts."

"Listen," Raine said, placing her hand on Emily's shoulder. "We've got this." She held up the folded newspaper. "It wasn't for nothing."

"It will be if we don't get out of here," Kay said.

"Leave it to me," Gina said, heading towards the parked cars.

"I'm not going back. I've barely looked for Jack," Emily said.

"Now isn't the time. We've got to be more prepared."

Emily could feel herself breaking down. She made no effort to stop the tears.

"But I can't leave him again. Let me stay here. I'll be fine."

Behind them, there was shouting as Gina shoved a woman trying to unlock one of the cars in the sparse car park. The woman hit the ground with a shriek, trying to keep hold of her handbag as Kay took it with both hands and pulled. They took the keys. Ethan made a dive for the driver's seat, but Gina pushed him aside.

"Emily, you have to come with us. You'll get nowhere by yourself."

"I have to try." She turned away, trying to work out which direction would take her out of town, towards the vast houses. There was a roar of an engine as the stolen car lurched backwards, then a mechanical grinding as Gina searched for first gear. Emily started walking, but felt Raine grab her again.

"Get off me," she said. "We've known each other three days. You have no right to stop me."

"Just wait, please."

The car pulled up beside them, music blaring from the speakers as Gina fiddled with the controls. Kay flung the rear passenger door open.

"Hurry up!" Ethan shouted. Raine got in the backseat, moving over to leave space for Emily. In the distance, the pervasive rise and fall of the CLE sirens was coming closer.

"Get a move on," Gina said. "I ain't hanging around."

Raine looked at her. "Please, we can do this together."

Emily slid in, feeling the last shred of hope that she might find Jack being wrenched from inside her. Finally finding the station she wanted, Gina took a grip of the wheel and pushed her foot to the floor. The car careened round a corner, joining the main road through town. Ethan was straining his neck, trying to spot the patrol cars.

"I ain't getting taken in. Come on!"

People gawped and ran, but Gina navigated smoothly out of town, still without sight of those pursuing them. They turned on to Galven Road, its wide, empty lanes and the cover of trees a welcome sight. Now they sailed, the car protesting loudly as Gina maxed the revs. Ethan was laughing, his face flushed, even Raine couldn't resist a sly smile as they neared the border gate.

"They've found us," Raine said, the flashing lights of the CLE cars now visible in the rear view.

"Straight through! Go straight through," Ethan shouted. They were close enough now to make out the wrought iron of the border gates open as a car began to idle through. They still had time, as long as they didn't slow. Black clad border guards were darting back and forth in a panic, some at the border, waving their hands at the oncoming car.

"They don't want to play chicken with me," Gina said. "There ain't no way I'm stopping."

Emily gripped the edges of her seat and felt herself pale.

"Won't we hit the car though?" she said, but Gina's focus didn't waver. They were travelling at a frightening speed. One of the guards stood his ground longer than the other, trying to gauge whether he stood a chance of intimidating the driver. He didn't. He jumped aside with moments to spare. Gina jerked the wheel as she made an effort to steer round the dithering car that had just passed the gates. The right wing mirror buckled as they glanced off it, breathing a sigh of relief as they flew through the border and left New Galven with the speed dial trembling at near its maximum.

"Yes!" Ethan shouted. "We did it!" The CLE cars were still on their tail, but they were in home territory now, cruising in fifth gear towards the old town. Emily was quiet, looking out of the window at the blur of landscape, trying to hold herself together.

"We'll have to ditch the car somewhere," Raine said. "Topside of the estate, dump it on one of the backroads."

Gina took advantage of the twists and turns, keeping ahead of the sirens. They turned onto an empty, dead-end road, stopping by a row of old garages, covered in graffiti.

"Quick! Get out," Gina said. They all bundled out and almost immediately, Gina, Kay and Ethan took off, running into the cover of woodland and scrub. Emily felt numb.

"Emily, come on. They'll be here any second," Raine said. But she barely felt like running, trying. What was the point without Jack? "If you don't get away now, you'll never get the chance to find him." It was as if Raine could read her thoughts.

She willed herself into motion, following Raine under the cover of the trees and leaving the car doors open, for the CLE to find. She stumbled over exposed roots and through overgrown weeds until they reached the other side and came out on the edge of the estate. Raine stopped to catch her breath.

"Pass me the paper," Emily said. Raine handed her the crumpled newspaper and Emily sat, unfolding it against her knees. She scanned the page again, trying to take in as much information as she could.

"It says the evacuees were taken in by people that volunteered, he could be anywhere." She kept reading, then saw Ronan's name. "I can't believe it."

"What?"

"He was behind it this whole time."

"Who?" Raine looked over her shoulder as Emily studied the picture again. His image did nothing to elicit any romantic feelings or affection. She felt as cold and impassive as his aloof professional stare into the camera. Mere business for him. Orchestrating an operation that would boost his career and leave her without the only person she lived for. "You know him?"

"Yeah. We dated back in college, a long time ago." She

looked up at Raine. "He's done this, just to get back at me."

"You don't know that."

"I do. I know it, and I'm coming for him. Ronan must know where Jack's been taken."

"Well we have this now." Raine put a finger to her temple. "It wasn't for nothing. Next time we go there, we'll get your son."

Chapter 12

"And what now?" Linda said. "Have them snooping round 'ere? Knocking on all our doors an' bringing god knows what. Oh, I heard all about it. Gina's been tellin' everyone about your car chase. Lucky you didn't mow some poor sod down while you were at it." They stood on the porch, Linda blocking the doorway with her large frame.

"Things got out of hand. We know we can get over the wall now, anyway," Raine said.

"Not for much longer. What would we 'ave done back 'ere if you'd been caught?" She huffed a large sigh, holding out a bag. "You two can take this to Helen, check if she's alright while you're there will you?"

Helen lived on the next street, a short walk from Raine's house. As the evening began to draw in, the temperature dropped. Emily drew closer to Raine, the narrow path pushing them closer together. Their shoulders brushed and knocked against one another. Raine looked at her, her face like a white moon against the backdrop of dark houses. Her eyes were bright pools of curiosity.

"I know it's not been long but I already feel close to you. I hope you feel the same, like you can trust me too."

Emily was quiet for a moment, thinking about the car, remembering Raine holding her.

"I do. I want you to help, but—"

"Then that's enough," Raine cut her off. They turned onto an unlevelled front path, through a gap in a stilted wire fence that was strung between concrete posts. Raine rapped on the peeling door. As they waited, Emily's phone vibrated in her pocket. She pulled it out and saw Ronan's name at the top of her brightened screen. Her stomach dropped as the door opened a crack and an overweight, nervous looking girl with greasy hair and flushed cheeks peered at them through the gap.

"Helen? Linda asked me to pop over. We've got some stuff for you," Raine said.

"Oh, ok. Come in." She stepped aside and let them squeeze into the narrow hallway. The air was hot and crowded. There was no more than two feet of space that was not occupied by some stray object or disorder. They were led into a small square of a living room, the epicentre from which toys spewed and a young boy played. An older child, a subdued slip of a girl, sat on the sofa. She appraised them with a sharp, inquisitive stare.

"This is my daughter, Sarah," Helen said, her weariness evident. "Kaden, my youngest. He should really be in bed." Kaden ramped up his enthusiastic truck noises in demonstration of his aversion to sleep.

He was so like Jack. The plump roundness of his cheeks, the soft brush of his curved lashes. His rounded chin and full lips, pouted in concentration. Raine handed Helen the bag.

"Oh, look Kaden. Linda's given us some sweets." Sarah

was straight at the bag, reaching in with an open hand and scooping out the contents. Kaden took the packet she offered him, clutching it to his bucket-sized chest with glee. Helen turned to them, frowning.

"Are there going to be more nights like last night? I don't have a very good blackout, and they were flying so low."

"I can't say. But we can help you with the windows?" Raine offered.

"If you would, I'd appreciate it."

They helped cover the windows, blacking them out, corner to corner with paper and sheets. While the children were occupied, Helen spoke to them in a quiet voice.

"You don't think they'd actually drop anything on us, would they? What value are we in all this? I don't know what it would achieve."

"Who knows," Raine said. "The Council seems to think it could happen. Maybe if Nemico can't get through Galven's defences, they'll take it out on us instead. Whatever happens, it's a good idea to take precautions."

Emily had been distant throughout the visit, distracted by the presence of Kaden. But she suddenly looked up.

"How come you've got your children? They weren't taken."

Helen looked uncomfortable.

"They weren't in that day, luckily. I got the letters, saw the announcements and what not, but I couldn't take them and be left on my own. And they didn't want to go either. Sometimes I worry if it's the right thing to do, keep them here in the estate when the Council says it's not safe. But we're sticking together no matter what."

She gave them both a closed smile as she ushered them out of the door, in slippers that were degrading underfoot.

CHAPTER 12

Did you enjoy your little outing? I watched you on the security footage seeing how the other half live, how you could be living right now if you'd made the right choice. You chose to stay in that cesspit with the likes of that lowlife that knocked you up. So enjoy it. Jack is better off here.

She read the text over and over. She closed her eyes, gripping her phone as though she held it over a clifftop. Every sentence had a new sting, a different poison.

She lay on the hard mattress, facing the covered window of Raine's airless bedroom. She'd declined Raine's offer of hanging out downstairs, wanting to be alone. She got up and washed her face in tepid water, over the sink in the bathroom where she studied the peeled grout of the tiles, the dark mould flourishing in the moistened space.

She replied. Though it pained her, though she wanted to scream and shout, call him names, she had to think of Jack.

What's the point in taunting me? I don't know what you want from me. I'll do anything, please.

She clocked the screen and climbed back under the covers. Raine came in, creeping on tiptoe in case she was asleep. She changed her clothes, putting on a baggy tee-shirt she liked to sleep in and nothing else. Emily closed her eyes at the sight of Raine's bare, white skin; the flash of rounded mounds, where her thighs turned to shadow.

Raine climbed into the top bunk and the room came to a still. Emily let her head sink into the lumpy pillow. Anger and frustration washed over her like waves, pulling at her insides, clawing at her throat and chest, looking for a release. Her phone gave a soft vibration and she brought the screen to her face.

You're not trying very hard.

She was woken by urgent fingers, pulling at her arm.

"Emily? Emily, wake up, planes."

Her mind was foggy with sleep and the war seemed like a faded memory.

"Emily, come on," Raine said, but the room was quiet and dark and the lure of sleep still held dominion. She felt Raine lie next to her, moulding around the shape of her back like a cushion. Her body came to life, inch by inch. She curled up tight, chin towards her chest. So many times, she'd done the same. When her bed had lain barren and the sense of waiting became unbearable. When the light was switched off and in a second her sight was wiped from the senses at her disposal, heightening all others. The clink of glass sounded like rocks hitting a window, the clearing of a throat like the great rumbling of a bus. His cologne, cloying and seeking like invasive, toxic smoke.

Someone else's hand fumbled over her body, finding her own curled fist. Raine used her thick, blunt edged fingers to loosen it, working at the taut muscles in small circles until Emily's slender fingers locked around hers. She let herself breathe and focused on the transience of night.

Chapter 13

"What d'you mean? They've all gone?" Raine said. They were at Linda's, in a kitchen that was empty for the first time since Emily had been to the house.

"All of 'em, this morning," Linda said. Her eyes were ringed red from where she'd been crying and wiping at them with the bundled tissue she still held.

"Wait, what happened exactly? I heard something about Jeff being dead?"

Linda nodded. "It all happened late last night. Jeff was in awful pain, all in his stomach, you know. Well, Julie tried calling the doctor, but she just kept getting passed around here and there, 'cos they don't have no insurance. It got so bad with him, when Gina got him in her car, middle o' the night, he could barely move. He was layin' there on the backseat, clammy and' cold as anything. Then when they got to the hospital, they still stopped them at the door. 'parently he didn't last long. Big bleed in his stomach, died right by the door, all because of this" She pulled out her brown ID card from the drawer next to her and flung it into the fruit bowl. She was still in her faded pyjamas, knocking into cupboards as she prepared a cup of tea. "Imagine it. Got the doctors there at the press of a button for the rich folk, while we get left to die on the street like dogs. I don't blame them for bein' angry."

"But where have they gone? I don't see what they can do that's going to help."

"They're gonna do something. Gina left with a good group of 'em, all riled up. They were talking about going to that upmarket food place in the retail park. I guess people are fed up with the rations already."

Raine turned to Emily with a sigh.

"Let's catch up with them. I know a shortcut."

They crossed the estate at a fast walk, cutting across the fields by the Aid Centre and slipping through the gaps between buildings to avoid trekking through the old town.

"They can't be that far ahead. They won't have cut through that bit like we just did," Raine said.

"What's Gina planning?" Emily asked.

"Impossible to say. She's gunning for a fight more than anything, with anyone as you can probably tell." She glanced at Emily. Neither had spoken about last night, when each had found comfort in the other and their hands had relaxed, minute by minute; what had at first been an electrifying tingle of a touch, morphed into a steady warmth.

"Hey," Raine said. "I wanted to ask, how did you and Noel meet?"

"I was doing photography at college, to my mother's staunch disapproval. She didn't think I'd ever get a proper job out of it. For part of my portfolio, I was taking photos of the estate. I was curious about life here, the rumours."

"We were your science project?"

CHAPTER 13

"No, no," Emily replied. "I wanted to see it for myself; living where I did, people liked to talk about it a lot, but you could never tell what was true. Plus, my mother had always told me to stay well away." She shrugged. "One time I was framing this shot of the terraces on Broadway and he just walked right into it, asked if I needed a model." A smile crept over her face. "He always had this thing about photos, he could never be on the side appreciating what I wanted to capture. He insisted on a human subject, usually himself."

She looked at Raine. Rather than catching on to her happiness at the memory, she caught Raine in a deep frown, her lips puckered inwards like she wanted to seal her mouth.

"Maybe he changed," Raine said. "Learnt his lesson. Some people say it can happen."

"Well, he never did anything bad to me. Me and Jack, we loved him," she said. "We love him," she corrected herself. "And when the war's over and the conscripts come back, I know he'll still be there for us."

"And this Council guy? The one from the paper? I'm gonna go ahead and guess there's some history there."

Emily was tight-lipped. "Not really. Like I told you, we dated. But he was too much for me, he wanted more than I could give him. He hasn't changed at all."

The retail park loomed like an oasis of shops and cars on an otherwise barren stretch of road that bordered this section of south Merredin. The large, square car park was lined on one side by shops, all different brands, all monotoned in size and colour. Each was the cumulative size of about five houses in the estate and, between them, offered a mix of necessities. It was a popular choice for the squeezed blue and red carded society and saw shoppers from both within and outside New Galven.

It was a far cry from the retail experience known by most of Shaw Hill, where on potholed roads frequented by the unable and inebriated and furnished with shattered glass and fag ends, they selected from 'Essentials' stores, where tokens could be exchanged for what the Council decided they might need. Though the park did have a discount store doing very good business for when an extra few quid was deemed flush enough for frivolity.

They could see the others, who were travelling at a far slower pace. They jogged to catch the rear of the group where the handful of teenage boys left on the estate carried sacks and various weapons, bats, clubs and posts. Gina was in the lead with Kay and Stacey. She stopped when she noticed them. She was staring at Emily.

"You finally joined us then Raine? Didn't manage to drag yourself away from your new love interest though."

"What happened to discussing stuff as a group, not just doing anything without thinking about it first," Raine said. Gina's still maintained her assertive, challenging stare.

"You can come." She nodded at Raine. "If you grab a weapon. She's not welcome though."

"What's your problem?" Emily said.

"It's you, still pretending like you're one of us. You showed your true colours yesterday in New Galven."

Emily saw Raine step forward, ready to react but she pre-empted her.

"I have every right to be here. I've been hungry too and suffered on my own with no support. My son's been taken, my partner too. I'm as angry as you are."

CHAPTER 13

"Really? Prove it," Gina said, dragging her bat across the stony ground. Emily looked around and saw Ethan. He offered her his golf club.

"This is stupid, Gina. She doesn't have to prove anything," Raine said. Gina smiled, still looking at Emily. Emily took the club.

"You're a long way from the Galven Girl's school now, princess."

Raine turned to Ethan. "You too? I thought you didn't like violence."

For a moment, Ethan's eyes cast downwards, but then he motioned towards a lanky teenage boy that was hunched in his shadow. His features were gaunt and furtive, like a wild animal caught in a trap.

"See him? This is Mark, Jeff's son. He's lost his dad, thanks to those bastards. It's not right, Raine. It's already gone far enough. We need to do something that'll make them listen to us, and if this is the way? Then so be it."

"Can we hurry up?" Mark said, his knuckles were white as they gripped a wooden post. Emily had never seen a look like his before, an expression of grief and compulsion, where loss and anger clashed with compliance, producing a desperate need to strike back, lash out.

"Let's get it done then," Gina called, and they resumed their walking, crossing the road and ducking under the barrier to get into the car park.

"What's the actual plan?" Raine asked.

"We're going to raid that fancy supermarket of theirs. Take our pick of the food they think's too good for us and send a message while we're at it."

"People might get hurt."

"Not if they move out the way."

They cut through the parked vehicles. A group of fifteen, they were already attracting attention. Shoppers either ran to their cars or clustered into groups and watched as they approached the wide, sliding doors of the supermarket. The lone security guard stood up from where he'd been sat with a jolt. Before he could say a word, one of Ethan's friends made a beeline to him and knocked him to the floor with a single blow to the face. The guard scrambled away, reaching for his radio.

Shoppers began to shriek and people were already running and diving for cover as the group surged forwards and split, clearing the shelves into black sacks. Emily was at the back, still by the doors.

"Get away from the doors," Raine said. "We need to be quick."

But the anger that had come so easily before now seemed to shrink beneath the bright strip lights of the supermarket. She saw a woman in her forties, crouching by the newspapers and clutching her leather handbag to her chest. The newspapers were stacked in great piles, side by side. On each of them, the headline: **THE BORDER IS BREACHED**.

She saw Mark in the closest aisle, standing before the bright selection of home décor. His face was slick with sweat; his hands were yet to relax their grip on the plank of rough wood he held. In a burst of motion, he bought the neat row of vases and candles crashing to the floor with one sweep of the post. As if now released, he moved in a constant arc of destruction, smashing and demolishing all the fragile ornaments in his reach.

"Emily? Now," Raine hissed through gritted teeth. "This

CHAPTER 13

way."

She ran past Mark and followed Raine into the next aisle where Ethan was directing those near him and scooping large armfuls of confectionary into his sack. Raine took a bag from her pocket and began filling it with food from the shelves.

"Are you going to help?" she asked. Emily scanned the packets of chocolate, sweets. Food that could make the difference between them surviving and being able to enjoy food, get the calories that the rations barely provided. But stealing still felt wrong.

She thought of her mother. A memory of the two of them, when her mother had sat in her chair, in the small pool of light thrown by the ageing fabric lamp. Her wheelchair dominated the south side of the living room where it presided in its down time, commanding the space much like her mother commanded her with a single look.

"I didn't take it!" Emily had said.

"Are you suggesting it merely vanished into thin air?"

"I don't know what happened, I just know I didn't take it." Emily's long hair had hung into her lap, imaginary worry bees in a high hum across her middle.

"I know I had fifty pounds cash in my purse and I put it on my dresser where it should be safe. Do you think the twenty pounds that's now missing happened to somehow grow legs and waylay itself? Or is it more likely that the only other person here, you, could have put your grubby fingers on it?"

"No, mother. I didn't"

"You probably think I lack the mental capacity to notice."

Emily squeezed her eyes shut, trying to stem the tears before they started. She heard the clack of her mother's long nails on the metal runner of the chair and saw the gliding approach of her mother's static slippers on the footrest.

She picked up packets of biscuits, dropping them into Raine's bag whilst all around them, the chaos grew. Sounds of shouting and destruction were gathering pace and approaching from the back of the store. Gina appeared, flanked by Kay and Stacey, all laden with full sacks. Gina, in high spirits, swept through the aisle, singing a tuneless song and knocking goods from the shelves in great falls of multicoloured boxes. Raine laughed but her eyes were hard and mirthless; Emily knew she was scared.

"Get your hands off me, worthless scum." By the tills, a suited man was facing Jordan. Shoulders squared, his face was twisted with rage as Jordan laughed at him and asked for his watch.

"You'll all get what's coming for you. You deserve it. Low-lives, the lot of you," the man said and was promptly knocked down with a swing of Gina's bat. She circled the tills and cowering shoppers with a masculine, broad shouldered swagger.

Emily's fingers flexed against the ribbed rubber coating of the club handle. The man's words echoing in her mind; not just his words, but his venom, that driving hatred fuelling all of the Council's treatment of them. All that she had. All that had been taken from her, yet she might still be held to her own morals. She raised the club and brought it down with frightening speed, taking out a display of cereal bars. The boxes and wrappers scattered on the pale floor but she still targeted them. All that she'd lost. Taken from her like the misshapen, beaten packaging on the floor, their crumpled goods spilt out and spreading in crumbs like a sea of waste and loss.

CHAPTER 13

"Emily!" Raine said. "Take these, we need to get out." She moved away, calling out to Gina and the others. Emily looked down at the black bags. One had collapsed to its side, offering a glimpse into its looted, dishonest gains.

I do not steal. I am not a thief, mother.

Mother could well be watching from beyond the grave, from a higher realm if her beliefs and rituals had been well met. She'd be looking down, not piqued with sadness as you might assume, but with her thin mouth turned up in a mimic of glee, and her working legs, lithe as a spring lamb, kicking with mirth. For her love of being proven right and having some frail understanding of the world was far greater than the unrequited love she imagined for a meek and faithful daughter.

She picked up the bags and followed the others retreating towards the door. Mark hadn't moved, still stood at the first aisle, but as they moved to leave, he erupted in a wail. He lurched upon the flower stand next to the newspapers, tearing and flailing his arms at the pots and oversized petals with utmost force. The woman who'd been hiding there pitched a tumultuous scream and lurched away with the kind of agility not known to her. Mark was a storm unto himself, slinging great swathes of dirt and ruin over the white stands and floor.

Ethan ran over. "Mark! Come on buddy, time to go." But Mark seemed fixed on the objects of his anger.

A hand cupped Emily's shoulder. "They're here, let's go!" Raine said. The sound of sirens and slamming doors came from outside. All around, the rest of the group joined them in running to the door, calling out and dragging their sacks. Those at the front collided with the unprepared CLE in a chorus of shouting, surprising them by both their volume and velocity. Raine put her arm across Emily's back and propelled her into a run.

"I don't care if you have to drop the bag. Just get out of here with me."

Emily let the club fall to the floor but kept her grip on the bag as they escaped into the sunlight and met a sight of thrashing bodies. A number of the group were tussling with the guards, not afraid to use their weapons, while others watched and jeered. But the backup was pulling up, and they were armed. Everyone began to scatter as a sense of flight took hold. Emily's feet found traction and she sprinted, fleeing with Raine across the marked ground of the car park whilst those left behind scuffled to break free.

Raine paused, looking back at the shop. Her hair was stuck across her face in wild strands. Emily dropped the bag like it was soiled.

Gina was whooping and high fiving the others. "I told you it'd be worth it," she said. "I told all of you. My idea, that was. Let's get all this crap back to the estate."

"Ethan's not out," Raine said. They watched from across the car park as the CLE converged on the door. They saw the slight figure of Mark stepping outside, still armed with his post. Ethan was pulling on his shoulder, one palm raised in a gesture of submission.

"Leave me be. Leave me here," Mark was slurring, his face had grown blotchy in contrast to his usual pallor.

"We've got to run for it. You and me," Ethan said into his bright red ear. But it was too late. Mark broke free, slipping from Ethan's grasp and running, but towards the waiting guards. Ethan, too, found his feet. But he was running away, putting as much distance between himself and the uniforms, the cuffs, confinement, as he could.

Behind him, Mark swung his post in wide, ungainly arcs at the black clad men, who represented all that had ruined his life, like the soft, biddable soil he'd displaced so easily before. There was a gunshot, like a crack of lightning. Mark fell.

Ethan reached them but slowed just a little.

"I lost him," he said, breathless with the exertion. "There was nothing I could do."

"You tried. You had to get away," Raine said.

It was time to leave and regroup, count their losses and their gains. Emily watched as more cars rolled in from the North. More of the same, clean, well-oiled parts of the machine. Mark was hidden in a huddle of figures, the life either ebbed out of him or about to be processed, digested by higher powers. She waited for Ronan's car to roll in on its slick, blacktop tyres with glinting alloys that shimmered in the sun like rows of endless teeth, its tinted windows blocking the watcher from the watched.

"Emily? Are you ok? You don't look well," Raine said. She bent under the outer fence.

Emily's phone vibrated in her pocket. It was Ronan.

And by your lack of reply, it seems you're not willing to. I'm a reasonable man, Emily. You have the choice to change this.

Chapter 14

"Just hold on a moment. Let me get these papers out, just a minute." Marsh ducked to retrieve a pile of papers from under his desk. The gathered council members watched in silence as he laid out newspapers, eyewitness accounts and a handful of photographs. His breathing was audible from across the room, vast swathes of air being drawn in and released from wide nasal cavities, a small pucker of lips sitting above a cascade of chins. He sifted through the papers, squinting at each one in turn.

"Commander, I visited the scene of the crime on both occasions. I can give you my account of the details."

Marsh silenced Ronan with the raise of his hand. A few seconds later, he looked at him.

"I'm quite aware of the events. If I want to know your account, I'll ask. A few more minutes please, gentleman." Marsh returned to his scrutinising.

Ronan clenched his teeth, biting back the urge to reply. His fingers drummed against the leg of his suit trouser. He scoped the room. Terry was staring at the curtains, his eyelids at half-mast. Gaz was trying to discreetly send a text, holding his phone just below the level of his chair. He looked over at Kyle, expecting to see the same, but found himself locking eyes for an awkward moment.

A sour taste burgeoned on his tongue. His mind again; why could he not control it. Thoughts of Emily, wandering alone, seeking sanctuary with those reprobates from the estate when she should have been with him. Desperation must set in soon enough. No better thing to break down even the most stubborn of spirits. If only she would make things easy, let him take her in his hold, smooth her hair. He could show her what she'd been so foolish to turn down. He'd overlook that, of course, in time. With the right gratitude and affection from her, trying to make amends—

"Right," Marsh said, clearing his throat. "Things have obviously gone a bit awry." Though his tone was authoritarian, his eyes were dull and his mouth was dry and sticking. He interlaced his fingers to stop them shaking or reaching for something to wet the tongue. "Something will need to be done about it, but it's a question of what."

"I couldn't agree more, sir. This kind of behaviour needs addressing with the firmest of hands. The people of Galven are crying out for some reassurance of safety and protection," Ronan said.

"This sort of crime is unprecedented though," Kyle said. "Other than the odd one or two giving us trouble, we've never seen a group attack targeting Galven residents before this."

"Exactly, I wouldn't put anything past these people now. If they get away with this, we can expect to see a mass mob turning up on our doorstep before we know it."

"Yes, I'm sure," Marsh said. "But what was behind it? Was there a genuine need for food? I know you've been taking cautionary measures since Kyle's run-in at the Aid Centre,

Ronan, but surely not enough to warrant this?"

"No sir, these people are your basic anarchists. An angry, unintelligent mob. Not even they have a clear idea of what their purpose is or how to engage in any reasonable action, they just have a hatred for people with more than them."

Marsh reclined in his groaning chair, bringing his Parker pen to his mouth and nibbling on the shaft.

"Perhaps the wall isn't as effective as we thought," Gaz said.

"The wall was never built with heavy-duty security in mind. It's there to mark the Galven border," Marsh said.

"Way I see it," Terry said, "the intruders that got over the wall, that was fairly minor, but it got people scared. What happened at the store was far worse and the residents are going to talk." His shoulders dropped; his input delivered for the meeting.

Ronan still felt riled. "You think they breached the wall just for kicks? How do we know what they were doing? I've already put in the drafts for improving the wall, adding extra measures to prevent anyone from getting over it again."

"We do need to improve security," Marsh said in a gravelly tone. No one spoke. Only the solemn tick of the clock filled the room for a minute.

"Can I give you my account, Commander?

Marsh's eyes had a watery glaze and a cough blustered up from his throat.

"Go on," he managed through sporadic bursts of coughing.

"When I went to the scene of the crime today, I found utter destruction. The perpetrators had managed to escape, except one, who'd been shot by the CLE after he ran at them with a weapon. Inside the store, not only had a large number of goods been stolen, but the vandalism was extensive. The manager told me it will be days before they can reopen, not to mention the cost incurred. Customers had been threatened, robbed and traumatised by these criminals, all of whom were very obviously from the estate as we know. This is more than just an incident. This is a direct challenge to the Council's authority. These people think they're untouchable."

"Thanks for that, Ronan." Marsh resumed his brooding.

Ronan struggled to sit still in his chair. He wanted to jump up, move around the room and kick the inactivity that had fallen over them like sleep. All he could do was wait. He felt for his phone in his pocket and slipped the screen out just enough to see if he had a new text. He hadn't.

"Any suggestions then on what we should do?" Marsh said.

"We need to arm the CLE," Kyle said. "There's enough justification for that," he glanced sidewards at Ronan. "Get them some guns, some protection. That'll make residents feel more secure and give these looters second thoughts about trying anything else."

"Yes, that might be an idea."

"I want to do a raid," Ronan said, without a breath's pause or a nod to Kyle. "I'm happy to lead it. I'll take a group of CLE right into the estate, see for ourselves if they've got weapons or anything being organised. While we're there we can take in some of those that match the descriptions from today, we know there's a few that avoided conscription."

"I think we should be careful about being overzealous though, it might provoke things as much as deter them."

"With respect, sir, you don't understand these people as well as I do. Aggression is the only language they understand. We have to come down hard."

Marsh sighed. "We can make a visit down there, see what

we find. But Ronan, I want any action to be thought out in advance and I want it to be passed by me."

"Yes sir."

"Let's wait for the reports and suffer the storm of tomorrow's papers. I'll do a quick review of your suggested border amendments, too. Probably tomorrow. Thank you all."

Everyone got up from their seats. Ronan was last, keeping his eyes on the floor as the other council members made their way to the door. He hung back, as was habit now. Marsh shuffled behind his desk, reaching down to massage his lower leg where a slip of his socks, blue with ducks on, was showing above his old brogues. Ronan cleared his throat.

"I'm starting to feel like you're pressuring me, Ronan. I've told you, talk about council stuff should be saved for meetings only."

"That's not what I'm here for. Grace wanted me to ask you to dinner tomorrow. She's making a big meal."

"She did?"

"Yes. I think she's been missing you lately, what with the challenges a new child brings."

Marsh's face softened. "Of course. I'd be more than happy to come."

"Is six o'clock ok?"

"Certainly. Thanks for the invitation, I look forward to it."

Ronan dipped his head and moved towards the door.

"Ronan?" Marsh said. "How is she? Is she ok, generally?"

Ronan paused, his hand on his phone again.

"Oh, she's fine." He gave Marsh a broad smile. "Just, doing as she normally does. I'll see you tomorrow."

"Grace!" he called. He dropped the keys on the polished

marble of the countertop, loosening his tie with his other hand. Quick, light footsteps signalled her approach. She entered the kitchen, her hair in a ragged bun. She smoothed her top.

"What is it?"

"Your father, tomorrow. He's coming for dinner at six."

"Tomorrow?"

"That's what I said." He leaned against the plush back of a chair while Grace processed what he'd said. "Can you get me a drink or something? I'm parched."

"You invited him?" she asked.

"Yes. I thought it would be nice, for you two to—" He finished the sentence with a vague wave of his hand.

"Oh, well yes, that would be nice."

"Make it a big dinner, won't you? We'll need plenty of alcohol too."

Grace went quiet. Ronan moved to her side and placed a hand on her lower back. Her skin was hot through the thin cotton of her top. She turned her head away from him. All he could see was the slip of her white neck, and wispy, breakaway strands of hair. He leaned in and pressed his dry lips against her fragile skin. She tensed. His other hand reached around to her stomach, wrapping her in a stiff, cold embrace. She twitched and then stepped away, distracted by an unwiped portion of the countertop.

"I guess I'll make my own drink then," he said. "Where's that kid anyway?"

"Watching television."

Ronan found him in the living room. Jack was sitting in the cream chaise lounge, perched on its edge amidst a pile of cushions and throws. His stunted hands were clasped in his lap, and his attention was fixed on the screen, his jaw slack and eyes enraptured by the bright cartoon animals, speaking in mellow voices.

He felt the anxious energy of Grace hovering behind him.

"Are you ever going to get me that drink?" he said. She bustled away. He stepped forward and blocked the television for a moment, before dropping to a crouch. Jack's eyes flickered to meet his and his mouth clamped shut. Ronan pulled his phone from his pocket and unlocked the screen. Once Jack had seen it was just a phone, he returned to watching his cartoons. Ronan opened the camera and raised it to frame Jack's face. After a second of stillness, the shutter sounded. Jack jumped.

"Ronan?" Grace was at the door, a cup of black coffee in her hands. He took it.

"Sod watching that crap all day."

Chapter 15

"Can I get down?" Jack asked. He'd eaten most of the trifle, only leaving the fruit uneaten in his bowl.

"Yes, you may," Grace replied. She reached a hand to help him but he pushed the chair back with ease and slid to the ground before venturing off to play, bunny in hand.

"He's a nice boy," Marsh began, pausing to hiccup. He put down his glass of wine. "Has he been good for you? I mean, behaviour wise."

"Oh, he's been wonderful. He's so well behaved. The only real problem we've had is at night time, he doesn't like to sleep in his own bed."

"Poor chap. I suppose some difficulty is to be expected given the circumstances." He glanced at Ronan, who sat back, staring at his empty bowl.

"If he'd just stop wetting the sheets," he said, his mouth hardly moving. "It'd be an improvement."

"It's no trouble, really," Grace said. "He was a bit better last night, so I'm sure it'll improve in time."

"I wouldn't worry too much. I've never had any doubt you were capable of taking up the challenge and providing lots of love and care." Marsh smiled a little sadly, and Grace flushed at the compliment. "Well, thank you for this lovely meal. It was top notch, splendid cooking and lovely to spend time with you both and Jack."

They rested in their seats, surrounded by used crockery and decanted wine bottles.

"More wine?" Ronan offered. Marsh raised a hand as if to pass, even as Ronan filled his glass with rich, red wine, no expense or volume spared eliciting a wry smile from Marsh. Grace got to her feet and started collecting the dishes.

"Best get the clearing up over and done with," she said.

"You leave that there. Ronan and I can deal with that."

"Thank you, Dad. I better get Jack to bed, it's already late."

Grace left the room. Ronan began stacking the plates without enthusiasm but already sensing an opportunity. It took a few minutes for Marsh to catch up with him in the kitchen. His movements were erratic and sloppy, his hiccups sporadic. He bashed against his chest with a fist.

"Terrible heartburn," he complained. They set to work at the sink, cleaning and stacking the dishes, putting everything back where it belonged.

"Long day at the office for both of us I guess," Ronan said, looking for where Grace kept the jugs. He'd only had one glass of wine, but was purposefully loose with his words, letting his tongue fill his mouth and the intonation drag a little longer on his lips. Marsh was facing away from him.

"You could say that. I've got paperwork and different requests filling up every damn space. I'll be glad when it all settles down."

"Me too. All we've done as a Council is try to improve people's lives, keep them safe and we've done a damn good job. It's crazy to think there are some on this island that would hang us for it."

Marsh made a noise of agreement. Ronan gave up trying to find a place for the jug, sticking it by the kettle instead. Marsh was drying the gravy jug in a heavy-handed fashion.

"Funny to think how one slip of the hand and that little problem could be wiped away, sod the red tape." Marsh looked at him with a frown. "Think about it, even after the hard work's been done and we've used up all our time and resources on placating those people, they'll do nothing more than continue to be a drain on our society, blighting our economy and the landscape." He paused, but Marsh was silent, occupied with the sudsy plate in his hands. "You could take that land you know. Sure, we'd need some new social housing, somewhere to house the conscripts long-term maybe. We need to think ahead, but do it in the right way this time and not end up with a pit like Shaw Hill, feeding and funding criminals that show contempt towards us."

"I'm not sure I follow you. You lost me." Marsh's eyes had narrowed and were coming into focus. He was sobering up. Ronan let go of the tension in his upper body and reached for another tea towel to help.

"Say we do find weapons on the raid," he said, "evidence that people are planning to try and take us down, what then?"

"You still need to show me the plans for this raid, Ronan."

"If the evidence is there, you won't be able to dismiss it."

Marsh rubbed his fingers against his forehead, trying to soothe his developing headache. "Look, I think you're getting ahead of yourself here. I was in a difficult position when I made you second in command. I put my faith in you, despite my doubts, largely because of Grace's faith. You need to put some faith in me now. I can handle this." His eyes were bright and his words coherent, but they still merged into one another.

"Think about it, anyway. I'm only trying to save you from a fall." Ronan was stony faced. He put the plate and the tea-towel on the counter as Grace came in.

"That's him in bed, for now. Is everything ok?" she said.

"Yes, fine," Marsh replied.

The kitchen was eventually deserted. After turning down a post dinner drink, Marsh made his bid to leave. He hugged Grace in the doorway.

"Be sure to message me, anytime. Anything you need," he said. He moved towards his car as Ronan watched, hands in his pockets.

"I'll see you tomorrow," he said to Ronan, who returned a brief wave goodbye. The door clicked shut and they heard the sound of his car die away.

"It was so lovely to spend time with him," Grace said, taking out her ponytail. Ronan picked up his car keys, ignoring her.

"Don't wait up for me."

He turned off the main road and approached the low, grey buildings of the compound. Fat droplets hit his windshield from the rain clouds that had spent the day gathering. He rolled past the corrugated fencing until he came to the turn in, stopping at the barrier. A military officer approached him from the small security hut. He wound down his window.

"I'm from the Council, C1. I have some business here." The officer squinted at him through the gap of the window.

"What business?"

Ronan searched his pockets for his ID. He so rarely needed it nowadays.

"Just a moment," he said, gritting his teeth. He had a quick look in the dashboard, it wasn't there either. He looked in the door hold and found it. The officer peered at his photo. "I'm familiar with the General, is he around?"

"I'll take you through to him." The officer returned to his hut, raising the barrier so that Ronan could pull in. He stepped out of his car and into the rain, ducking his head. He was shown to a nearby brick building, where inside, a handful of military personnel sat at desks. They appraised him with cold disinterest, all except one, who jumped from his seat and went to clap Ronan on the shoulder.

"Been a while," he said. He lowered his voice. "What brings you down here? You need more reports?"

"No, actually. I wanted you to take me to a conscript."

"Oh, one in particular?"

"Yes, indeed."

"Follow me then." They slipped through the rain and into the cover of one of the indistinctive, low grey buildings that occupied the majority of the complex. They reminded Ronan of chicken sheds—rows and rows of uniform, intense farming blocks. Couldry unlocked a door, shutting it behind them before he spoke again.

"It's been one thing after another lately ever since you were last here. Mind you, you've never been in the blocks, have you?" Ronan shook his head. "Well, it's not the men giving us grief, it's my own staff going at me. I don't know if I'd still be in this job if it wasn't for that pay rise you got me."

"Well, don't quit yet. I need you." Ronan hunched his shoulders and glanced around the dim cabin-like interior of the empty room.

"They're a bit further in, we keep them in the dorms. Say, I was going to message you and see if you and Emily fancied coming out for a drink with me and Steph sometime. She misses seeing Emily Been on at me to set something up, you know how she gets."

Ronan suppressed a sigh building in his chest like a balloon. "Sure, I'm booked up though."

"Whenever you're free. Did you want me to do another report by the way? It's been about a week."

Hold off for now, I need to work some things out. Do you have a man named Noel Carson?"

Couldry frowned. "Not under my supervision, but wait here a minute and I'll find out where he is."

Couldry left through another door and the room fell quiet. There was a distinct odour of commercial cleaning fluid, mixed with fresh cut wood and the stale musk of inactivity. What was the point in waiting? His body was tight with a nervous energy, ready to uncoil. He approached the door that Couldry had disappeared through, but as he pressed his weight against the handle, Couldry burst through from the other side, knocking him back.

"Have you found him?"

"Yes, come with me."

They proceeded down a corridor, deeper into the cavernous recesses of the building. After going through another door, the space opened out into a warehouse floor, full of empty work stations and machinery. The great static of so many machines was unsettling. The sound of their footsteps seemed to reverberate off every sheet of metal and stack of crates.

"I have to say, when I saw you, I assumed you'd be coming to take the new fella off our hands, the one they brought in from that looting."

CHAPTER 15

"Has he been difficult?"

"I'll be relieved when he goes for his trial, put it that way."

"He'll be off your hands after we've stuck two ton of charges on him, I'll make sure of that."

They came to a corridor that must have been the dorm area. Numbered doors lined each side. Couldry stopped at number seven and pulled out a key. Ronan tried to suppress the twisting in his stomach. It wasn't excitement, and it was far from fear. It was a world away from what others might describe as butterflies, timid little flaps in his midriff. No. It was the great unfurling of a behemoth; its wings, like his anger, struggling to be contained in such a small space. Just a little while longer.

"What do you want with this Carson guy then?"

"Privacy," Ronan said.

The silver handle dropped with a press and they entered a narrow room with bunks on each side and small huddles of men either relaxing on the beds or sitting at one of the tables.

"He's at the end, on the right." Ronan nodded. He'd already spotted him.

"Is there a room of some kind where I can talk to him?"

"There are a couple of staff rooms I can probably find."

"What about that door, down at the end."

"That goes outside I believe; I can unlock it for you."

"Please."

He waited for Couldry to sift through his keys and unlock the metal door in the corner. He ignored the curious glances. Couldry paused by the door as if he wanted to say something else.

"That will be fine, thank you." Couldry still hesitated. "I'll come and find you after."

Couldry left the room and Ronan waited for the latch to click. He looked at Noel; a man who regarded him with the same casual disinterest you'd afford to any stranger. But his face was familiar to Ronan. He had the same dark, narrow eyes and thick eyebrows as in the pictures. When his face turned away, Ronan saw the same, sculpted profile that Emily must have fallen for.

He advanced through the room, his patent leather shoes, pointed and polished, were at odds with the dirt ridden, industrial floor.

"Noel?" he asked, standing over him. His name was like acid in his mouth.

"Who are you?"

"Step outside." He flashed his Council ID. Noel didn't get a chance to read it, but the black edging was enough to get him to his feet.

It was dark and wet outside. The door opened onto an empty patch of ground between the back of the dorms and a high perimeter fence.

"Am I in some sort of trouble?" Noel asked. Ronan paced back and forth, muddying his shoes. He stopped in front of him. They were about the same height, but any similarity ended there. Where he was stocky and thick around the middle, Noel was slim and willowy. His own neat, red hair carefully styled each morning, couldn't be further away from Noel's wispy, unkempt hair. Noel was arty, a dreamer. Ronan appraised his long, slender fingers and wondered where they'd been, which parts of her they'd touched and traced over.

His shoulders broadened. "Why don't you tell me a little about yourself. I believe this is the first time we've met."

CHAPTER 15

"What's this about?"

"Just," Ronan flapped his hand. "Just do it."

"I work in the factory, making shells mostly. Like everyone else here, I'm just trying to earn enough to move back to my family, once the war's over."

Ronan went still, rain running down his face.

"Tell me about your family."

"Are they ok? What's happened?"

"Emily. What's she like?"

"Um," Noel swallowed. "She loves taking photos. She used to at college. She loves dancing and taking our son to the park. She doesn't see her other family, same as me."

"And?"

"I'm not sure what you want to know."

Ronan was suddenly upon him in a burst of movement. He gripped the hem of Noel's shirt, their noses mere millimetres from touching.

"And she's not yours. You're never going to touch her with your grubby hands again."

He let himself release. The knuckles of his right fist connected with Noel's jaw with a satisfying crack. Noel flew backwards, skittering in the mud as he tried to get away. But he didn't get far. He stopped by the fence and put his hands up.

"You're crazy. You can have her, I don't care." Ronan pressed him back by the shoulders before he could recover.

"You're nothing to her, you never were."

Noel tried to resist, but before he could twist away Ronan delivered two more punches to his face. His hands smarted with the sting of ripped skin.

"What did I do? I've never even seen you before."

"You took her from me. You took her even though she's worth so much more than you."

Their eyes met and Noel moved fast. He kicked Ronan in the shin, trying to duck out of his grip as it loosened with shock and pain. But Ronan still had strength enough in one hand to keep hold of him. He struck him again and again. He tried for a third, but Noel dropped to the ground and squirmed away. He cut off his escape, kicking and kicking as Noel tried to cover his head with one hand and scramble for a hold in the mud with the other.

He stopped, catching his breath as he stood over him. Noel tucked his knees to his chest, writhing in pain.

"You're worthless, like everyone else in that hole of an estate. But you deserve that more than the rest of them. You deserve that for ever looking at her and thinking she could be yours."

Noel groaned by his feet. With a rattly intake of breath, he spoke.

"She'll never be with someone like you, either. If she finds out what you've done."

Ronan gave him one last hefty kick, feeling the brittle resistance of his ribs give way against his shoe. Noel wasn't speaking anymore. He writhed on the ground; his face covered by his arms.

"She's already with me," Ronan said. He left, walking around the back of the building to get back to his car. Soaked through and with throbbing hands, he drove away.

Chapter 16

"Least you guys have stayed behind to help," Linda said, scanning the bags and boxes strewn across the floor and dining table. "Rest of 'em seem to 'ave either dumped it 'ere or just gone off with what they took for themselves."

Raine rubbed her forehead.

"We can't just store it all here like this," she said.

"You think they'll do a raid?" Emily asked.

"Probably. We'll have to split it up, store it in a few different places, make it harder for them to pin all of it down."

Emily grabbed some of the empty bags discarded on the floor and started packing the loose items. Her stomach had twisted at the thought of a raid, at the thought of Ronan seeking her out.

"Leave some of that chocolate here, and the coffee," Linda said. She spotted a bag with candles and picture frames, most of them smashed or damaged. She carefully picked out an undamaged candle, placing it on the windowsill and admiring it in quiet contentment for a minute. Emily and Raine stuffed some of the bags in cupboards, taking the rest to the door. Linda said goodbye to them from the kitchen table, a cup of tea in front of her and chocolate in her hand.

"See you soon, kids. Watch out for 'em guards. If they's coming, they's gonna come in hard."

Outside, dark clouds were gathering.

"I can't believe she's done this."

"Who?" Emily asked.

"Gina. She has no idea what she's done, and with no thought given to a long-term plan." Rain began to fall and Emily wondered if Jack was warm and dry, if he had his coat to wear. The doors to the neighbouring houses were all shut and dark. Where windows were open, thick off-white netting swayed with the wind.

"Will we have any way of being warned? If they raid us?"

Raine shook her head.

"No. If they do, Gina's responsible, and if we lose people, that's on her too."

"Hey!" Ethan approached from the top of the street. They put the bags on the ground and waited for him to meet them. As he came closer, Emily could see worry lines etched on his face. "I've got a bad feeling," he said. "The other lads, they won't hide the weapons. They want to use them for when the CLE come looking for us."

"Are they stupid?" Raine said. "We got lucky back there. If they come here, they're going to be taking us in or trying to. What if they're armed?"

"I know that. I'm not getting taken, I'd rather they kill me."

"But if you went to where they keep the conscripts, you could talk to Noel," Emily said. Raine and Ethan turned to her with surprise. "I know he's not well-liked, but he'd do anything for me and Jack, I know it."

"Noel?" Ethan said. "The rapist?"

"What?"

"Ethan, wait," Raine said, but he continued.

"Carson, right? Was a big deal when it happened. I got told she was his girlfriend at the time; overdosed not long after. Don't think I ever saw him around here after that."

Emily turned away to hide her face. Everything was blurry and out of focus.

"I don't understand," she said.

"Take the bags," Raine said to Ethan. Emily felt Raine's arms wrap around her, the bare skin of her biceps pressing against her hunched shoulders. "Come on."

Emily lay in bed. The pillow was too flat, too low down. The duvet was heavy and hot against her chest.

"Are you ok?" Raine asked her from the top bunk. Emily didn't answer, watching the dark shapes of the bedroom with an anxious fervour. She reached for her phone, unlocking it and reading Ronan's message again. Her thumb hovered over the letters on the screen. It would only take a few taps, but what could she say?

"Emily?" She heard Raine get out of bed. The mattress gave way as she slipped in beside her. She tucked her phone under the cover beside her. Raine smoothed her hair with the tips of her fingers, her black nail varnish chipped and wearing away.

"Did he ever do anything to you?"

"No," Emily replied, her mouth angled into the rough fibre of her pillow. She desperately wanted to sleep, for the day to melt away. Her body ached for it, but her mind would not cease. Their respiration merged in the silence, but it did nothing to quell the memories. The darkness of the room was too familiar.

She remembered a night back at home when, like now, she

had been desperate to seek the reprieve of deep sleep. She had lain in bed, facing the thin strip of light from the landing. Jack was already stirring. Soon he'd be awake and complaining, disturbed by the light being on.

And then the room was plunged into darkness and Emily's heart lurched. She'd forgotten the meter was on its last reserves. She reached for her phone on the side table; without Noel to take it from her, it never left her side. But in her haste, she knocked it to the floor. Her hands found her camera, relieved to feel its solid familiarity. She clasped it to her chest and sat upright, primed to run. The totality of the darkness around her brought about a fear so permeable that it seemed to penetrate her deepest core. Not even a standby light or the glow of a digital clock could aid her bearings. She knew where the door was though, how could she not? But no one now, only Jack, could push through it with seeking fingers. He couldn't touch her anymore.

Her lips had gone slack, but a single sensation brought them to life. She felt the soft wetness of Raine's lips, pressing against hers and seeking to shape them, tease them into a response.

"What are you doing?" Emily pushed Raine back, one hand moving to her mouth to cover it.

"I'm sorry," Raine began, her body becoming as tense as Emily's. All at once, the sheet felt binding, and the space between them begged for an increase, for release.

"Why would you do that? Can you get out and let me sleep?"

Raine left the bed without a word, settling in her own sheets and letting the room return to its drowsy stillness. Emily took out her phone again, this time letting her fingers move across the keypad without too much thought. A few minutes passed, and its tremulous vibration told her he'd replied.

CHAPTER 16

She slipped away, in the slumber of the pre-dawn, quiet enough to escape Raine's notice. She walked to the border, the sun rising as she travelled in the half-light. The peace allowed her plenty of time to think and with every step, her forethought—*For Jack, For Jack, For Jack.*

Chapter 17

The border gate loomed like a sluice in the road. She read his message again.

Meet me at the border. Let's see how sorry you really are.

She stopped at the barrier, waiting for one of the guards or Ronan to appear. She sent a message again, telling him she was here.

"Can we help?" One of the guards approached, bleary-eyed and disinterested.

"I'm waiting for someone, he told me to meet him here."

"Really? Funny kind of meeting place for this time of day." He came closer, waking up a little. "I'll need to see your ID card."

She unzipped her backpack and looked for her ID. It was stuffed at the bottom, its brown edging defining her as lesser, underclass.

"Show it to me please," he said. She held it out, her palm covering the card. He leant closer, squinting.

"He's from the Council," she said. She wasn't sure if he'd want her to say his name. "It's important that I meet him; he should be here any minute."

The guard reached out and took her card. It took one glance

at the colour for him to give it back.

"Nice try. Unless you can give me a name or some kind of proof, you're not coming through."

"Let me wait here then, he'll come."

The guard scanned the long, empty road behind her with suspicion.

"I don't know about that," he said. "Some funny business been going on lately."

The sound of a car approached and to her relief, it was the familiar black Mercedes that Ronan drove. He pulled up at the gates and got out, flashing his card in the guard's direction. His eyes were locked on her from the moment he stepped out of his car as if he thought she might leave again if he let her out of his sight.

Emily felt a wave of self-consciousness. How must she look? After so much stress and lack of sleep, without a slick of makeup to brighten her dull complexion or well-fitting clothes to compensate for it, she hardly felt attractive. Still, the way he looked at her, it had been a long time since a man had looked at her like that.

Ronan hit the barrier twice with his hand. "Let her in."

The guard disappeared and the barrier opened. He led her to the car and held open the passenger door. This time he watched a little more closely as she got into the seat and fastened her belt. Cream leather and chrome surrounded her. The pervasive smell of polish rode roughshod over her senses.

"It's good to see you," Ronan said as he pulled away from the border with a heavy foot. Emily couldn't quite bring herself to say the same. His eyes kept straying from the road, looking at her, looking at different parts of her. "How come the change of heart?"

"I realised you were right. I don't belong there and I need to give us a chance and stop running away."

Ronan sniffed and brushed at his nose.

"That's all I've been asking. You won't find happiness there, with those people. I can give you a good life."

They were in the residential area now. The houses passed like great monoliths of stone and brick, with winding drives and numerous storeys, each mounting the other as if accolades to wealth.

"And Jack?" Emily asked, holding her breath. "You'll find him for me?"

Ronan smiled. "Of course." He was quiet for a moment.

"I need to know he's ok."

"Sure. We'll get to the house and get settled in and then I'll need to speak to the Commander." He checked his watch. "I can probably take the day off, but I'll still have to make some calls."

Emily's heart surged with a sickening mix of wild hope and dampening disappointment. The car slowed; he seemed to be concentrating on the houses they were passing. He swerved into a driveway with a garage at the end.

"Here we are," he said, getting the keys from his pocket. "I bought it just recently. I've been working so much, though, I've barely been able to get set up but we can make it ours."

They were outside a modern, detached new-building with dark windows. Ronan killed the engine, enveloping the two of them in the quiet of the early morning. Inside, the house smelt of fresh paint and gloss. There was nothing on the walls and the furnishing was scant. He'd left a couple of gym bags by the back door.

"You can probably tell I've just been crashing out here," he said, disappearing around a corner. Her footsteps echoed through the kitchen. "It's a blank canvas," he called, returning to join her. "For you to make your own." He reached out to her, slipping one of his arms across her lower back and curling the other around her hip.

"Can you call the Commander now? Or someone who might be able to look up where Jack is?"

He checked his watch. "It's early. Come here." He leant in and pressed against her, moving his mouth to hers. They kissed. Emily could feel the excitement emanating from him. He pushed into her, seeking every part of her tongue with his.

"You don't know how long I've been waiting for this," he said into her ear. She was looking for the door, looking past his shoulder and breathing the clear air that wasn't thick with his cologne.

"I'm so tired," she said. "I've barely slept in days."

He smiled. "I'll show you to the bedroom."

She woke up in an empty bed. Though she lay under plush covers, her head resting atop two plump, freshly laundered pillows, the room was cold and devoid of any furniture or belongings. She was still dressed; Ronan's wandering hands had only got so far before she'd been overcome by the need to sleep.

Downstairs, she found Ronan on his phone, pacing the kitchen.

"I will when I get a chance to." He paused, his eyes straight on Emily as she came in. "Possibly tomorrow, maybe later, I can't say right now." Another pause. "No," he said, a little terser. "Marsh needs this advance summary like yesterday. Let me focus on that and then I'll give you a call when I can help. Ok, ok bye." He pointed towards the counter. "I brought breakfast."

She took a bagel from one of the greasy bags.

"You're going to give this a chance then?" he asked.

Emily wiped the sleep from her eyes.

"We haven't had much chance to talk yet. All I can think about is Jack; when he's with me again, then I'm willing to talk it over and be open to possibilities."

He moved towards her, pushing the food aside.

"I don't want possibilities, Emily. I want you to commit to this, live here with me."

She tried to swallow her mouthful too quickly. The dry bagel caught in her throat.

"We will, I want that. Just don't rush me too much into certain things."

"I understand." He picked up one of her hands and held it in his. "You need time to adjust, it's been difficult. Living in that place, with those people, it's got you all muddled." He pressed the small pucker of his lips into the hair just above her temple. "You're not going to run away again though, are you. You won't just leave me after I find Jack for you."

"No, I meant what I said."

His breathing became heavier and he kissed her neck. She felt him press against her, asking, wanting. She pushed him away.

"Please. You said you'd call the Commander." She looked up at his face, but his eyes were dark and his jaw was a hard block against her forehead. He turned away, dialling a number on his phone.

"Commander? How are you this morning?" He laughed. "Feeling the wine? Listen—" He went quiet for a second, his pacing taking him closer to the back door. "To speak about the upcoming plans, yes." He gripped the handle. "Really? I guess it's common behaviour for their kind. I wanted to ask you about something while I have the chance." He opened the back door and stepped into the garden, shutting it behind him.

Emily watched him through the window. He was pacing outside, consumed in his conversation. She thought of Raine and all the talk that would be going around at Linda's house and all over the estate. She was happy to leave it behind, a community she'd never felt part of, not completely. She entered the living room. Like the rest of the house, it contained neutral, characterless furniture and little else. One of Ronan's gym bags was by the coffee table. She sat next to it and let her hand drop to the zip, teasing it open while she listened for the creak of the door. It contained a few changes of clothes, some trainers. The scant, impersonal belongings of a bachelor. She felt a stab of sympathy for him. She knew too well what it was like to be lonely.

She unzipped one of the inner pockets. Inside, she felt a small plastic bag. She lifted it into view and saw that it contained fine white powder. The back door opened and shut again with a bang. She returned it to its pocket and zipped the bag closed before he could catch her.

"I spoke to Marsh," he said. "He's got a lot going on, but he'll look into it for me. It might not be 'til later though, or tomorrow."

Emily stood. "Are you serious? I can't hang around here all day waiting. Let me go out and look for him myself, I need to do something." She stepped towards the door but he blocked her.

"No, not without me. Marsh did say we could try the compound. Some of the children have been going there in the day, in place of school."

"I want to go, now."

The road was busier now that the day was in motion. As they approached the perimeter of the compound, Emily looked through the window at the security fencing. Boundaries within boundaries. It seemed everyone was trapped in their own kind of prison. She got a first glimpse of the uniform buildings that Ethan so feared; that Noel and so many others called home.

They pulled into the entrance, but rather than stop at the barrier, Ronan pulled up at the side and switched the engine off.

"Are we not going inside?"

"There's no point unless there are evacuees there today. I'm going to ask."

He got out and Emily followed. A guard met them at the barrier.

"Hi there," Ronan said, flashing his card.

"Can I see her card please?" the guard asked, but Ronan stopped her before she could reach for her pocket.

"She's with me. I just wanted to ask if you have any of the evacuees here today."

The guard raised his eyebrow and glanced at Emily again.

"No, not since last week."

"Can you look up details of them? Do you have some kind of register or something?" Emily asked, stepping forward.

"I'll give you a name; if you could look this up on your system." Ronan took out a paper from the car and wrote down details. He handed it to the guard.

"I'll have to pass it to the General."

"Can you do it now?" Emily interrupted again. "Please, it's really important we find him."

Ronan turned to her, placing his hands on her shoulders.

"Give them a chance, Emily. We'll find him. I was with the General just yesterday and he told me he's caught up today."

Emily moved away from him. She couldn't stand his touch or the thought of getting back into the car. Despite what she'd told him, and the fruitlessness of it, she couldn't help but feel the urge to run.

"I heard about what happened last night," Ronan said to the guard. "The Commander told me. What was the guy's name?"

"Carson, I think." Emily perked up, now listening intently to every word. "Noel or something like that. Yeah, it was quite bad. We've put the guy that did it, the new guy, in isolation."

Ronan looked at Emily. "I didn't realise it was him."

"What? What happened to him?" Emily said.

"He's dead," Ronan said. "Marsh told me this morning."

"Really?" the guard said. "I didn't know."

"Come on," Ronan said, guiding Emily to the car. She was shaking. Every bit of security in her life, all that she'd relied on. How could it all have fallen apart in such a short space of time? Noel seemed like a distant memory. All that he'd meant to her had been wiped away. There was only Jack.

Emily sat at the small dining table. Every passing minute felt like an hour, and as the day slipped by outside, so did her hopes of finding Jack today. Ronan silenced his phone for the third time.

"I need to head out for a bit," he said. "They want me at the

Council, it shouldn't take long."

Emily stood, her chair scraping the floor.

"I need to get out of the house, for a walk, anything."

"No, you can't."

"Why? You can't keep me trapped here." She went to the door but Ronan stopped her.

"Because you forget, Emily. You've got a brown card. You try and go anywhere and someone asks to see it, you're going to end up either getting arrested or kicked out. You need to be patient. Let me help."

"How long though?"

"As long as it takes," he shouted, his voice filling the room. "I don't even know if I can trust you yet. I still don't know if you're just planning to use me and then leave me again like you've done twice before."

"No, that's not why I'm here. I want to be a family like you said."

"Prove it then," he said and took her in his arms. Emily was knocked back by the force of his lips. This time, his hands had a new kind of urgency, one moved by determination. His fingers pushed and pulled at her body, her hips, her jeans. She couldn't breathe for the intensity of his body upon hers. He finally pulled away.

"Come upstairs." He took her hand. "Come to bed with me, now."

"Ronan, I'm not ready for that."

"Bullshit," he said. His breathing was heavy as he went to the table and picked up his keys. "You might as well go then; you know I can just kick you out. I can get you put away if I wanted. How are you going to find Jack then? Is that what you want?"

CHAPTER 17

As she watched him go to the door, Emily was hit by a surge of panic. To be out in the cold again, with no one to call on and not even anyone to believe in was worse than anything she could imagine.

"Wait," she said and went to him. She pressed against him, letting her lips find the delicate underside of his jaw and his hands, once again, began to explore her body unhindered.

She went with him to the bed and let him mould into her, find every part that he'd so longed for, in her. One moment, as though she was watching someone else, the sights and sounds of the ceiling, his shoulder, his pleasure, were things that occurred in the third person. And then it finished, and he lay next to her, skin to skin. He was hot and clammy against the cool of her arm. He caught his breath.

"Was there any need for you to be so scared? We're done with the games and the running around. There's no need for that anymore. I know I can make you happy."

Emily didn't reply. She lay watching the ceiling, thinking of Jack.

"Emily?" She looked at him. His eyes were looking for clues, seeking a different kind of intimacy. "Let me love you." He kissed her cheek and got out of the bed. "Are you ok?" he asked as he buttoned his shirt.

"Yeah."

"I'm going to head out. Sort out this business at the Council. I'll chase up the Commander as well, ok?"

"Ok."

He stopped by the door. "Where's your ID?"

"Downstairs, on the counter."

He left. She didn't move until she heard the back door slam shut.

Chapter 18

The local park was busy with bright movement and the sounds of birds and people, all enjoying the green space. For Grace, it appeared like some kind of utopia; an exclusive area, which she'd never received admission to before, not properly at least. Ronan would laugh at the idea. A stroll or a picnic with her was like a particularly unpleasant chore forever avoided. Her dad was never available, and solo trips were a painful reminder of her loneliness, the empty space on either side of her where she longed for small hands to clasp her own.

Now, she had a child. They'd wandered down the path, Grace perhaps keener than Jack. Ahead of them, a blissful picnic area was spread out in the sun, bordered by trees and flower beds. Beyond that, lay a busy playground next to the road.

"Keep going, we're almost there," she said. But he wasn't by her side. She looked around and saw him a few paces behind, stood on the edge of the tarmac with his hands over his ears, his bunny squashed against his cheek.

"What's wrong? It's not that loud." She tried to loosen his fingers and lower his arms, but he resisted, screwing up his face and turning away. "Hey, we're almost at the park, Jack, look at this." She picked a dandelion and held its delicate white florets by his face. He took it, feeling the soft stem and studying its fluffy head.

"You can blow on it, they'll fly away."

Jack looked at her with a question in his eyes, a murmur on his lips, but before he spoke, a large truck honked on the street. Jack's hands flew back to his ears, this time pressing them and tossing his head as though sound became pain.

"Jack? Jack. It's alright."

"I want to go, I want to go!" he shouted, his words trailing off into a wail as his panic reached a peak.

"No, stop." Grace grabbed him. He went still for a moment and opened his eyes. But they were cast towards the ground and he saw his now crumpled dandelion, its miniature flower heads broken and detached amongst the stones. His wail became a shrieking. An awful, high pitched sound that drew concerned and annoyed looks.

"Jack, Jack! Stop making that noise." She held him as loose as was possible without letting him break free and run. He turned and twisted in her arms. "Look, over there, there's swings."

Jack looked towards the playground. There were swings and slides and children and a lot of shouting.

"Where's my mum? I want my mum," he said. Grace wiped the sweat from her forehead, ever more conscious of the attention they were attracting. With only one hand to hold him, Jack broke free and made a run for the nearest gate. She dashed to grab him, so scared of him getting on the road that she produced a burst of speed she'd never experienced before. She caught hold of his top.

"Why do you do that?" she shouted. "Why run? Do you

want to get killed? I'm trying to look after you, do you not get that?"

He wouldn't look at her, too distracted by the movement and the sounds of the people nearby.

She entered the house and felt a wave of relief. Jack went to find his blanket in the living room. He'd taken to sitting in front of the TV, his bunny propped beneath an arm with a blanket covering them both. She was almost finished making a cup of tea when a car pulled into the drive.

"Dad? I wasn't expecting you," she said as she let him in.

"Just a pit-stop," Marsh said, hanging his coat. "I wanted to check how you and Jack were. I know I haven't been able to come over a lot lately."

"Oh, well we're fine. Would you like a drink?"

"Sure." Marsh cleared his throat as he followed her into the kitchen. "Is Ronan around? I didn't see his car."

"No," Grace said as she filled the kettle. "I assumed he was at work."

"Not that I know of." Marsh waited for the kettle to finish boiling, then he cleared his throat again.

"How are things with Jack? Is his sleeping any better?"

Whether due to physical exhaustion or the vulnerability of having her dad here, Grace knew from the moment she opened her mouth to reply that the tears would come.

"No, not really. I just tried to take him to the park, and like every other time, he tried to run away. I don't know what I'm doing wrong."

"I'm sure you're not doing anything wrong. He just needs time, that's all."

"I feel like I'm failing." She wiped her tears with a tissue.

"It's not easy. But I can see that you love and care for him, and that's really all you can do. Don't put too much pressure on yourself." She felt the clumsy touch of his hand on her arm. "Is Ronan not helping?"

"Not really. He doesn't do anything with Jack and he's not interested in supporting me or talking about it." She sipped on her tea and scorched her tongue. Marsh gazed out of the window at the driveway, where the sky was darkening with heavy clouds and the gravel stretched to the open gate.

"Is he looking after you?"

"He's working. He's out of the house all of the time it seems, focusing on his career."

Marsh took a sip of his tea and grimaced at the temperature.

"Well," he said. "It's your birthday next week. I'm sure he's got something planned, something to look forward to."

Grace smiled but couldn't look at him. From outside, the sound of tyres hitting gravel announced Ronan's arrival.

"I better go," Marsh said, setting his cup down by the sink. "I guess I'll see you on your birthday, let me know of any plans."

"I will," Grace said, showing him to the door. Marsh passed Ronan on the driveway, just as he stepped out of the car. He raised his hand, as Ronan looked from Grace to Marsh with a frown.

Grace returned to the kitchen, waiting for Ronan to breeze in and make his coffee.

"What's going on?" Ronan said as he walked in, still in his shoes and coat.

"He just stopped by. Where have you been?"

"I've been at work, where else would I be?" He pulled out his phone. "I've got a lot of important stuff I'm dealing with, Grace. I don't know why you ask me these silly questions."

She felt the approach of tears again. She had to turn away, focus on something else.

"When's your Dad around again, anyway? I could do with talking to him."

"My birthday, probably. It's next week." Ronan was too occupied with his phone to reply. "I thought about what I'd like," Grace continued. "I'd like a new necklace. I've been looking at some online."

"Yeah?" He looked at her properly, for what seemed like the first time in days. "Show me."

She took out her own phone and pulled up the website she'd been browsing while waiting for Jack to sleep, trying to cope with his wailing.

"This one." She pointed at the one she'd been coveting; an opal solitaire pendant hanging beneath a diamond on a nine carat, white gold chain. He studied it for a moment, taking in the website name and the product details.

"They have a store in town, don't they?"

"Yes, I think so."

He kissed her on the forehead and went back to his own phone.

"I'll see what I can do."

Chapter 19

It had been a long evening by herself. After Ronan left, she'd crept downstairs, half expecting him to jump out and surprise her or be watching from a darkened corner. He'd locked the doors; it was the first thing she'd checked. Wandering around the empty rooms, the windows might well have been barred for all it felt like a cell. She had to trust him, put faith in a man who'd only ever let her down.

A heavy gloom settled outside and still he hadn't returned. He'd not left anything other than clothes in his bags this time. She'd sifted through them with a different kind of caution, but the zip pockets came up empty and all that languished at the bottom was his socks and underwear. She'd turned to the kitchen, looking through the drawers, unsure of what she wanted. Scant cutlery and pans filled most of them, but in one, a pile of letters lay underneath the tea-towels. They were utility bills, council charges. All addressed to a Mr Peter Barnett.

She'd gone to bed, hoping to pass time with sleep but ended up at the bottom of the stairs again. Feeling the silence of an empty house, she'd leaned on the latch, letting her weight sink into the metal mechanism that kept her here. She pushed her fingers through the biting brush of the letterbox, feeling the nip of the evening air. There was a world with Jack in it, a space bigger than her own. She promised herself she'd get there.

Anything was better than her hopeless, anxious pacing. She'd lain immobile in bed, like a sentient vessel between crisp covers. She watched the hallway light beyond the door with an incessant focus, waiting for approaching footsteps, hands that felt for her vulnerable body.

She must have fallen asleep because without warning, a heavy weight pressed into her, shocking her into alertness. Ronan pulled her into the mound of his chest, surrounding her with the smell and feel of him. Physically, she was still. But her mind was in chaos. How could she find rest or happiness in him, in his body? Everything was wrong.

She woke to the sight of him dressing in a suit again. He was by the door.

"Wait."

"Come downstairs," he said. "I haven't got long."

She got out of bed and joined him in the kitchen. He was searching for something to eat.

"You're going to work?" she asked.

"I have to. Marsh is on my back." He turned, looking for cutlery. His face was dark. "We're running low on supplies. I was thinking I could pick up some stuff later on my way back. Something nice for dinner? Some wine?" Emily tried a smile, but food couldn't be further from what was on her mind.

"How did you get on yesterday?"

"I put in the papers for your ID," he said between bites of toast. "It's not ready yet though. Maybe later today. I did, however," he paused to find his jacket and search the pockets, "get you this." He pulled out a small jewellery box, wrapped in fine paper and tied with a ribbon. She unwrapped it and lifted the lid to find a delicate, white gold necklace with an opal pendant beneath an impressive diamond.

"It's beautiful," she said, tracing the crystal with the lightest touch.

"I wanted to give you a present to celebrate the start of our new life together." He kissed her then returned to his toast.

"Thank you, it's beautiful." She paused. "But Ronan, I really need to know where Jack is. I can't focus; I can't feel happy without him."

Ronan stopped eating and placed both his hands on the counter.

"I told you I was dealing with that. I've sent out emails to the relevant departments and I've requested the paperwork. It turns out there's a lot of forms to be filled out before they'll move an evacuee."

"How long? You said it wouldn't be much longer than a day or two."

His phone began to vibrate. He silenced it.

"I know." His teeth were clenched. "I know that's all you care about. Is it not enough to be with me? To simply enjoy some time together on our own?"

"Ronan, please. You said you would."

His breathing was heavy. He picked up his plate with one hand and threw it into the sink. The sound of its shatter made her jump.

"Give me your phone. You've no doubt been messaging those Shaw Hill bottom feeders."

"No, I haven't messaged anyone," she said. But he came

straight towards her, grabbing her phone from her hand and turning away to search through her messages. "There's nothing on there, I've not lied to you."

He put it in his pocket.

"I'm finding it hard to believe anything you say right now. You're only interested in using me for what you want." His phone started vibrating again on the counter. "I have to go. You need to have a serious think about this. You're nothing here without me. Nothing. And if you're not going to give me what I need, what I want, then it's over."

He went to the door.

"No," Emily said. "Don't leave me here. Leave me a key or something. Let me look for him, please." She tried to squeeze beside him and block him from getting out without her, but he shoved her back, pressing his nails into her arm.

"You're not going anywhere," he hissed. "Wait for me to get back, then we can talk." She saw him take the house key and move it towards the lock.

"No!" she shouted. "Don't lock the door." But he ignored her.

She watched his car roll out of the drive and leave. A feeling of panic engulfed her. There was no way she could wait another day, waiting for the pain in her arm to subside, and for him to return, and ask for more.

She made a quick assessment of the windows. The ones in the living room were built with narrow panes, but the kitchen windows were wide and opened into the small garden. She took one of the heavy-based saucepans and clambered onto the counter. It took two swings. She shielded her face from the glass as it shattered outwards, leaving space enough for her to fit through. She cherished the breeze from outside,

CHAPTER 19

and the garden's fresh scent of freedom. She used tea-towels, bunched up in one of the drawers, to line the jagged edge, but the glass still cut into her hands as she pressed down to steady her drop onto the slabbed garden path. But blood was nothing. She unlatched the gate and left.

Chapter 20

Liz and Viv were enjoying some light conversation in-between the irregular snipping sounds that came from Viv's side of the rose bush. Liz's feet were aching and the sight of Viv in her front garden had offered her the perfect excuse to rest her feet. Her dog, Quinn, sat panting on the pavement. At a glance, it looked like she was talking to the shrubbery until the peak of a wide brimmed cream hat rose above the leaves and Viv's face came into view, a shine on her rosy cheeks, and hedge cutters in one weathered hand, resting against her slacks.

"I mean, it's just monumental the amount I'm paying out. I know they have to pay for all this extra security and it's good they're taking it seriously, but it's extortionate," Liz said, scanning the bush for errant leaves.

"I say, stop paying for supplies and aid. Use that money instead for the defences."

"That'd be an idea. Oh, are you coming to Pilates this Thursday? We missed you last week."

"Should be," she said, going back to her pruning. Liz was left to look around the quiet residential street, searching for something else to talk about so she could further delay her

CHAPTER 20

walk.

Emily turned down another street, another drowsy, pristine street with postcard houses and pristine lawns. Locked doors, blank windows. She'd been looking for what felt like hours. Without any ID, she was too afraid to go into town. Maybe she would spot him or find some sort of clue. He had to be here somewhere, tucked away.

At last, she saw people. Two older women, talking. One crouched behind a rose bush whilst the other stood on the street, frowning in the sunshine. She approached them.

"Excuse me?" The snipping sound stopped and Viv stood up to look at her. "I just wanted to ask if you could help me. My son made friends with one of the evacuee children, but now we've lost track of him and my son is very upset. I was wondering if you'd be able to help me find him."

Liz stared at her. Emily saw her gaze move over her clothes, her shoes.

"I—" she started. "Well, Viv, I think you'd have more of an idea than me, do you?"

"Yes, I suppose."

"His name's Jack. I can write down his details." Emily tried to relax and act as though it was a trivial matter, but her breathing was getting faster and she was starting to sweat.

"I could ring my friend, Julia. She works in the local school. She might be able to find out," Liz said. She put down her shears and took off her gloves.

"If you could, that'll be so helpful, thank you."

"You just wait here; I'll see if she can help first."

Viv wandered towards her house to make the call. Emily heard her bright hello and then nothing more. Liz was still looking at her, lingering on the loose stitching of her top, the grey scuffs on her shoes. Emily clasped her arms together in front of her.

"Do you live nearby?" Liz asked. Quinn began to whine.

"Not far."

"How did your son and this boy become friends?"

"Oh," Emily paused, scrabbling for something to say. "They met at one of the after-school clubs. The other boy left before I had the chance to speak to his carer."

"But you have his details?"

Emily bit down on her lip. "Yes." Viv was still by the house with her phone pressed to her ear. She was making sweeping gestures with her hands. An awkward minute of silence passed until eventually, Viv re-joined them.

"My friend recommended that you go to the school in person, there's not much she can do over the phone."

"Oh, ok." Emily could feel the tension. She knew they were waiting to talk about her.

"It's just that way," Viv pointed. Though she smiled, her eyes were guarded as she picked up her shears again.

Emily walked away. She got as far as the next street before the familiar sound of the CLE sirens sped towards her. She turned and tried to run, but the gates and hedges blocked her from escaping the street while the CLE cars prevented her from running back. The guards were swift. They took her by the arms and restrained her with handcuffs, searching through her pockets.

"No ID," one of them said.

"Must be her," said another. "Put her in the car."

He pushed her towards the open door, where the black inside of the car appeared like the end of everything.

CHAPTER 20

"Wait! Please," she pleaded. "Ronan. Call him for me, tell him it's me."

"No point, he's already authorised the pickup."

"Tell him I'm sorry. Tell him it's the last time, please."

The guard looked at the others.

"Might as well ask him how he wants us to process her," he said. He was on the phone for a mere minute. Emily watched as his expression remained cold and immobile, only his hand around her shoulder provided some warmth. He hung up.

"Get in the car."

She watched through the window as the car passed through the border gate, her cuffed hands in her lap. Back in that derelict no man's land, she felt more at a loss than she ever had. The car stopped and the door opened. She could feel the watchful, armed gaze of the CLE and the border guards, smirking, approving. She was the bottom rung on the stratum of society, without even her phone now, or ID.

"Move on, lady," shouted one of the guards. Her wrists were released and the CLE withdrew to their cars again, waiting for her to move away. She looked up at the newly erected watchtower, where one of the guards was holding a gun.

"Get out of here or I'll shoot," he shouted.

There was a sudden cracking noise and a sickening high-pitched ping somewhere to her right. He'd fired. There was laughter. What else could she do, but walk back to Shaw Hill.

Chapter 21

He hadn't been gone for long. He'd been to the shop first, picking up some single malt for Marsh, amongst other items, to soften him up. He'd planned to go straight on to the Council, but the house was only a ten-minute drive away and he wanted to see if she'd settled down. He needed her to be in an amenable state of mind for what he had planned this evening.

He took his shopping bags out of the car—wine, steaks and accompaniments, chocolate for her, condoms for him. When he saw the state of the kitchen window, most of it spread in shards, he put the bags on the floor carefully. Now she'd know what it was like to fear him. There'd be no more chances. He made the call.

She'd gone by the time he got there. He passed through the border without a word to the guards, his ID said all it needed to. He parked by the trees, facing the road to the old town. His tinted windows shielded him from curious eyes as he watched the bleak landscape of the road, crops of untended trees and scrubland left to grow wild. She'd gone. Whether to the estate or into the wilderness, she could be anywhere. He knew though. She'd be back into the arms of the same people who'd trapped her there years before.

He took a small plastic bag from the glovebox and emptied it onto the concave surface of the armrest. He used his platinum credit card to cut and organise the fine white powder. One short, sharp inhale. Fire and gasoline. Then nothing, except for the growing sensation of something building inside him, kickstarting his heart, reaching a crescendo. There was a tingling in his scalp and around his chest that pressed like a band. Everything was brighter, more vivid. The clothes against his skin felt electric as though he himself powered them. Oh, everything was clear now.

He brushed away the pale remnants of his fix and turned the key in the ignition.

Coming back through the border gate, a small crowd made the road narrow. He rolled down his window and stopped. There was some commotion between the border guards and a group of women who were standing in front of two range rovers. He got out of his car. The lead guard, who was suffering the brunt of the complaint, looked relieved to see him. Although most of the guards recognised him by now, he still took out his ID and held it up.

"What's going on?" he said.

"Perhaps this man can authorise it," the woman closest to the guards said. She was approaching her fifties, wearing a long skirt and hoop earrings. The expression on her face read trouble and Ronan's mind spared a second of sympathy for the no-doubt brow-beaten husband she had at home.

"Why are you here? The border's no place for gatherings."

"We're a small group of local women who've organised a

community collection to give to the underprivileged in Shaw Hill living without vital supplies. We've put together some packages for donation—clothes, food and toiletries for the women there and we just want to drop them off, and see if we can be of any help."

Ronan looked at the other women, who were holding shoe sized boxes, wrapped in decorative paper.

"Ladies," he began, and just the tone of his voice was enough for the woman that had spoken to him to drop her hopeful expression and crease her brow. "It's not advisable for anybody to go to the Shaw Hill estate at this time. The Council has received significant evidence that residents there are both armed and willing to attack anyone associated with New Galven."

"Is that so?" she said.

He looked at her with piercing eyes.

"Madam, these people won't be grateful for anything you give them, they'll just look to take more and more, by force if necessary. They are a violent, ungrateful breed of people down there, and once you pass these gates, you are outside of our immediate protection." He let out a breath and forced a smile. The woman didn't move, but glanced towards those with her, looking uncertain.

"May I see one of those boxes please?" Ronan said. A stout woman came forward and handed him a box. He inspected the flowery wrapping and ran a finger over the twee little card that was taped to its front.

"Could you place them all in a nice pile here, next to me, please?"

The women hesitated, but the guards set them into action, helping to empty the cars and put all the packages together on

CHAPTER 21

the ground. Ronan took the last one from one of the younger women and in his carelessness, ripped the paper. He tossed it with the others, watching it scuff against the ground. He spoke to the guards.

"Search the boxes for weapons or information. Anything that the Council might be interested in." The guards began to rifle through the boxes, being no more careful with them than he had been.

"I can't believe this," the woman at the front said. "We're still at liberty to pass through the border even if we are advised to avoid the estate." She emphasised the word 'advised'.

Ronan leant towards her, his teeth like a snarl.

"You are. But there's no guarantee you'll be let back in."

He left them with a smile, watching in his rear-view mirror as they bundled back into their cars. His foot was heavy on the accelerator. A female pheasant was bobbing about on the road just ahead of him, too slow to notice the impending car that was destined for the same piece of tarmac. It raised a foot, twitched its head and then placed the foot. Its eyes rotated this way and that as it assessed the world around it.

Ronan felt the small knock and momentary bump as the pheasant met his front wheel. A puff of mottled brown and downy white feathers flew up behind him. He drove on.

Chapter 22

Emily walked until her legs ached with every step and the last light faded from the sky. She had nowhere to go. The thought of going home was too painful; the place where Jack's memory lingered in every room. On the fringe of Shaw Hill, she assessed the empty houses that had once been the pride of their owners. Selecting one with no car, a fallen sold sign and lightless windows, she got in through the already breached back door and lay down on the nearest soft surface.

She woke to birdsong, leaking in through the smashed glass panel of the patio door. She had no food in her bag, nothing to wash with, less than a handful of things she could call her own. She went upstairs, looking into every room as though she haunted the place, imagining this other person's old life, surveying what had been deemed the unessential debris of someone's life. She spent a few idle minutes in the nursery. It was decorated in a similar way to how she'd imagined Jack's room might have looked in those bright early days of pregnancy. In reality, they'd just about scraped together the bare necessities in time for his arrival.

In the main bedroom, she looked in the wardrobe for new clothes. She opened the white doors, but there were only some bare hangers and crumpled old t-shirts that had been dropped into a corner and left there. She lifted them to examine them and uncovered a small cardboard box. A fabric strap was peeking through the opened folds. It was a camera in pristine condition, a more recent edition of the one gifted to her years ago by her mother. Although this one had seen very little use in contrast to her old one's worn detailing through countless presses and the fraying neck strap.

She pressed the power button, not hoping for much other than the black screen of the digital display, but it turned on, the view of the lens covered by its cap. She looked over her shoulder at the empty room and stood up on shaky legs. She slipped the strap over her head and cherished the feeling of a camera in her possession once more. Who knew why it had been left behind, hidden in a corner. A brief flirtation with the idea of an artistic rendezvous? Cast aside on the realisation that no such ideal could be attained with work, learning and time. It didn't matter. She put it in her bag and left the house.

She was sitting on a patch of grass beside someone's vacant driveway when Raine found her. Emily was focused on the camera, first framing the cloudless, afternoon sky, then pausing to adjust the settings and look at the lens before switching to study the house across the street, its door on its hinges and weeds reclaiming the driveway. Raine sat beside her with a rush of air and began picking at the grass. They were quiet for a minute. Emily was adjusting the aperture.

"You got hold of a camera then?" Raine said. Emily kept her head down.

"It's not too different from my old one. See that number?

I'm making it higher; that way I can reduce the amount of light that reaches the sensor and get everything in focus." She put her eye to the viewfinder and framed a shot of the house.

She felt Raine's hand on hers, pulling to aim the camera towards her. Emily adjusted the settings again.

"For portraits, you have to widen the aperture." She checked the view. "Hold on, I need to adjust the shutter speed as well."

Raine sat motionless whilst Emily adjusted and checked, adjusted and checked. And just like that she put the camera on the grass and broke into tears. Raine put an arm around her and leaned in close. Emily could smell fabric conditioner and stale smoke, could feel the rough, worn cotton scratching against her cheek. It was safe though, a small safe space.

Linda took her in a hug as soon as Emily entered the kitchen.

"We were so worried about you. What happened?"

Emily paused, noticing Ethan at the living room door.

"I went to see someone who I thought could help me."

"In Galven?" Raine said. Emily nodded.

Linda took a slow sip of her tea.

"I went there and I thought it could work, but it didn't. Now things are worse. I've lost my phone. I don't have my ID and I still don't know where Jack is. I couldn't even find a trace, nothing." The tears came again and Linda's well cushioned hands came towards her.

"They're coming after us," Ethan said. "I know it." His fists were balled by his sides and he was pacing by the stairs. "We have to get ready."

"We will," Raine said. She looked at Emily. "If it's who I think it is, who you went to, we'll prepare. We're expecting it anyway."

CHAPTER 22

"I know, but he's so angry. I can't help thinking, what if Jack Isn't there? Not anywhere? How can there be no trace at all?" Raine was next to her still. She looked at her. "We're going to do something, aren't we? Whatever it takes?"

"We are. We're going to take those bastards down."

Chapter 23

A convoy rolled through the border gates. One long line of black rolling steel, each with an engine heart. They thundered down Galven Road, armoured military trucks with newly equipped CLE inside, eager for action. Behind them, a sleek Mercedes with tinted windows followed, the driving force. They didn't slow as they reached Shaw Hill, providing no warning other than twitching curtains and the departure of birds. Like an autonomous machine, the convoy split into three, each group descending upon separate streets.

Ronan turned down a murky looking street named Carter Close. He was behind three of the trucks, lining the length of the road as they came to a stop. The residents watched out of windows or wandered out of their houses, still with suds on their hands, worn slippers on their feet. The younger ones kept more of a distance, ready to run and many did run to gather the others.

He stepped out, putting on his sunglasses and appraising the street. It was the first time he'd done more than see the estate from a distance. It was as dire as he'd anticipated; peeling paint and an air of neglect. Everywhere he looked he could see the ugly electric meter boxes, with rusty doors left to swing open in the wind, and overfilled bins and abandoned pieces of furniture melding into the greenery as they grew thick with mould, marring the gardens. One house still had its Christmas lights up. Without any power to brighten them, they were just a dull remnant of happy times passed.

The people were no better; a shabby, dubious sort. The odds and ends of society and all possessing that crude, brusque quality of the unrefined. They watched with undisguised and shameless interest, a challenge in the posture and defiance in the fold of their arms. Next to him, the guard examined their list of addresses still housing men of conscription age.

"Start at the top, we'll work our way down. Make sure you have a good look around and take anything that's of interest to the Council, even if it seems like nothing. If there are any kind of weapons or evidence of group activities or plans, seize it," Ronan said. He'd had to speak progressively louder in order to make himself heard over the commotion already burgeoning at the other end of the street. "I'll need a couple of you to stay with me while I talk with some of them. Don't let your guard down with these people."

They went to the first door of the long line of terraces on the right side. A series of shouts sprung up from behind them, where a brawl had broken out between the officious CLE, their confidence bolstered by their new equipment and the small handful of lacklustre youths, too careless to have run away with the rest of them. Now, their cocksure arrogance prevented them from retreating. Some of the guards still had bitter memories from the recent looting and came in heavy. They had no interest in civility or conversation as the closest ones were handcuffed by force and pushed towards the open trucks with no regards for an explanation.

One in particular was full of vigour. Ronan had marked him at first sight as a troublemaker, a ringleader. He stood with his sizeable feet planted wide, chewing furiously on a piece of gum. His mouth was open, planted like a tree, his roots in the concrete, surveying his options. He waited until the guards were bold enough to come for him, trying to bring his wrists together across the great expanse of his midsection. He burst into motion, shaking men off his arms like they were bothersome children. His face contorted into further shades of deep red as he twisted and turned, pushed and kicked at the growing number of men who set on him.

With one great lunge, he shoved away the two men in front, freeing himself for a second so he could turn and escape. But his broad and slovenly legs were not built for speed and within a few short strides they were upon him and brought him back to the ground. The whole street watched as Lee fell, his gum flying out from his mouth and sticking to the dry, dusty grit. He roared, a guttural noise of injustice and rage. His wrists were cuffed, and as they got him to his feet and led him away, his eyes fixed upon one of the other boys who hovered by the houses.

"Go and tell the others! These bastards are takin' us," he shouted and with desperate comprehension, the other boy retreated at a sprint and disappeared.

Ronan turned to the guards.

"I guess that's how it's going to be. I didn't think they'd want to come easy."

At the first door, an elderly woman was clutching her dog, a scraggy haired terrier.

"Good afternoon, Madame. I'm Ronan, First Council." He flashed her his card. "We're here to conduct an investigation into recent crimes and see how any further incidents can be prevented."

"You're bloody brave to show your face around 'ere," she said with a cold stare. The dog was yapping in her arms. Ronan laughed without humour. One of the woman's arthritic hands moved to grip the edge of the door.

"I'm going to assume that you weren't directly involved with the latest attacks near Galven. You don't look like you'd be up to it. Nevertheless, I'd like to ask you about some people that are of interest to the Council."

Emily watched with cold horror from Linda's kitchen window. Linda had gone to the door and Raine had run towards the garden, calling for Emily on seeing the black vehicles pull into their street. She was frozen though, shielded by the half-shut blinds. She watched the door of the Mercedes swing open, polished loafers setting foot on the street. A suited Ronan, his dark red hair slicked back and large shades obscuring his eyes stood less than twenty feet away.

She dropped beneath the level of the counter and tried to keep a hold of her rising panic.

"Emily," Raine hissed. "Come out the back, we'll get somewhere safe."

Emily was still frozen in her dark corner of linoleum, shielded by the false wood of the cabinets, a shelter she didn't want to leave.

"It's him," she said.

"The one from the Council?"

Emily nodded.

"Get 'er out through the back gate," Linda shouted. "No one

will be coming through this door either way, but you guys get safe. Go. Hurry."

They ran through the back garden and the back gate, which opened into the next street. Raine paused, checking the road.

"We have to tell the others. They're doing a search, I bet."

"What if he's coming for me?" Emily said. She had her back to the thin wooden fencing of Linda's garden.

"You think he would?"

"He went crazy the last time I left him, back in college."

"Was it serious between you?"

"No, we only went on three dates. But he got way ahead of himself, talking about our future and everything else. It scared me. There was all this stuff going around about him at the time, and then when I ended it, he wouldn't leave me alone for months. He turned nasty."

"It's ok, he can't get you here, not with me."

They heard pounding feet coming from the alleyway. A pale, nervy looking boy of about nineteen appeared, sprinting like a hare from hounds. He saw them and shouted.

"They've got Lee!"

"Come on," Raine said, urging Emily to run. "Let's get to Gina's."

"Hi there, my name's Ronan, first officer of the Council. I'm here as part of an investigation into suspected illegal activities." He motioned with his hand to convey his impatience with the matter. It was only the fourth house, yet he was already tired of the insipid conversation. Now, the woman in front of him seemed already set against him. She occupied the entire width of the doorway, her wide-legged stance looked solid as an ox. She looked down at him with the expression of someone that has stumbled across something both repulsive, yet with the potential to provide some facile entertainment. Despite the mutual contempt, Ronan kept smiling.

"You're 'ere to round them boys up?" she said, with not the slightest effort to moderate her tone or enunciate her words.

"Some of the young men who unlawfully didn't present themselves for consignment before are now being forcibly conscripted, yes. It's a Council order, for the benefit of the nation."

Linda raised her chin.

"Best you try and get on with that then, and get the hell outta here."

Ronan smiled again.

"Believe me, I don't wish to stay here any longer than I have to. But while the guards are taking care of that, I'm making enquiries as to the whereabouts of some people of interest."

"That so?"

Ronan took a piece of paper from his suit pocket and scanned it. He glanced up to check the house number.

"Someone named Braydon lives at this address, correct?"

"Hardly see him. He hasn't been here in days."

He tried to look into the house behind her, but she blocked him.

"I'd like a look inside the house, if I may. The Council has issued a right to search the homes of all the addresses I have written down here."

"Try it. See what happens."

He was on his own. The guards had gone to help detain the ones already rounded up. They were causing as much noise and difficulty as the guards could manage. He returned the paper to his pocket.

"Look, I'm trying to be polite. You really don't have a choice. Stand aside, let us in and we'll make it as quick as possible. If you deny us access, I'll be led to believe you've got something to hide and in that scenario, we might end up having to do a comprehensive search of the premises."

Linda stepped forward, leaning into him.

"Use all the fancy words you want. I'm telling you, you ain't coming in this house without going through me."

He'd had it. Screw them all. He tried to shove past her but she was ready, leaning her weight towards him so that he could do nothing to gain ground. He stepped back, trying to reign in some control. He knew she was smirking at him, mocking him. It took all his strength to mask his anger enough to be able to give her a parting smile and a nod of the head.

"We'll see you soon then."

Chapter 24

Raine and Emily got to Gina's and found the door open. The sight that met them was one of chaos and preparation. The people who had successfully avoided the CLE chase, along with some of the others who had participated in the raid, were regrouping. A band of seven or eight women were bringing in the weapons and equipment that Gina had stored in her shed. A few were assembling and distributing the same amongst themselves. Raine and Emily made their way across the hustle and found Gina in the kitchen, shouting directions as the others took armfuls of clubs, bats, knives and anything sharp-edged they could find out through the garden gate to stash somewhere new.

"What's going on?" Raine said.

Gina turned her attention to them, looking at Emily with a sneer.

"You've got a nerve bringing her here."

"I'm nothing to do with the Council," Emily said. "They're after me too."

"That's your story, is it? What's in it for you? Being a mole?"

"Stop acting like an idiot," Raine said. "She's one of us. Now's not the time anyway. Everyone needs to get out of here and get somewhere safe. There was armed law enforcement just outside Linda's, they'll probably be here any minute."

"You would say that, wouldn't you? She can do no wrong in your eyes."

"Stop!" Emily said. "We're wasting time. Yes, I went to see someone I know from a long time ago; he's in the Council now. He told me he could get me to my son but instead, he just took my phone, my ID, locked me up and tried to keep me there, trapped. He's coming for me and I don't know what he'll do."

Raine took a knife from the cluttered countertop and put it in her pocket.

"Let's get moving, now," she said.

"I'm taking care of the others," Gina said. "They're dividing up the weapons and hiding them in different places. Then they're gonna split up. We'll make it as hard as we can for those bastards to get any of us." She looked at Emily again, her expression softer this time. "You'd be best off going to Ethan's. He's holed up there no doubt."

"Let's go then," she looked at Raine.

"Don't let 'em get you, and if they do, don't tell 'em anything," Gina called out as she gathered up her things.

Back on the street, they cut across the gardens to the right, coming out of the small close where Gina lived and took another right onto Moorland Avenue. They ran downhill, keeping close to the wall as they watched every car, every corner for the appearance of the CLE. They reached Hillcrest Road, the main road intersecting the lower portion of the estate, without seeing anyone. Raine took her hand.

"We have to go straight across. If we head down there, we

can take a shortcut to Ethan's," she said.

"Will they not come looking for him too?"

Raine shook her head. "No, they have a different address for him. His place should be safe." She peered around the corner to look down the street. "I can see them, but they're not close. We'll just have to run."

"Is he there? The one in charge?"

"I can't see him."

Emily looked at the road and saw parked trucks about ten doors down with residents grouping by the open doors of their houses.

"Ok, I'm ready."

Raine dropped her hand and they sprinted across the road. They ran down another street passing more terraced houses as they approached a left-hand bend in the road.

"This side," Raine called, crossing the road. Emily stepped off the pavement to follow, but from around the corner, the wide, black bonnet of Ronan's car appeared. He blocked her path.

"Emily!" he shouted, leaning out of his window. Raine was calling her, desperate for her to get out of the road.

"Quick, we'll have to go this way," she said, forcing Emily to look away and move. Ronan was opening his door. She was too scared to look behind her as she followed Raine at a sprint, running towards the last house on the right, where a small gap concealed a rough path. Her arm burned from where she'd scraped it against the rough brick in her haste. Ahead of them, the path opened out into a dreary wasteland, filling the void between two streets.

They heard the roar of an engine from behind, as Ronan stepped down hard on the accelerator.

"Are you ok? My street's just over there," Raine said.

"He's coming for me. I knew it."

"Don't worry, just follow me. Let's go to my house. I doubt he'd come there."

They crossed the sparse land and were at the lower end of Raine's street. Emily kept an eye on the top of the street, feeling like a trapped animal.

"We're too exposed, we need to get off the road."

"Over here," Raine gestured with her hand. She led Emily to the rear of the first house on their left, where low wire fencing marked the border of someone's garden.

"Wait," Emily said, her breathing heavy. "Should we be going this way? It feels wrong."

Raine stopped and looked at her. "There's nothing wrong about it, they won't mind." She looked at the house. "I know everyone here anyway; they'd rather we use their garden as a cut-through than get caught by anyone from the council." She swung a leg over the fence and waited for Emily.

"I just, I don't know if it's worth all this running. When it seems like he's going to catch me anyway. How can I escape him when he has all this power?"

"Stop it," Raine hissed, glancing over Emily's shoulder. "You can, and you will. Your route to Jack isn't through him. If he can't keep you for himself, he'll just lock you up, make it impossible for you to find Jack out of sheer spite. We can do this without him, and he won't catch you if you just get a move on and follow me."

Emily hesitated, but the distant sound of a car made her decision easier. She followed Raine over the fence, keeping a careful eye on the dark houses of the neighbours they intruded on, but they were either quick enough to escape their notice or the occupants were too distracted by the raid.

They came to a hedge that, although only waist height, was full of sharp looking branches. Emily managed to partly climb over, partly squeeze through one of the sparser sections. They were in a small back garden. Discarded, rusty bikes occupied one corner, and the rest was a mixture of patchy grass and gravel. Raine crept towards the back door, trying to see through its frosted window.

Emily waited by the thin wooden fence in the garden's right-side boundary, looking for any cue to run or follow. Raine was still until they heard someone kicking the back gate with force. Raine joined Emily and took out her knife, waiting for the unbearable sound of another kick.

The rickety gate burst open, almost breaking off its hinge. It was Ethan, dishevelled and pale faced. He was holding a cricket bat.

"I've been looking for you," he said, checking behind him before he pushed the gate close with his elbow. "Have they not been here yet? They're carrying out a search in lots of houses."

"I don't think so," Raine replied. "We were going to go to your place, but one of them is after Emily and he cut us off. You're not with your uncle?"

"No, he's gone to see what's happening, like everyone else. I went to Jordan's; they're all gearing up for a fight."

"What? That's the last thing they should be doing. We need to spread out and stay out of their way."

"I know, but they're angry. They don't want to wait around. I wanted to find you guys, see what's happening out here."

"They'll take all of us if we're not careful," Emily said. Ethan shook his head.

"Not me. I'd rather die before they turn me into some soulless machine."

Raine looked troubled. She paced between them.

"We're going to have a look at what's going on. I thought Gina would keep Jordan's lot in check, but by the sounds of it, they're planning on getting themselves into more trouble than we're in already. You'll need to be careful, and stay close to me though," she said to Emily.

"I will. I feel too restless to sit still. I can outrun Ronan if I need to," Emily said.

They went through the back door and straight through Raine's house. Emily couldn't see Raine's father but they could hear the low drone of the television set coming from the living room, and a strong smell of stale cigarette smoke was seeping into the corridor.

"Quickly," Raine said as she held open the door, checking the road constantly for black cars or trucks.

They headed left, passing through the same alleyway that Lee had appeared from earlier in the day, that brought them to the bottom of Linda's street. They couldn't see Linda but the street was filled with commotion. Five trucks now took up the road and residents stood by the neighbouring houses, talking and watching as the events unfolded.

They soon saw the focus of everyone's attention. One of the last houses on the left was hosting a standoff. Five CLE officers were grouped around a doorway as a lanky, shirtless man with cropped hair and grey, oversized tracksuit bottoms blocked their entry. Those on bikes were circling like buzzards, shouting at and taunting the guards.

CHAPTER 24

Emily moved forwards with the others, close enough to hear the exchange.

"I have the necessary papers in my possession," the guard at the front cautioned. "We're going to be conducting a search of the house

and you'll need to come with us for consignment."

"I ain't going anywhere with you pricks," the man growled, squaring up to the guard. "So you can get off my property now, all of you."

More of the residents were getting braver, moving in to see what would happen. Emily saw Jordan on a bike, calling to others at the top of the street.

"Gina's here," Raine said. She was. Emily could see her by the first truck, involved in a heated discussion with another CLE.

"Last warning. If you don't step aside and let us in, we'll be coming in with force," the guard said.

"Get out of here!" came a shout from the crowd, and jeering ensued. The man the CLE was threatening slammed the door in their face. The crowd became louder as more CLE moved in and started to spread out. They waved their arms in a sweeping motion, calling for the residents to disperse whilst behind them, two guards got a firm grip on the compact battering ram now in their possession, preparing to take down the door.

The boldest ones at the front were playing chicken with the guards, unwilling to move back, daring them to enter their personal space. Emily recognised a cohort of Jordan's becoming increasingly animated.

"You don't belong here," he spat at the closest CLE. "Get on and leave. Go! You can't touch any of us." He lurched forwards and took hold of the guard's bulky shoulders. A short struggle ensued with much shoving and swearing as the other guards moved in to help overpower him and pin the young man to the ground.

There was an instant reaction from the crowd. Rocks flew through the air, hitting the guards as they now faced violent attacks from all sides. Raine saw Jordan throwing stones and whatever else he could grab. She tried to intervene.

"Jordan? Call them off! This isn't the time; you'll just make things worse!" He was impervious to her warnings. More trucks pulled in, and following them was a Mercedes.

"Raine, I have to go," Emily shouted. Ethan looked ready to run. Raine turned to look at her but was distracted by the events unfolding.

"Emily?" Ronan called, and all at once he was there, cutting through the crowded street in his suit, oblivious to the chaotic scenes as the guards tried to contain and cuff those attacking them.

"Go with Ethan," Raine shouted. "Run!"

She turned and ran, chasing after Ethan as he disappeared down the alleyway. As she turned the corner and launched into a full sprint, closing the distance between her and Ethan, she heard a gun fire somewhere behind her.

It felt like endless running. Every step was torturous as her feet hit the ground like rhythmic pistons. Ethan didn't let up his pace until he'd twisted through the gate that would take him to his street. His house was the last one on the estate's farthest edge, where beyond the road, desolate scrubland occupied the far vista. She caught him. Pain burned beneath her ribs as she bent forwards, still moving to stay with him as they darted inside the corner house. He locked the door behind them.

It was a full minute before Ethan had caught his breath enough to speak.

"This is my uncle's house," he said. "They won't find us here. It's safe."

She followed him upstairs to a bedroom. The house was dark. Brown carpets and low lighting contributed to a claustrophobic atmosphere. But his room with its minimalist furniture, just a bed and a wardrobe, gave them enough space to relax.

"Will Raine be alright? What if they take her?" Emily asked.

"She's alright. She's smart enough to stay out of serious trouble."

"I wish she'd come too, though."

Ethan sat beside her on the bed and put his hand on her back.

"It's fine. We'll be ok."

"What are we going to do? What about the others?"

He stood up and went to his wardrobe.

"Come here," he said. She went to his side, close enough to smell his deodorant and see the small details of his patchy facial hair. He opened the double doors and searched through the pile of clothes that were lying on the shelves. He moved them to the side, piece by piece, until he found what he was looking for. He lifted an old hoodie, a faded navy. He reached into the pocket and pulled out a set of keys.

Emily looked at him, puzzled.

"The car, remember? They never took it. I kept the keys. Now we have a car we can use."

"But, today—"

"Not today." He leant in closer to her. "When we need it.

When we finally do what we need to do, to get what we want, to end all of this."

Emily tried to hide her disappointment. She turned away, feeling a wave of loss at the reminder that Jack was out there, somewhere far from here, this room, from her. She felt his clammy fingers twisting around hers, coaxing her to join him where he'd crouched.

"What is it?" she asked, but he was silent as he eased open the bottom drawer of his wardrobe. He pushed aside the boxers and socks, clearing out the furthest corner. As he moved the last pair of socks with a gentle sweep of his hand, she saw the gleam of a short metal barrel, the curve of a trigger. Their eyes met, but as she was about to speak, two loud raps on the front door echoed through the house. Emily was too stunned to speak, certain that Ronan had found her.

"Wait here," Ethan said, pushing the drawer close. She listened to his descent on the stair, and held her breath as distant voices carried upstairs.

It was Gina. She burst into the bedroom with all of her usual poise, dumping a handful of jewellery and watches onto the bed.

"Why aren't you with the others? Was there fighting?" Emily asked.

"They want the men," Gina shrugged. "Let them sort it out; me and my girls are safe. "We were putting stuff away in safe places. The fancy stuff we don't want to part with. Thought if we spread it out, they can't pin too much on us and we'll be sitting pretty for a good while." She looked at the two of them. Ethan had gone back to the wardrobe to stand by Emily. "Did I interrupt something?"

"No, we were just talking," Ethan said. Emily felt the drawer push back further and sealing shut as he let the weight of his foot press gently against it.

Her lips parted, but the look in his eyes silenced her. It was their secret.

Chapter 25

The car cruised with a low purr, slow enough to let its driver get a good look at the hideous streets on the off chance that a young woman may have taken refuge in one of the dark cubbyholes. Ronan pressed the brake. Another road that had yielded nothing. His tension filled the small car interior with grunts and huffs and the incessant drumming of his fingers on the wheel.

He did a three-point turn, hardly bothering to look where he was driving until he was ready to try another street. With one hand on the steering wheel, he straightened, ready to accelerate, but had to press hard on the brake. A brazen woman, dressed in a grubby, off-white vest top that accentuated the musculature of her upper body, stood a mere foot from the tip of his bonnet. His commitment to braking was more in fear of her touching the recent wax job rather than for fear of causing her injury.

He wound down his window and did little to look polite.

"Please move out of the way and don't touch my car."

The woman strode to the open window, leaning close enough that he could see the green shade of her eyes amidst the deep lines and flaws of her bare face. He realised how little he'd seen women without make-up, even Grace. He was grateful for it.

"Are you looking for someone?" she asked, in a vulgar, coarse voice.

"A young woman, she's called Emily. It's important that I find her." His right foot hovered above the gas pedal and his left thumb tapped against the handbrake release. "Have you seen her? Or do you know where she could be?"

"What's it matter to you?" Her eyes moved from his face to the collar of his shirt to his chest and back up again. His own gaze had settled on the garish bows on her visible bra straps. No decorum.

"Is she a friend? Do you know her?"

"Sure, I know her. Probably know where she is, too. But why d'ya need to find her?"

Ronan sat back in his chair.

"I'm from the Council. She's not in trouble, but I do need to pass on some very important information."

"Must be important, for a fancy guy like you to come all the way from the border just for that." Ronan shrugged. She was wasting time.

"What'd be in it for me?" she asked.

He pulled out some crumpled notes from his pocket.

"For valid information only, that leads me to her."

She was looking at his wrist.

"Nice watch."

"Are you going to tell me where she is or not?"

The woman shrugged.

"I can, for payment. But I can't guarantee she'll still be there" She popped her gum, letting it stick against her teeth for an unbearable second. "You don't have much choice."

Ronan looked at the cash in his hands. He held it out to her, watching as she snatched it from him.

"Well?" he asked.

"Somewhere that way on the next street I reckon."

"Is that all?"

She walked away, patting his bonnet twice as she passed it. He jammed his fist on the down button halfway through the letting the window up. No. He couldn't take the aggravation anymore. He flung open the door and unclipped his seatbelt.

"You! You stop right there! Council order!" She looked back with a smile and ran. He had no hope of catching her. He sunk back into the driver's seat and closed the door with a slam. He took deep breaths. Frustration was getting the better of him, fogging his mind. These people were going out of their way to get a rise out of him.

He started driving again with gritted teeth, heading back up to Hillcrest Road, but once again he had to stop. This time though he was happy to. His target was caught mid-run, her long hair blowing in the wind as she registered his presence with a look of surprise and fear. She was perfect, still. How could she be? Even after what she'd done, she was all he wanted. But rage stirred beneath his longing. It deepened when another woman, her hair completely shaved on one side of her head and wearing shapeless men's clothing began to pull Emily away.

She had ignored his calls, of course. Once again, he watched her retreat. He didn't need to chase, not on foot. His net was closing in.

He turned back down Carter Close, surprised to see the number of trucks still there. It should have been cleared out a while ago without issue but he soon saw why they hadn't. The lower half of the street was chaotic. Residents of all sizes and ages were wrestling and attacking the CLE with an array of home-sourced weapons; it was a barrage of projectiles. The guards were fighting back, making use of their new equipment as they grouped together with their shields and struck the protesters with their batons. They were managing to bring some of the frontrunners to the ground and subdue them with cuffs, but it wasn't without significant opposition.

He opened the glove box and took out a small wrapped package before he got out and approached the crowd, ready to direct the guard and get as many of them he could in the vans. All at once, the residents seemed to split down the middle and a loud whizzing erupted from the back of the group as fireworks were shot straight at the guards. There were whoops and shouts as the crowd watched the guards fall back.

The residents surged forward again, not seeing the gun that Ronan held in his outstretched hand. He fired into the sky, watching people scatter in all directions as the explosive crack rang out. The residents dispersed, retreating into their houses and down dark alleys on their bikes, leaving the guards to deal with those they'd managed to restrain.

He joined the guards as they moved in on the loudest, most active resident on the ground. It was a man in his early twenties who'd been brought down in a rather unfortunate manner, left with his cap hanging from his forehead and his bottoms in desperate need of a good tug north. With some considerable effort, the man rolled onto his back, clearing the obstruction from his eyes and sparing everyone the sight of his white backside.

"Dun' take me, dun' conscript me, I've got a disability," he rambled.

Ronan was holding the gun by his side, his hands shaking.

"Get them all in the trucks. I want to get out of here," he said.

The man locked his legs and tried to find a grip against the crumbling tarmac.

"You haven't got no right to take anybody," someone shouted from a doorway behind him. Ronan spun and held out his gun. The door slammed shut as around him, the guards stopped and stared.

"Sir?" one of them asked.

"What?" he snapped, lowering the gun again. "I said get them in the trucks."

Chapter 26

Emily stood bereft in the shower. The hot water scalded her chest and found the dark plughole between her feet. There was a deep ache in her neck as she looked up at the pattern of black mould on the white ceiling. Thoughts began to slowly coalesce from out of the sinkhole of her mind. A memory from the time before Jack had been frightened of the camera flash.

"Hold still, look at the camera." Jack ceased all movement with some considerable effort and faced her with a wide, toothy grin. His wet hair hung in thick cords across his forehead and rainwater collected in beads on his porcelain skin. With a short burst of laughter, Jack pulled her close to him, into the wet, vibrant warmth of his delicate body, urging her to hold out the camera so it could capture them both.

If only she'd been able to keep the pictures. The cost of printing had always been too high and inaccessible. The photos had been lost when she'd had to sell the camera. She tried to recall the exact image of Jack's happy, carefree face, wet from the impromptu lashing of rain on their walk back from the shop. But the shortfalls of her memory could not summon the disarray of his hair, the slight squint of his features and the lopsided set of his mouth. Only the digital image had been able to capture all of that in a feast of detail.

"Emily? Are you in here?"

Emily looked beyond the shower curtain and saw Raine in the doorway. She hunched forward and tried to cover herself with her hands.

"Get out, why are you looking?"

Raine stepped back and let the door close. Emily turned off the shower and reached for the towel. She did a poor job of drying herself in the confined space. As she guessed, Raine was waiting in the bedroom, looking pensive as she sat on the lower bunk.

"What did you want? Can't it wait until I'm dressed?" Emily scowled as she held her towel tightly with one hand.

"We've got a plan. We're going to take a hostage but we want to move quickly."

"Now?"

"We have to do something."

"Is Ethan going?"

Raine studied her face. "Yeah. Are you ok? What happened between you and him yesterday?"

"Nothing, I'm fine. Let me get dressed and I'll be there."

Raine was smoking outside in a dark hoody. Emily stepped out of the house, dropping her shoulders and squinting.

"How are we doing this, then?" she asked. Raine threw her used cigarette to the ground and raised a hand in a greeting to Gina. She was flanked by Stacey and Kay.

"We're taking the car... You'll see."

Gina joined them on the path.

"Are we ready to go then? I've got some more people to

come and help. They're walking. Ethan's gonna meet us at the car."

"We brought these," Stacey said, holding out a club, an iron bar and a cricket bat.

"Just for show, hopefully," Raine said. "We're going to take the car up so we can get the hostage back here quick. Once news gets to the Council, they won't just hang around."

Emily thought of Ronan coming back at the estate, realising what she'd been part of. She'd be stronger this time, with the leverage on her side. He'd be under her control for once.

They met Ethan by the garages. The car was where they'd left it, partly submerged in the dense overgrowth that bordered the scruffy patch of tarmac. Some other boys were gathered around the car, watching as he put the key in the ignition.

"She's on," Ethan said with a smile, as the dashboard lit up in a wave of bright lights and a digital display. Gina shoved past the two boys trying to get a look inside.

"Get a move on, you lot," she said.

"I'm riding in the car," Jordan said, climbing into the passenger seat.

"Nah, you're not. The girls and I are driving." Jordan was about to protest, but she grabbed him by the arm, digging in her nails. "We outnumber you guys now."

Jordan got out with a scowl and picked his bike off the ground.

"We'll meet you up there," Raine said. "Get a block ready where we said, yeah?"

He nodded and sped away.

"Are we all fitting in there?" Emily asked.

"Yeah, squeeze up," Raine said. Emily just managed to fit in the backseat between Raine and Kay. Ethan pulled out of the disused lane and found the road into town.

"Is that the radio? Can you turn it up?" Emily said. Gina moved the dial, and clipped voices, speaking in received pronunciation, filled the car.

"News of the new living arrangements for the Shaw Hill children near the military base has been welcomed by many Galven residents, some of whom have reported increasing disruption and negative influence on their own children. We have another caller this morning who wants to share their opinion with us. Charlotte? Are you there?"

"Yes, Margaret. I wanted to speak to you because this has been on my mind all morning."

"How do you feel about the news then?"

"Well, I feel torn, really. I took in one of the Shaw children, a nine-year-old. When I signed the forms, I was fully prepared to take on the commitment of having her in my home and the thought of the upheaval and her having to move to a strange place all over again makes me feel terrible. But I really am at a loss. The behaviour has been challenging, to say the least. Now my own child has started to repeat some of the crude words that she uses, at liberty it seems, and there are all sorts of other problems with manners and what not, which is just such a shame, as I wanted it to work."

"Do you think the Council has made the right call?"

"They're reacting to the situation at hand. Who knows? Maybe it'll be better for the evacuees in the long run, to be with their own kind."

"Well, it's definitely not an easy thing for a lot of people. But the results of our own phone survey show that over eighty per cent of residents agree with the Council's decision. So maybe this is the right course of action."

"I hope so."

"Thank you, Charlotte. So that was Margaret, weighing in on today's debate. If you'd like to call in, you can dial 99 88 543 for a chance to be on the show."

"What a load of shit," Gina said, reaching for the dashboard.

"Wait," Emily said. "Let me listen for a minute."

"An update on yesterday's news," the radio continued. "The Council has released a press statement indicating that the findings of their investigation into illegal activities in Shaw Hill have confirmed the need for them to introduce new measures to ensure New Galven's safety. Whilst they did not disclose what the nature of this action will be, the Council have reassured residents that all offenders will be held to account and preventative measures will be heavily enforced."

Gina turned it off.

"I can't listen to this anymore," she said. Emily watched as Gina leaned out of her window. She held the bat out against the wind and watched as her bony hand erupted in goose pimples at the cold and wind resistance. They came to a stop on Galven Road before the view of the border, in the middle ground where there was only the straight road, lined with trees on both sides.

Emily was glad to get out, finding some space again. They began to gather branches from the nearby trees, dragging them towards the road to create a road-block. Helen and Sasha joined them, having set out on foot earlier. Twenty minutes later, Jordan and his mates arrived on their bikes.

Emily felt full of nervous anticipation as Sasha and Helen joined her where she stood waiting by the trees.

"Hi," Sasha said with a warm smile. "Helen wanted to join

us."

"Linda's looking after my kids," Helen said. "Giving me the morning off. Thought I better make myself useful and all, help out where I can."

"How's this going to work? Isn't it risky?" Emily said.

"Yeah," Raine said. "But fewer people are going to the shops here after what happened, so we're hoping to catch one of the cars on their way out. If it goes wrong, we'll just have to get out of here quick."

"If we can pick up someone though, the Council will do anything to get them back." She thought again of Ronan.

"Pretty much."

"I think it's about done," Gina called, stepping back and appraising the pile of branches now obstructing both lanes.

Chapter 27

The pristine, white SUV rumbled along Galven Road. Inside, the woman in the passenger seat made low noises of irritation as she adjusted and readjusted the heated seat settings on the touchscreen dash. The man next to her kept his eyes on the road, drumming his fingers on the leather steering wheel and resisting the desire to hum. She hated his humming.

"It's a real pain having to come all the way out here again, Craig. The armchairs still need plumping and the table needs to be arranged. You know I like to get that done first."

"I told you I'm sorry. I thought I'd got everything."

"Well, you managed most of the main, although the recipe does specify vacuum-packed chestnuts, though I don't suppose it matters too much. It's my fault. I should have known not to trust you with the shop."

Craig zoned her out. He began a quiet but cheerful hum as he navigated a gentle bend, but Bernice shot him a look so severe that it died in his throat of its own accord. She carried on.

"If it had just been some trivial thing, I might have been able to send you to the small shop up the road, but you wouldn't find polenta, sourdough or tarragon in there." She huffed.

"They *should* have those things, but that's another matter."

"I thought you weren't doing polenta?"

"I changed my mind; I forgot to tell you." Craig raised his eyebrows, nonplussed. "I'm serving it with garlic and basil butter. We'll need a whole nutmeg for that too, remind me."

He nodded in servitude. The road straightened out again, wide and smooth.

"I'm not happy with the wine you bought, either."

"It was on special offer."

"Shiraz is a terrible accompaniment to partridge. And it's cheap. I can't offer that to Bernard and Wendy."

"I thought they were coming to enjoy our company, not judge our wine."

"I'd rather die than hand out cheap wine to guests. I need a nice, quality Rioja."

There was a blissful quietude for a few minutes. Then she spoke again.

"You're absolutely sure that Cecelia's no longer vegetarian?"

"Pretty sure. She ordered a steak at the business dinner last week."

"If she is then she'll just have to fill up on bruschetta. You won't make any stupid comments, will you?"

"I'll be on my best behaviour, making no noise and pretending I don't exist."

"What?" she snapped.

"It's a reference, the Dursleys, you know… never mind, don't worry, it doesn't matter."

She scowled at the windscreen.

"Well don't do that, either. I need you to keep Bernard occupied enough that he doesn't try to join me in the kitchen."

Craig didn't reply. He was distracted by an obstruction up

CHAPTER 27

ahead. A large branch blocked most of the road and at the other end, a young woman was attempting to drag it away. She looked up and raised her arms in a universal stop gesture.

The others watched from their hiding places. Gina and Raine were behind the nearest trees, wide enough to offer cover as long as they stayed pressed against the bark. Emily was crouched behind the car, full of nervous energy. Beside her, Ethan surveyed the empty road. Helen and Sasha were on her other side.

"Feels so strange being out without the kids," Helen said, her face a vivid pink. "We've barely gone anywhere for ages, but this mornin' I was really stuck for food. Had nothing for breakfast, an' as it is they'd gone to bed on some tinned hotdogs and the last bits of bread. Went to Linda's an' she sorted us out, told me I should've gone sooner. Then she said I ought to have a break. I hardly get any time to myself."

"Imagine if the car we stop has food in it," Sasha said.

"Should have got a car coming back from the shops, not goin' there," Kay said in a low voice.

Ethan made a shushing sound as a car approached. The way the midday sun hit the blacktop made it appear like some great metal entity rising out of the ground and growing before them.

Emily had been chosen to play a lone, helpless woman to help divert any oncoming traffic.

"Can't someone else do it?" she'd asked, but the consensus had been that she was the least likely to make someone suspicious or scare them away.

"Go, go!" Ethan said, giving her a gentle push.

She grabbed a branch and started to feign pulling on its end, making it look as though she was trying to clear the road. As the car slowed, she stepped to block the only free space in the other lane and raised her hands.

It came to a stop. After what seemed like a very slow few seconds, the driver's door opened and a well-dressed, greying man with some cushioning around the middle and a trilby tipped jauntily on his head walked towards her.

"Do you need a hand?" he asked, and for a terrible moment, Emily looked into his eyes and saw only concern. She wondered how she'd got here. Then somebody shouted.

"Now!" And from the trees, Emily's remaining party rushed at them forming two groups. Gina, Raine, Sasha, Helen and Ethan went straight to the car where the driver's door hung ajar. Bernice screamed as they reached at her from both sides to take her ID and phone.

"He must have the keys," Gina called to Jordan, who stood in front of Craig with the two other young men, blocking his route back to the car. The man glanced at Emily, but she could do nothing to help him. She moved away from him and watched all of it unfold.

"Hand them over," Jordan said.

"What do you want? That's my wife in the car, let her go," Craig said.

"Your wife's coming back with us," Raine said. "She won't be harmed as long as you and the Council do as we ask."

"Taking her where?"

From the car, Bernice began to scream again as Gina ripped her handbag from her hands.

"None of your business," Gina called but at the same time, Raine said, "To the estate," earning a glare from Gina and her sidekicks. The man went pale, looking from Gina to Raine, not knowing whose response was worse.

Jordan moved closer, eyeing up his pockets.

"Look, there's money in the car, let me get it and you can have all of it if you let us go."

"Already got it," Gina said, holding up a handful of notes.

"Give us the keys or we'll take them ourselves," Raine said. But Emily could tell, whether out of bravery or fear, the man had no intention of giving them anything. Jordan and his friends tried to grab him, but he brought his fist out of his pocket and lashed out at Jordan's arm and chest. They began to panic knowing another car could be approaching at any second.

"Ow. This is not just his hands," Jordan cried in pain. "Cut it out, you're crazy. Ow." Jordan tried to grab the man's hands.

"What's he got, a knife or summat?"

They moved back to see what he had. It turned out he was using his keys, held between his fingers.

As the boys struggled, Gina yelled. "We've got to move."

"Grab him." They brought him down, easing free the keys from his hand and getting a few good kicks in as he tried to protect his head.

"Enough," Raine said, moving them away. She helped the man up, handing him back his fallen hat.

"What's happening Craig?" Bernice called.

"This is what you need to do if you want your wife back. Go straight to Galven, it's not too far to walk from here. Tell them that the residents of Shaw Hill have taken your wife as hostage, and if you want her back, they need to negotiate a solution with us."

"Please, don't do this," he said, looking wistfully at the car.

He went to take a step towards it but Gina blocked his path, raising her fists.

"You want some more? Bet it's been a while since you've seen this much action." He shrunk away from her. Emily watched, frozen. They had to get out of here.

"Raine? This is taking too long," she said.

"Yeah, let's wrap it up." Jordan passed her the keys.

"Craig?" An elongated, sorrowful call came again from the car.

"Go," Gina said. She picked up a rock and threw it in his direction. He began to run up the road, back in the direction of the border. Though no stones hit him, they were an effective motivator.

They had a harder job extracting Bernice from the passenger seat and getting her into the back. Emily held the door open as they tried to manoeuvre her. Her legs seemed to have lost their strength, dragging stiffly against the road. She emitted a keen wailing noise.

"Shut up," Gina said. "Or I'll give you something to cry about." As she hauled Bernice up from the ground that she was trying to sink into, Gina landed a swift kick to her shin. Bernice cowered and climbed into the back without more struggle. She made less of a fuss after that. Emily sat on one side, Raine on the other. Gina sat up front, rifling through Bernice's handbag as Ethan drove, wide-eyed with excitement and focus as he got familiar with the new car.

There was a squeal of tires as the rest of the group sped back to the estate in the other car. Bernice seemed to shut down and remained passive yet stony-faced. Emily could feel her slight tremble; the lack of space in the back seats pressed their legs and arms together at every turn and swerve. She tried to block any sympathetic thoughts. Bernice was a hostage now, their captive. If it got her closer to Jack, then Bernice's short-term fear would be worth it.

"How much time will we have?" she asked, looking in the rear-view mirror.

"Enough to be prepared, hopefully," Raine said.

Bernice began to cry.

"Why would he just leave me like that? He barely put up a fight."

"Because men are shit sometimes," Gina said. Bernice sniffed. "Never rely on 'em. That was your first mistake right there."

Two hours went by before there was any sign of the Council arriving in Shaw Hill. The car had been parked on the grass at the bottom of Linda's street. The hostage was more than secure in Gina's bedroom, tied to a chair in the spare room and under constant guard. Though curtains twitched and conversation over garden fences was rife, there was never any concern that their position would be given up.

Linda's was one of the central streets; Emily, Gina, Raine and a few of the others waited there. They sat on kitchen chairs having dragged them to the road, with weapons by their feet. The other residents watched, cooling drinks in their hands. They stayed far enough away to avoid being implicated. When the fleet of Council vehicles descended on the street, some residents backed away, and all of them put down their cups.

Emily wanted to run. She could see nothing of the drivers through the tinted windows. Gina watched them like a cat that observes a flitting bird who has not yet noticed the cat is there and comes closer. Raine looked at Emily and gave her a reassuring smile.

Her resolve was a thin sheet, stretched yet further. The door of the lead car opened, but it wasn't Ronan who got out. He wasn't there at all. The man that approached, flanked by guards, was the one that had tried and failed to dictate orders at the Aid Centre. He had the same small stature and habitually combed hair, wearing the same blue suit as before. He addressed them from a short distance.

"The Council have received reports of a New Galven resident being abducted and brought here. Would you ladies happen to know anything about that?"

"We've got her. She told us her name is Bernice," Raine said.

"She's being held in a secret location," Gina said with a smirk. "If you try to pull summat shady, you won't be getting her back, not unharmed anyway. One call and it's game over for your precious red card holder. Let your residents chat about that on their fancy radio shows."

Kyle held up his palms.

"There's no need for anything like that to happen. The man that spoke to us, the hostage's husband, told us you have some requests."

"We want supplies. Give us our tokens back and let us spend them again. But extra this time," Gina said before giving anyone else the chance to speak.

"We also need to contact our children. We want to know where they are and that they're safe," Raine said. Emily leapt from her chair.

"Wait, No." Kyle raised his eyebrows. She moved closer to him, ignoring the guards. "We need the children back here, with us." She lowered her voice. "I want my son, Jack, back."

CHAPTER 27

Gina and Raine came towards them. The guards raised their weapons.

"Please," Emily said.

"The children were evacuated for their own safety," Kyle said. "I'm sure you're all aware of the recent flyovers from Nemico planes. They're not safe here."

"No," Emily said, moving forwards. Raine tried to hold her back, but she shrugged out of her grip. "I don't care. My son's safest with me, he needs me." Kyle checked his watch.

"Can I see your identification cards, please? If you want your requests to be met, we'll need a point of contact."

"Do you know Ronan? I know him, he's part of all this."

"Yes, I do, and of course he is. He's first Council."

"He's involved with me, or he was, he wants to be."

"Emily, let us deal with this," Raine said.

"No, I need to speak. Ronan is using my son against me because he wants me to be with him. He kept me trapped at his house. He took my ID."

"Really? That's interesting. I know he took in an evacuee."

"Kyle?" One of the CLE behind him said. "The Commander's calling."

Kyle's gaze returned to Emily.

"I'll investigate further, thanks for sharing that information. But for now, we need the Galven resident to be returned safely. If you don't comply, there's likely to be grave consequences." He took the phone and held it near his ear.

"We need supplies, double the amount we've had so far. And we need a way to contact the children," Raine said. Kyle spoke into the phone while they waited. He looked over the nearby houses.

"She ain't in these," Linda said, hands on her wide hips.

"Are you going to disclose the location of the hostage?" Kyle asked.

"What do you think?" Gina replied.

"And if we give you what you've asked for, you'll release the resident straight away?"

"You have our word," Raine said. Gina handed him a piece of scrap paper.

"You can use that contact number," she said. He was still listening to whatever the Commander was saying on the phone. He hung up after a brief pause.

"One hour. We'll drop off some supplies and provide a point of contact for those with evacuated children. In return we expect to see the resident released, unharmed, immediately. If that doesn't happen, you can expect this place to be levelled or the like." He turned to the guards. "Let's go."

They got back in their trucks.

"No!" Emily shouted, trying to get to Kyle before he could shut his door, but her path was blocked by Raine.

"Emily, let them go. We're going to be given a way to contact the children, that's something, right?"

"It's not enough. I need my son with me. You said we'll get him."

"We will. We'll get them back. But not now, like this. If we ask for too much, they'll use force, people will get hurt."

The vehicles retreated and began to drive away. Emily made to follow them, but Raine reached for her arm again.

"Don't touch me," Emily said. "Leave me alone."

She tried to catch up with Kyle, but all she saw was the receding tail-lights.

It was just under an hour before they got the call. A large drop

CHAPTER 27

of supplies had been delivered to the Aid Centre, and people were already waiting. Some papers were included with the supplies, providing not only a list of children's names next to phone numbers for contact but also an address where letters could be sent to them. The hostage was released, blank-faced and trembling, back to the waiting CLE trucks on Galven Road.

Emily had no interest in the food. She snatched up the papers and scanned them quicker than she could read. She made herself slow down, reading from top to bottom and studying every name. He wasn't there. Jack was missing from the list as though he'd been wiped from existence.

Chapter 28

Since the new influx of conscripts, there had been growing unrest and a sense of discontent within the ranks of the warehouses. The fragile balance had been upended and any remaining complacency had been kicked to the dust. New ones, young and old, brought with them stories of the events in Shaw Hill. They gave life to rumours that before had been no more than speculation, and when one or two began to speak up, others found their voices and followed suit. The words 'Them' and 'Us' gained capital status among the hushed conversations of darkened dormitories.

News had spread about Noel's death. A man not popular whilst alive, unable to escape his past from the estate, was now talked about with reverence, someone who didn't deserve to die at the very least. The last person seen with him that night had been a Councilman in a suit. That much had become common knowledge.

Tensions rose, and some of the bolder ones began to advocate the idea of leaving. Never mind the promised ID, the security or the money; or the fact that they were kept here, under guard.

CHAPTER 28

The state of Ronan's week had been in a rapid decline. He couldn't prevent his mind from returning to the meeting after the raid, the point at which things had started to slip from his control. Kyle had sat next to Marsh, vying for Ronan's spot, ready to question every valid point that he presented. And though he'd tried with facts, detail, reasoning and argument, Marsh was just too stubborn to acknowledge the truth or accept the logical course of action.

"You can't just dispel this kind of attitude, their willingness to commit acts of violence against the Council. It's like a disease," he'd said. "And it will spread unless it's stopped."

"What about the identification register, could we use that somehow? Take in those who are likely to pose a threat," Marsh had said. It was Kyle's arrogance that was catching, bolstering Marsh's aptitude for an argument.

"That's hardly a reliable system," Ronan replied, enunciating every word. "Next to none we captured had their ID with them and their information was outdated. The system relies on residents to update it themselves, therefore it's an accurate record of those living in New Galven and not much else. I didn't design the thing." He shrugged.

He'd tried, but Marsh was averse to reality. It was too easy for him to give in to the comfort of Kyle's rash reassurance, promising yet more useless security reviews.

He got out of there before saying something he'd regret. But ever since, rather than the usual personal, casual interaction that he'd come to benefit from, Marsh had insisted on a more formal procedure of documenting any query, complaint or communication by way of email, replying that he would look at it when he had time. He was avoiding Ronan. Marsh probably intended to let him simmer off, provide a bit of distance to give emotions a chance to settle, but the longer he was dismissed, left with admin work or scolded like an insolent child when he requested a meeting or reply, the more his anger and resentment grew.

It was Tuesday evening when he pulled up outside his house. There was a car he didn't recognise in the drive, a dark blue saloon. He went to the front door, squinting to get a look through the kitchen window, but there was no one visible. As the door swung open, he heard Kyle's voice coming from the living room. He appeared with Grace, both smiling.

Ronan threw his keys onto the sideboard with a clatter.

"I didn't know you were visiting?" he said.

"I'm just stopping by." Kyle glanced at Grace. She looked away. "Marsh asked me to pass this to you. Everyone else has already signed it, we just need your signature at the bottom." He handed Ronan some stapled sheets of paper.

Ronan studied Grace's face for a second. She hung back by the living room doorway. He flicked through the papers.

"This is your security review, I take it?"

"Yeah. Marsh has talked it through with me and he's pretty satisfied with what I've done."

"Is that so. He's at the office now, is he?"

"I came straight from there."

Ronan put the papers on the wooden surface of the sideboard and smiled at Kyle.

"I'll take a good look at it later. Let me see you out."

Kyle said goodbye to Grace, leaning close to her for a hug, but it was Ronan that she looked at, wide-eyed and nervous. Ronan waited for Kyle to shut the door and accompanied him

CHAPTER 28

to his car.

"Don't stop by my house without an invitation, is that clear?" he said. "What do you think you're doing?"

"I told you already," Kyle said with a casual expression. "Well, to be truthful, Marsh wasn't too bothered about your signature, but I didn't want you to be left out."

He had to turn away, let out his breath. He flexed his fingers, hoping Kyle hadn't caught his momentary expression. He didn't deserve the satisfaction.

"I wanted to check up on Grace, as well," Kyle continued. "I had a rather funny conversation when I was in Shaw Hill today."

Ronan turned back to face him.

"What conversation? With who?"

"A woman there, she looks very similar to Grace actually. She said some interesting things about you being involved with her. Something about her son and that you'd kept her trapped." He looked towards the house, scanning the upper floor windows.

"This is exactly why you shouldn't be sent anywhere near that place if you're stupid enough to believe the ramblings of a crazy woman."

Kyle laughed.

"I'm not going to engage anymore in this. I can see why Marsh feels the way he does about you." He unlocked his car and opened the door. Ronan put a hand on the door's edge to block Kyle and moved close to his face.

"I don't want to see you here, ever again. Is that clear? If I do, you'll be leaving in an ambulance."

Kyle got in. "See you at the office."

Dusk was setting in as he pulled up outside the Council building. He gathered the security review that he'd tossed on the passenger seat and went inside. He knocked twice before opening the office door without waiting for an invitation. Marsh was reclined in his leather chair, his straggly beard sprouting in all directions. Two empty whiskey glasses were on his desk, one of them in a small pool of honey-coloured liquid. Ronan threw the crumpled review onto his desk.

"I suppose you think Kyle's done a great job, what with this," he gestured at the papers, "and his dealing with the hostage today?"

"Ronan, steady on." Marsh eased himself upright with some effort and rubbed his face with his hands, trying to blink through his weariness. "It's not appropriate for you to come bursting in here like this without arranging an appointment." He poured himself another drink, squinting towards the clock. "It's not even working hours."

"Sod all of that. You'll listen to me if you care at all about the state of this nation. You do realise that what happened today with that hostage would have been avoided entirely if one of the sensible courses of action I suggested had been carried through? And now, Kyle's gone in there and just given them what they asked for, essentially rewarding their actions. You watch and see it happen again, every time they want something."

"Ronan—" Marsh started again, and as Ronan looked at his face properly for the first time since entering the office, he noticed his bloodshot eyes and pallid, sagging skin. "I was provided with some of the details regarding that business with the conscript that died, this Noel fellow."

"By who?"

"That's not relevant. I noticed just how quickly this other fellow, Mark, was tried and acquitted for the thing, all within a single day. And it's got your signature at the bottom."

"It was a clear-cut business." Ronan shrugged. Marsh took another long draw of whiskey and motioned towards the chair.

"News has got around to me that you were there that night, there are even rumours that you were the last person seen with him."

"Couldry would tell you differently."

Marsh put down his glass a little too hard, adding to the spreading puddle.

"I'm sure. But I'm not entirely sure I can trust him anymore either."

He retrieved another glass from his desk drawer and poured Ronan a double. He slid it towards him and carried on.

"It's funny, I was just thinking about your father. His situation was similar, wasn't it? What he did?" Ronan's jaw tensed.

"My father acted, I believe, with the best intentions. Things didn't go to plan."

"Did you ever speak to him about it? After his sentence I mean."

"No."

Marsh took a sip, and then another longer one, wiping across the stubble on his chin with the back of his hand. Ronan took his own, tight-lipped sip, watching Marsh's eyes draw further into shadow, his cheeks flowering in a deeper rouge.

"Is that the kind of solution you believe in? Because, let's be blunt, that's what you've been advocating from the start of all this—violence against our own citizens. You see nothing worth saving outside of the border." Marsh's words blended at the end.

"I only ever wish to solve the problems put in front of me. That's my job."

Marsh reached for the bottle again. His arm came to rest midway across the table as if it lacked the energy to move further. Ronan took a long mouthful of his own drink, tapping his thigh with the fingers of his free hand, the pressure just hard enough for it to hurt. Marsh made the extra effort and decanted what was left of the bottle.

"I'm getting old," he said. "I know I've not been as involved, or active in this job as I should be. Naturally, I'm thinking about what the future holds."

"Of course. What of it?"

"With the way things are, I think it may be better for you to take a backseat for a while. I know this will be hard for you, but someone with a cooler head, like Kyle, may, I feel, manage all of this turbulence a little better. Don't view it so much as a demotion, but rather an opportunity to spend more time with Grace and any other projects you might want to take up, not involving Shaw Hill."

Ronan sat motionless, trying to process. He felt cold like his muscles had frozen. Marsh had avoided looking at him whilst speaking, and he still did now. He brought the glass to his whiskered lips, but his breathing was heavy and his eyes no more than pink slits. He eyed the golden liquor, then lowered it, rubbing his right temple.

"I'm going to have to call it a night," he said. "My head, I have such an awful headache."

"Would you like some painkillers?"

CHAPTER 28

"Yes, please. I think there might be some in that cabinet, in the corner." His voice was muffled by his shirt sleeve. "I ran out of what I had in my drawer, but I'm sure there were some in that cabinet."

Ronan stood on stiff and unwilling legs and went to search the messy, disorganised cabinet. While he was looking, Marsh called out.

"Do you love my daughter, Ronan?"

"Of course. She's everything to me," he replied. With his back to Marsh, he felt for the breast pocket of his suit jacket and took out a small, plastic packet.

"I can only find some soluble painkillers," he said without turning. He glanced over his shoulder, but Marsh's head was still in his hands, his reply unintelligible. Ronan went to the desk and took his glass, still half full. He turned away, tipping the contents of the packet into the glass with shaking hands. It was a lot, a week's worth for him. He watched it cloud the whiskey as it dissolved.

Marsh reached with his hand.

Ronan gave him the glass and watched him knock back the contents. Marsh pushed the empty glass away from him with a careless shove.

"You've reacted better than I thought you would," Marsh said. "Do you understand my decision? I want you to be ok with it."

Ronan was still standing. He kept his distance.

"I think it'll be fine. That's not to say I don't think I serve the Council best in my current position, or that it's the right choice, but I respect your opinion."

Marsh slumped further on his desk, squeezing his eyes shut.

"I will leave you to recover, sir."

He closed the office door gently behind him.

Marsh was found in the morning by the cleaner. She always began the day with a heavy-duty sack, ready to clear the empty bottles she'd come to expect. She found him on the floor, frothy bile staling on the carpet by his face. They later said it had been a heart attack; whatever it was, within a matter of days, talk had moved on to Ronan's new leadership. He'd taken on the post with a solemn servitude, reassuring the media that he'd carry on the wishes of the Commander. Top of the agenda was the issue of Shaw Hill, and first on his to-do list was to call Couldry.

Chapter 29

Helen squeezed through the gates of the Aid Centre, left open in the haste of the last drop. Her children were with Linda, safe for now, but she couldn't dispel the guilt and urgency that had brought her here. The attack warnings had been increasing since the raid, acting as a constant reminder of the threat of Nemico and the vulnerability of being where they were. She'd not spoken to anyone except for Linda, urging her to keep it quiet.

"I won't be long, I just have to get everything ready," she'd said. She'd almost finished packing.

She couldn't stomach the thought of their faces when they realised, when she'd say goodbye and pass them up for more privileged, more affluent hands.

It wasn't so much the thought of getting caught by the Council that worried her; the thought of anyone seeing this, the lengths she had to go just to give her children what they needed, would be the final humiliation she could do without.

She smashed the window with a crowbar, flinching at the sound of shattering glass. Inside, she found the main room where the children used to stay before the evacuation. She knew it must be here, the generous box of spare clothes—her children had frequently borrowed from it after various mishaps. She'd always been diligent about washing and returning them, but now she needed a more permanent loan. At home, even with the drawers emptied and the still damp washing flung together and sorted, the suitcases were pitifully half full. How could she send them to the care of a stranger with so little to clothe them, let alone clothes that were well-fitting or looked nice.

She entered what must have been a staff room. Shelves and cupboards lined the walls. After a short search, she found it, a plastic container fitted neatly into a cubbyhole, with folded clothes stacked inside. She began to take them out, one by one, so consumed with her methodical piling and sorting that the low hum of an aircraft took a minute to strike her as a concern.

Harry and Miles were inches from each other in the cramped cockpit. Beneath them passed the frothing sea, the sliced chalk cliffs and then the stretch of green fields that blanketed the outer edges of Merredin.

"Is fuel ok?" Harry asked, gripping the control wheel.

"We've not exactly flown very far, so I'd hope so." Miles glanced at the panel. "Yeah, it is."

Harry was silent as he turned the control wheel, raising the right aileron and rolling the plane back inland. His gaze lingered on the radar. Through the small screen of plexiglass, they could see the grey mass of the Shaw Hill estate, situated like a sprawling tumour beneath the rest of civilisation.

"Everything alright?" Miles asked. "You're not as talkative as usual for a training run."

CHAPTER 29

Harry nodded, but his jaw was clenched. "Did I see you speaking to Couldry before we left? What did he want?"

Harry flexed his grip on the control wheel again. "Oh, just—" he paused, squinting at the view in front of them. "He was talking to me about the training."

"Right," Miles replied.

The radio receiver crackled as Couldry spoke.

"Raise the altitude," he said. Harry raised the elevators without replying, prompting Couldry to ask, "Are you there?"

"Yes, sir."

"Remember what I told you."

Harry nodded, ignoring the questioning looks from Miles. They were steady at 15000 feet; below them, the houses looked like a mesh of tinderboxes.

"We're going to dive," he said to Miles.

"What? Now?"

"Your duty, Harry. See it through," Couldry said.

"Close the oil and radiator flaps and get ready on the dive brakes," Harry said,

"What's going on? You didn't tell me we were doing this?"

"It's just practice," Harry said through his teeth, but the split second he looked at his co-pilot was enough for Miles to register the frantic fear and panic churning just beneath Harry's surface expression. With trembling hands, Harry moved the throttle to idle and began to tip the nose into a dive.

"Dive brakes," he growled.

"We're not loaded, are we? Harry? Why are we doing this over an area with civilians?" Miles shouted as he fumbled for the switch and leaned back in his seat, watching as the speed shot up and the elevation dropped. The rising whine of the engine and air resistance drowned him out. The houses were approaching fast.

"Do it, Harry," Couldry said again on the radio.

It was time. Harry reached for the release button that would open the hold and drop the missiles that had been loaded in secret. 'Just like training'—that's what Couldry had said. He thought of what he'd been promised; an extra pay-check, early release. Was it worth it?

He pressed the button, releasing the hatch that held the bombs.

"What have you done?" Miles said. But Harry was trying to pull out of the dive.

"Retract the brakes," he said, battling to raise the nose again as he began to apply the pressure again. "We're losing thrust. The brakes, Miles!"

But Miles was turned in his seat, looking through the small window behind them as the previously peaceful vista now exploded into fire and ruin. The blood had drained from his face and a sensation of nausea overwhelmed him.

"What have you done?" he repeated, turning back to face Harry and reaching out to grab him. He knocked the control wheel as Harry reached for the brake control and all at once the plane pitched and rolled.

"We're going to stall," Harry cried, as the flashing sensor for the insufficient angle of attack filled his vision. They were falling, sinking, too low for him to push the nose down. A building loomed, one with a car park; it was on their trajectory. Miles had passed out, and Harry was frozen, watching the instant justice approach.

In the quiet before the bomb hit, before the overhead plane

CHAPTER 29

came hurtling towards the ground to drop devastation, all had been still. And then, a cacophony of collisions, noise and ruin became all-consuming and tore through the peace of the estate. For Emily, the hit had struck like a hammer blow, shattering the reprieve she'd found in Raine's gentle company as she'd been showing her the camera. Great billows of thick, choking smoke curled towards the sky above the rooftops, just a few streets away.

She stepped out into the street with the camera still around her neck. Everyone else, too, was stumbling out of their houses and looking at the sky. Raine ran past her.

"Are you coming or not?" she called over her shoulder. Emily followed her, past the other residents, past Linda's house, where Linda was standing with her arms around Sarah and Kaden. Emily slowed.

"Where's Helen?" she asked.

"She went to the Aid Centre," Linda said, clutching Helen's children closer. "See if she's ok, please."

Emily nodded.

"Emily? Keep up," Raine said from further up the street.

They found the scene of the hit—it was one of the streets connecting with Shaw road. The usually uniform row of houses had been obliterated. The houses had become cracked shells, fronts torn open, offering a window into the thick flames pillaging their insides. All across the street, rubble and wreckage lay strewn in a thick heap, smoking and dusty, as though the bomb had wiped out not only the buildings but their colour too, casting a claggy grey over every surface.

"This is Stacey's house! She was here. I can't find her?" Gina pushed her way over the rubble and suddenly stopped short. A short distance away, near the shattered base of the building, a dusty arm stuck out limply from a mound of broken, displaced bricks.

Ethan was there too, phoning the hospital. Emily became painfully aware of the faint, distressed mewling of others who had been injured.

"They can wait, they're makin' noise," Gina shouted, summoning others to help Stacey first. More residents were showing up to help with the rescue effort and to satisfy their shocked curiosity. Raine and Ethan clambered through the rubble towards Gina. Their expressions were blank as they helped her free Stacey.

She wanted to help, but Linda's request was at the forefront of her mind. The Aid Centre was a short distance away, in the direction of the second column of smoke.

"Did you see?" A stunned, elderly man next to her said. "The plane went down; I saw the whole thing. Come crashing down it did, straight after it dropped them bombs. There's no way they survived it, and people say God dun't exist."

She looked away. She had to go.

Emily cut past the wreckage and headed towards Shaw Road. From behind, she heard Gina cry out; she knew what it meant.

She reached the park next to the Aid Centre. Beyond its border fence, where the Aid Centre had been, now lay the scene of a vast wreckage. She could feel the heat of the fire, but it didn't stop her from moving closer. The plane had crashed into the building, demolishing both the main portion of the Aid Centre and spreading charred fuselage amongst budding flames.

She heard rapid footfall approaching. It was Raine and

some of the others, coming to see.

"Helen was in there," she said to Raine as she passed. She gripped Emily's shoulders.

"Are you sure?"

"Linda said, she was here on her own."

They got closer, picking a careful path through the rubble.

"Helen?" Raine called. She began moving some of the larger pieces of debris that were blocking their way, concealing the remnants of what used to serve as day care for the estate children. Emily noticed Raine's arms, streaked in blood and coated in grime. She tried to help, but it was a hopeless task. There were no cries, no signs of life.

"She's gone," she said. "If she was in there then she'll be gone. There's no point."

Raine was breathing hard. Emily moved away from the mound of wreckage, not wanting to watch as the realisation hit her; Helen couldn't have survived.

A few metres away, she noticed a portion of one of the plane's wings, laying on the ground. She examined it, looking closely at the part still shiny and smooth, undamaged by the collision. The Council's insignia was on one end, a small blue shield, with a red, eight-pronged star at its centre. It was one of their own planes.

She raised her camera and adjusted the focus. She took the shot, capturing the unbroken part of the wing, the number decal and the unmistakable embellishment of their own Council. In the distance, the sound of sirens grew.

Chapter 30

That night, the communal fire burned again in Carter Close. Surplus wood and flammable debris had been gathered and piled to fuel the flames. They licked at an ever-distant sky, its air a choking mix of tension and grief. Most of the estate had come to join in the fireside vigil, some on bikes, others on wheelchairs, stools, chairs, boxes and old cushions.

Gina sat on a low, upturned carton with her knees spread wide and her elbows resting on her upper legs. She studied the ground without any of her usual character. Raine stood by her, alert and bare armed despite the chill. Emily watched them from the kitchen chair she was sat on, her camera hanging from its neck-strap. Her gaze kept wandering to Raine's face; the fire cast flickering patterns of light and shadow across her cheekbones and the subtle curvature of her jaw.

Linda came out from her house, leaving the door ajar. A silence fell over the group as she approached the fire. She watched the flames as she spoke.

"Do I need to name the ones we lost today? We all knew 'em. We know everyone here, in this place, where we've lived, suffered, an' gone through all of this together. This isn't right, we all know it. Getting killed like that, in our own homes, while over that wall they know nothing of bein' hungry, being scared. Those children of Helen's are askin' me why it happened. How am I meant to answer that?" She shook her head.

"They've divided us by money and class, by circumstances we were either born or thrown into," Raine said. "They've stripped us of our rights, taken our children, family members, and now left us to be bombed, at will. Why should we sit and do nothing? We deserve protection too, and the rights to a decent life with the people we choose." A murmur of agreement passed through the group. "So, I say, now we strike. Now's the time to take a stand."

"And if it goes wrong?" Gina said with a husky voice. Raine turned to look at her, shocked, but Emily wasn't surprised. She recognised Gina's expression of defeat, the remorse in her shaking hands. "If they take it out on us? We're just going to make them less likely to help us and more likely to make it worse."

"It can't get worse than this," Emily said, getting to her feet. "Look at this photo I took, it's part of the wreckage from the plane today. You can see, it had the Council insignia on the wing, it was one of the Merredin planes." People gathered around her, leaning in to look at the photo on the camera display.

Those closest to her fell silent for a few seconds, processing the image. Gina pushed through and took it from her, bringing it to almost her nose.

"This was the plane? From today?" she asked.

Emily nodded.

"Does anyone need any more evidence that the Council isn't on our side? It's fight or die. Why should we make it easy for them when they don't value our lives?" Raine said in a sombre tone.

"Out the way, let me see," Linda said. The others fell away as she closed in on Gina, squinting at the picture of the wreckage. There was a quaver in her voice when she spoke, scanning the crowd's watching faces.

"We fight. After they've done this? We bring the fight to them with everything we have."

Fiona was sat next to Paul on a high-backed chair, his jumper clad arm curled tentatively around her lower back. She watched the others through the body of the fire, impervious to Paul's incessant stroking. They remained seated, their voices low enough that no one else could hear their discussion.

"We've got to help," Paul was saying, his voice reedy and strung out. "After all they've done for us, without any obligation. We'd have been left on our own without their help."

"No, I'm not doing it. I've said it before; I'm not getting riddled with bullets or banged up like common scum for some gung-ho crusade against civilised society." She clenched her hands, pressing her long nails into her palms.

"You won't be shot. I wouldn't let that happen. There are many ways we can help that don't require active combat." A hint of his old joviality crept into his voice and the start of a smile played on his lips. "I have to say, I quite fancy a bit of action myself." He started to laugh but soon ceased seeing the flash of fierceness in Fiona's eyes.

"I'd rather die than go to the border associated with this lot. I'm sure it's all fun and games to further destroy your life and lose your dignity, but I won't forget where I belong and it's not here with these people." She spat the last word with particular vitriol. Paul drew his arm back to his lap, looking at the marked leather of his shoes.

"Please don't speak to me like that," he said quietly. She glared at him.

"Don't let me stop you. Go then. I always knew you would leave me."

"That's not what I want."

"You don't care about me at all, admit it. You were lying when you said you'd look after me. All you care about is yourself."

"Fiona, come here. That's not true." He tried to reach out to her and turn her back to face him again, but as his fingers touched her shoulder, she lashed out with her hand, striking him in the diaphragm. He recoiled in pain, watching as she began to sob.

"You don't care about me at all," she said with shallow breaths.

"I do, Fiona. I do." He was more careful this time as if reaching for a neglected puppy. He tested the water with some light pressure before easing the hardness of her body into an embrace.

"If it upsets you this much, if you don't want me to go, then I won't. I'll stay with you."

"I don't want you to," she stated with a sniff.

He made soothing noises, staring at the mesmerising movement of the flames as he savoured the gentle pressure of her against him.

"How you gonna do it then?" Linda asked with a critical eye.

There was still a small group gathered around Emily.

"It's by no means a fine-tuned plan, but I want to involve as many as we can and coordinate a multi-angled attack on the border, and if we can manage it, the Council too," Raine said.

"We've still got weapons stashed away, haven't we?" Emily asked. "If we can distract the guard and get behind them, there's enough of us to cause a major problem."

"With the conscripts, maybe" Raine added. "If we manage to get to them and have them help us somehow, we'll be at a major advantage."

"Maybe we could send them a message," Linda said. "With all of us, and them, we could make enough protest, enough noise, that they'll 'ave to listen. At the very least, we 'ave to make their voices heard, bring it straight to the Commander and show him that we ain't gonna just conveniently disappear, while he makes out it's Nemico that's doing this. That they're not at fault."

Raine was scanning the group, calling for people to be involved and agree to join them. She wrote down their names, organising a meeting place. Emily's mind was working hard. All she had thought of was Jack; finding him, holding him. But now there was an added fire in her. She wanted revenge.

"It could work, or at least achieve something," Raine said with a frown. "If enough of us can make a scene at the border, if anything, just to draw the CLE's focus there, then with the right people on the other side," her eyes met Gina, "maybe we could take control of the camp."

"That's ambitious," Linda huffed.

"It is, but if we can get a message to them, there must be enough there to overrun the guards. Or at least make a scene." She threw her hands up. "Scare the fuck out of the Council."

CHAPTER 30

"And then we can move in," Emily said, just loud enough for Raine to hear her. A silent dialogue passed between them as their eyes met, the firelight still dancing on Raine's creamy skin. Find the Commander. Find Jack. Emily knew she understood, waiting for her to dismiss those who persisted with questions.

"We're doing it. It's happening," Raine said with a smile.

Emily noticed Ethan lingering on the periphery, anxious to listen but too nervous to be involved. She could sense his eyes on her, waiting for something.

"Ethan?" She went to him, happy to get away from the jostling of the others. "Are you ok?" He looked past her. Something was on his mind. "What's wrong?"

"Come with me," he said. "There Are too many people here."

They passed through the alleyway. On the next street, Ethan scanned the shadowy area by the back fences, where the litter strewn concrete hid all manner of illicit activities come nightfall, but residents were still huddling by their doors, swapping gossip with their neighbours and young people passed through on their bikes, spreading messages throughout the estate. He put up his hood. "Let's go to my house."

She followed him in silence. At his front door, she waited for him to dig out his key and let them in. He gave her just enough room to slip past him, still silent as he locked the door behind them.

"We shouldn't be interrupted this time," he said.

"Ethan?" A weak, throaty voice called from inside an open, chipboard door. It erupted into a volley of coughs. "Ethan?" it gasped again. "What's gone on out there? Are there more of those blasted planes?"

He sighed, kicking at the frayed edges of the carpet. "No dad. There won't be any more, not tonight." He paused. "People are going to take a stand, dad. They're planning it now, everyone's joining."

She could hear raspy breathing, the clink of a mug. "Don't you be so stupid. You'll play into their hands, you will." The coughing started again, and he urged her to follow him up the stairs before his dad could say anything else.

She stayed by the bedroom door, too agitated to sit down. He dropped his backpack on the bed.

"What if there are more?" she said.

"What? Bombs?"

"Yeah. How can you reassure him like that?"

"It's the only thing I can do. I can't protect him or tell him the truth. We've never been safe, not a single night in this place."

She shivered, not from cold but from the sudden sensation that she was so displaced from home, from who she loved. In this sullen box of a room where not even the window offered the solace of brightness. Ethan was right; her only safe space had ever been, ever would be, the feeling of Jack close to her, and the knowledge that once she held him again, nothing would ever bring them apart.

He came closer and took her by the shoulders, pulling her gently to his chest. To be held again by a man was something foreign. His body was hard, coiled. She felt the bone of his sternum against her cheek, the soft washed cotton of his top was like a blanket tossed over a stone. She pulled away.

"Are you going to be part of this then?"

"Yeah, I think so. Whether it's a good idea or not, I want

to help." He returned to the bed, opening his backpack and pulling out a folded blanket. "I wanted to give you this. I had it with me, out there, but I didn't want anyone else to see."

He unfolded the blankets and opened his hands. She saw the smooth, black barrel of a gun, the same one that had been in his wardrobe.

"You're giving it to me?"

"Yeah." He placed it in her hands. The weight of it surprised her.

"Is it loaded?"

He nodded. "Yeah, be careful. It's quite simple to use."

"Have you fired it?"

"No." He went quiet, staring at the trigger. "That's why I think you should have it. I'm pretty sure I'm not brave enough to point it at someone and pull the trigger."

"And you think I am?"

He dropped his head close to hers. She could hear his shallow breathing.

"I think if you needed to, you'd do it without hesitation."

She felt the press of his cold fingers against the soft underside of her jaw, lifting it slightly.

"Stop," she said, letting out her breath. He backed away, avoiding her stare. "I'm sorry. It's not what I want, right now."

"Don't be sorry," he said. "Just focus on tomorrow."

Linda walked at a steady pace as she approached the border gates. A child on each side, she squeezed them to her broad hips, Kaden's hand clasped warmly within her own. The straps of her sandals bit into the flesh of her feet and she rocked side to side with the pressure on her feet, but her sole focus was on the border.

At the checkpoint, one of the guards sauntered towards her. "Can I help you?" he asked.

"I have two children here who should have been evacuated. They need to be taken into Galven for their protection." Anyone from the estate familiar with Linda's usual casual drawl would have noted the difference in her speech; she was putting on her airs an' graces as she would have termed it.

The guard took a careful look at the bewildered children. Sarah leant closer to Linda, trying to stifle her desperate anxiety. Kaden tried to pull away, scared of the strange man in uniform.

"Do you have their identification cards?"

"Right 'ere," Linda said, pulling two brown cards from her back pocket and handing them to him.

"Wait here just a minute, I'll need to make a quick call."

He left them by the gate, disappearing into one of the cabins.

"When will we see our mum again?" Kaden asked. "I don't want to go too far away."

"It's not for long," Linda replied, but she had to swallow, settling the uncertainty she felt so that it wouldn't show on her face before she could look down at her. "Your mum loves you very much but she can't be with you at the moment. You'll be safe across the border."

Kaden began to cry again, sensing that something was happening but not understanding what it was or what it meant. Linda crouched, hugging him as she looked Sarah in the eye.

"Remember what you have to do." She angled her back towards the cabin, touching the padded pocket of Sarah's jacket with a single, light press. "You know how to tell if they're one of us, right? People working, wearin' different clothes. The ones with them brown cards. You have to give 'em this message, ok?" Sarah nodded, sucking her lips with her teeth. "But most of all, you keep you and your brother safe."

"Hello?" The guard was back. Linda stood and watched him raise the barrier. "Come on, you two. Come with me."

She watched them follow him across a border she could not breach, and with a weighted heart and a churning worry in her stomach, she returned to Shaw Hill.

Chapter 31

Ronan sat with his feet resting on the desk. He'd been on the phone with Couldry for the better part of half an hour now and still, the Captain wouldn't stop.

"Questions are going to be raised, Ronan. There already are."

"And?" he replied. "Direct them to me if it's an issue for you to handle some inane talk."

He could hear Couldry's agitated breathing as he examined his stubby fingernails, tempted to pick at them.

"Was that the only time?" Couldry asked.

"What do you mean?"

"Do you intend to do it again? Attack the estate?"

"I think I've made my feelings about it quite clear, haven't I? And you can't say you haven't been compensated well for it." He paused. "Have I paid you well? Or have I not?"

"You have."

"So, I'll give you instructions as necessary and you'll hold up your end."

"Right."

He hadn't smoked for years but on his way into the council building he'd picked up a packet of cigarettes. He lit one and brought it to his lips.

"Tell me about the casualties. Did you recover their ID cards?"

"Yes. Two females, three males."

Ronan slid his feet down and sat upright.

"What about the women? Do you know their names?"

"One was—" Ronan could hear shuffling papers. "Stacey Dower. The other was Helen Moor. Do they mean anything to you? I'll send you the report, of course."

"No that's all. Wire it over and I'll speak to you tomorrow."

He tossed the phone onto the cluttered desk and looked at the locked door. Still, she persisted in his thoughts; in the quiet moments when he had nothing to distract him. This is what she wanted, wasn't it? No more warning, no more chances. Perhaps there was nothing that could make him happy now. No way out of this torment, unless she ceased to exist. No hope or alternative.

He let himself in and checked his phone again as he waited for Grace. She usually came scurrying out to greet him as soon as the front door swung shut. He hung his jacket on the hook.

"Grace?"

She appeared in the doorway. He could hear the faint sound of children's television.

"Don't I get a kiss anymore? How was your day?"

She came towards him but there was no smile, no affection. She felt cold and impassive as he embraced her stiffly.

"Grace?" The high pitch of Jack's voice came from the living room. She turned away from him as though repelled.

"I'm here, sweetie. Ronan's back, do you want to say hi?"

Ronan followed her.

Jack looked at him with an expression of apprehension, his small hands bunched by his sides. He moved past both of them to get to the kitchen.

"Go back and watch your show, sweetie," he heard Grace say. "Stay in there, ok?"

She hung back by the doorway and watched as Ronan made a cup of coffee. She had the same cautious expression as Jack had. Her careful assessment of his every move, like a wild, cornered animal, began to irritate him. He tossed his spoon into the sink and faced her.

"What? Is there something wrong?"

"Yes, actually." The coldness of her voice sparked an instant fear. He put his coffee down and watched her pull some folded paper from her back pocket.

"What is it?"

She didn't reply. She went to put them on the counter but he snatched them from her hand. She went quiet as he scanned them. He folded them again. "And? Will you not just tell me what's got into your head this time?"

"Don't you have anything to say about those?"

"About what, a receipt? Is Kyle behind this?" She wouldn't look at him. "Is he?"

"He told me about a conversation he'd had when he went to Shaw Hill. A young woman there had quite a lot to say about you."

"I'm sure they all do in that cesspit. Even if some crazy woman did mention my name, you'd believe Kyle?"

Grace didn't answer. She watched the pieces of paper as though they'd disappear if she didn't. He moved closer. The guilt was written on her face. "Really? You fell for his games," he said, shaking his head.

"He was worried, that's all. Why would he lie?"

"Worried? Grace, you can be so stupid sometimes. Kyle's been jealous of me for a long time and he makes no secret about being after you, too. Obviously, he's going to twist whatever he can."

"Then how do you explain that?" Grace picked up the papers, pressing them towards his hands. "That's a receipt for the necklace I showed you, but you never gave it to me, so who was it for?"

There was a momentary pause, but he kept his gaze on her, the paper still in his hand.

"Of course, it was bought for you. I just haven't given it to you yet."

"Where is it then?" He picked up his coffee. "Well? Because it wasn't with the receipt."

He sighed. "Grace, this is ridiculous."

"Kyle was right," she said, her composure beginning to slip.

"No, no." He put a hand on her arm, searching for the softness that she usually had. "If you insist on knowing… Your father wanted to see it. I took it to the office to show him and he suggested I keep it there so you didn't find it. With all the chaos after he died, I forgot to pick it up in time for your birthday."

Grace's eyes began to water but her mouth was still set in the same, firm line. She pulled away.

"That still doesn't explain the messages," she said, reaching for the other piece of paper. "I printed out the email conversation you had with someone called Peter Barnett about renting a house? Why would you need to rent a house? And this woman said, according to Kyle, that you kept her trapped? That you were using her son?"

"Kyle doesn't know what he's talking about," Ronan spat. And his anger came rushing to the surface, beyond his control.

"So what's true then? Have you been involved with someone else?"

"No, not like you're imagining. I told you, he's taken something someone said and twisted it to suit himself."

"The evidence says otherwise. How can I believe anything you say?"

She backed away but he took her wrist in his grip, not letting her leave.

"You don't understand. Grace? Listen to me." She pulled back, trying to get him to release her.

"Don't lie to me."

"I'm not, listen. I was going to tell you. I haven't done anything wrong, in fact, I've been trying to do the right thing."

"What is it?" She went still and studied his face, watching for any sign of deception.

"I was involved, briefly, in trying to help a woman whose son was evacuated. I know I should have told you, but I got sucked in. I was trying to do the right thing."

"That doesn't make sense? Why this woman? How did she even get in contact with you?" There was silence for no more than half a minute, but long enough for the expression on Grace's face to change from a wavering sadness to grim resolve.

"Grace," he started, but she slipped free from him. "Grace! Look at me."

His eyes drifted past her, towards the doorway from beyond which Jack would be sat mutely in front of the screen.

"Jack?" Grace said. "I don't understand."

CHAPTER 31

"Let me explain. It's a long story—"

"You had a child, with someone else?"

"Grace. Don't leave without giving me a chance to explain." He made a grab for her hand again, but she was too quick, hurt consuming her features. She stopped by the door.

"I don't know who you are anymore," she said. "Our marriage can't go on like this. I can't trust you."

She turned and left before he could stop her. He heard the thumping of her feet on the stairs. He listened in the hallway, trying to slow his racing heart. He thought of Emily, her heart shaped, innocent face. He thought of Kyle. He heard the thud of one of the suitcases being dropped onto the wooden floorboards of the bedroom, then the faint zipping sound of it being opened. His breathing began to settle and his skin turned cold. He was decided.

"Jack?" He found the boy, as expected, sat cross-legged a mere metre from the television. He'd been watching his show with his head tipped back, plump lips parted in an expression of soft rapture. "Jack, come with me. We're going in the car."

He didn't have time to wait for a response. He could already hear Grace calling him from upstairs. The boy was looking at him with cautious apprehension, his small mouth now a thin line of consternation. He took his hand, pulled him upright. "Come on, to the car."

He didn't bother to look for Jack's shoes or jacket. Instead, he hurried him along by the hand towards the front door, pausing only to pick up his car keys.

"Where are you going?" Grace was behind them, her eyes darting between the two of them.

"I'm taking him to the conscript base. Then we won't have to speak of him again."

"What?" Her mouth dropped open in shock. "Please, don't do this. I don't want him to go. What will happen to him there? He won't have anyone to look after him."

"He'll be with the others. Either way, that is none of your concern," Ronan said, gruffly. Grace reacted with yet more questions, rushing forwards with pleads for him to stop. But he shut the door behind them. The car kicked up gravel in a stony farewell as she watched from the house.

"Put your seatbelt on," he said for the fifth time. Jack was huddled on one of the back seats, his face drawn and pale. Ronan took his eyes off the road and reached around quickly, trying to show the boy. "It's there, it's right there. Just put it on, will you?" But Jack flinched away from the sight of Ronan's hand as the car hit the rumble strips.

Ronan gave up. Ronan pulled his phone from his pocket and clicked on Kyle's name. He'd meet him at the office where the two of them could settle this, or rather, Kyle could finally get what he'd been so desperately asking for. The answer from Ronan, to the question he'd posed in every challenge. In his job, his life, and now his wife. Are you brave enough to do something about this? Are you going to sit down, buckle up and submit to my behaviour? He had the answer. And delivering it to Kyle would provide him immense satisfaction.

"I want Grace," Jack said from the back, his whispered voice barely audible. Ronan sighed and returned his phone to his pocket. He didn't reply. The boy posed a more complex set of questions.

The turn to the conscript base was up ahead and his decision was mostly set. He picked up his ringing phone, expecting to see Kyle's name, but it was John, the one he'd put in charge

CHAPTER 31

of the border law enforcement. He pulled over, aware of the growing mewling coming from the back.

"Quiet," he snapped as he answered the call, his irritation growing. But his thoughts of Jack were soon occupied by something more pressing. He listened in disbelief.

Chapter 32

In Shaw Hill, the quiet roads and still houses suggested a state of calm that had settled on the estate; but behind closed doors, gathered in the confines of Linda's house and spilling into her back garden, various residents had come together and were waiting, abuzz with a growing sense of anticipation.

"Is everyone clear on the plan?" Linda called out, rising to her tiptoes to look over everyone that was gathered. There was a general murmur of affirmation.

Emily stood by the radiator in the kitchen. She had her jacket on, grateful for both the extra padding and a place to put her hands. She had her back to the wall, much like the first time she'd stood in Linda's house. But this time was different, there were no ifs or maybes now, no suggestions or radical ideas. They were doing it, and they'd do it together.

She pushed off the wall and went to Raine, who was moving through the group, distributing the stashed weapons and equipment.

"Are we ready to go?"

Raine stopped and turned to her with a soft smile.

"Pretty much. I think everyone has what they need. Do you feel ready?"

CHAPTER 32

Emily nodded. "I need to have Jack back by the end of today. I can't wait any longer."

The residents began to move outside, congregating on the shared front gardens like a ragtag parade made up mostly of women, young and old. They were grim-faced, but still found laughter and excitement in each other. Emily squeezed through the doorway behind Raine. They joined Ethan, who stood leaning against the stolen car, keeping plenty of space from the rest of the group.

"Looks like we've got nearly everyone out here," he said. "Guess there's not much left to lose anymore."

"How did you get on? Were you seen?" Raine asked.

Ethan shook his head, kicking his toes against the loose asphalt. "No one saw a thing. The only trouble I had was hauling it up there, but it's ready. They won't see us coming."

Gina, Sasha and Kay appeared from the alleyway. Emily noticed the guns before anything else. Each of them was armed with gains from their raids of the more affluent houses or some place she didn't know, but Gina brandished hers with a frightening boldness, happy for everyone to see. Raine went to meet them.

"Do you have it?"

Emily jumped; Ethan's voice interrupted her distant worrying.

"What?"

"What I gave you. You might need it."

"Oh." Emily's hand moved to her jacket pocket. Through the thin denim, she could feel the smooth hardness of the handgun. "Yeah, it's here."

"Good. Don't let anyone or anything else distract you." He lowered his voice. "My Dad isn't happy with me being here.

He'd have stopped me if he could."

"Then you should have stayed. What if you don't come back?"

Ethan shook his head, but she saw his eyes darken. "I told him I had a commitment to keep. That I wouldn't leave the same people who've been there for me my whole life to go into this alone. But really, I want to see you get your son back. Whatever happens to me or anyone else, I gave you the gun so you can take care of yourself, if you have to."

"Thank you," Emily said, but gratitude was a poor word to describe how she felt. Maybe it would come later, at the day's end, when she'd either be afforded the luxury of reflection or the agony of failure.

The street was full of residents now, even those who couldn't participate had made the effort to leave their homes and partake in the send-off. From the top of the street, another pair approached.

One of them, a sparse haired, oversized man with an air of determined resolve, looked as though he was intent on ignoring the well-dressed, anxious looking woman who followed him. She was shouting after him.

"Paul? Paul!" She called insistently, like someone trying to recall an impertinent dog. He tried to shake her off as she caught hold of his arms, pressing her long nails into the fleshy part of his arm.

"Fiona, I told you. I'm going." His voice trembled with uncharacteristic boldness. Despite his assertion, he couldn't meet her eyes.

"What will I do?" she wailed. "How am I expected to survive by myself."

"You can wait here, sit it out. Whatever you choose to do,

CHAPTER 32

I'm going to help these wonderful people."

"Stop!" She watched him join Linda, who stood on the gathering's outer edge, with a bemused smile. "If you do this and leave me here, that will be it. We'll be over. You'll be on your own and lonely forever, you know. No one else will ever love you."

"So be it," he replied and turned his attention to the active conversation around him.

Ethan held open the front passenger door and waited for Emily to get in.

"Hurry up, if I'm going to die today, then I want to at least drive one last time," he said. He managed to nip back around to the driver's side just before Raine returned. She slid into the back without a protest, stretching her legs across all three seats.

Emily could hear the tap of Raine's fingers against the door and Ethan's low muttering as he manoeuvred the car in a tight turn at the end of the street. She kept her eyes on the road, no one mattered now but Jack.

A dark blue saloon car cruised along New Galven road, its speed beginning to level off as the long, dark stretch of the border came into view. The radio was playing quietly, the air con was turned on low and in the rear footwell, Kay was tucked beneath a large picnic blanket.

"Is it close?" Sasha said from the boot, her voice muffled by the surrounding bags. Kay shifted her legs, trying to ease the cramp.

"Well?" she said, addressing the driver.

The driver, Julie, tried to speak but all she managed was a hoarse affectation of a cough as she cleared her throat.

"Just a little further. We'll be there in a minute." She gripped the wheel tighter, unable to prevent thoughts of being shot from pervading her mind. A cheery, popular song started to play on the radio. She turned up the volume slightly, anything to ward off the recurring image of the gun, aimed at her chest as it had been in the car park of the retail store, too far from the guards to shout for help.

"Make sure you look nice an' pretty now," Kay said, her voice frighteningly close. "Don't want them to suspect anything. Remember, I can stick a bullet through your back quicker than any guard can call for help."

Julie pulled the visor towards her with a shaky hand and glanced at the reflection of her face in the vanity mirror. Her makeup, freshly applied less than a few hours ago, had been ruined. Her eyeliner had smudged with tears and her lipstick was dull and patchy.

They were at the barrier. She fumbled to find her ID, lifting it to the lowered window.

"Tell 'em you're in a rush. You wanna get us straight through, got it?"

Julie nodded, trying to keep her fingers from trembling. She kept the car in first gear, resting her foot on the clutch. The guard motioned for her to wind down her window.

"Morning, miss," he said, peering at her identification.

"I'm in a hurry." She pretended to be distracted by the dashboard but the strain in her voice was easily detectable.

"Everything alright?"

"Yes, quite alright," she replied in a clipped manner. The guard examined her face. "Please hurry," she paused. "I- I have

CHAPTER 32

to get home, urgently." The involuntary wetness of her eyes was spoiling her mascara further. She knew if she blinked, its dark smear would spread.

The guard straightened, letting his gaze wander over the rest of the car.

"Just hold it there a moment; put the handbrake on."

The guard took a step back and began to stroll around the side of the car. In front of them, the gates began to slide apart. He waved his hands at the security booth but still, they continued to open.

"Wait a moment." He leaned towards the window. "You wait here a minute, 'til I say you can go." He went to the boot.

Julie did as he asked, barely able to breathe. She could sense the movement of hands beneath the blanket. The thought of feeling for the cold press of metal, the hot destruction of a bullet, was unbearable.

Gina, lean and agile as she was, had no trouble tucking into the narrow space of the car's footwell. She used a heavy-duty winter coat for cover but had positioned herself in a way that meant she could peek between the front seats and up at the road ahead in brief intervals. She held a knife in her right hand and used it, without an ounce of guilt, to motivate the driver, Richard, to do as she asked.

"There's a car ahead, the guards are checking it," he said. Their speed had hit forty miles per hour and close to the border as they were, there was little time to think.

"We'll have to wait," he said, letting their speed drop.

"Put your fucking foot down and go straight through. It's open, isn't it?" she said with a sneer, slipping off the coat and raising her knife.

"I can't, I can't!"

"Well, get the hell out of here then." She climbed over the handbrake in one smooth movement, taking control of the wheel as Richard unbuckled his seatbelt in a frantic hurry and opened the driver's door.

He suffered a momentary panic at the sight of the moving road beneath him. With no one pressing the accelerator, their speed was decreasing. Still, it seemed little more than a terrible, grey blur that could only offer a hard impact. Gina pressed against him as she shifted into the driver's seat, commanding the car's direction and reaching for the pedals. Feeling her so close, knowing the knife was mere centimetres away, he made the jump, hitting the tarmac with a thud and rolling away as well as he could manage.

Gina settled in the driver's seat and leaned back, pushing the accelerator to the floor as the car picked up speed and roared forwards. The guard by the stationary car straightened, staring with an expression of surprise as the impending car that moments ago seemed to stall and meander about the road, now sped towards him like a bullet. She swerved onto the empty, right lane, paying no attention to the guard's frantic signals to stop. The gates began to close again, sliding slowly to narrow the gap. More guards appeared like bees from a hive, alerted by their comrade's shouts. But they weren't quick enough to stop the car as it aimed for the space between the gates.

Gina made it through, skimming the gate's edge and wiping out the driver's side wing mirror. She wound down her window, barely watching the road.

"That's how you do it!" she shouted, sticking her middle finger to the wind.

CHAPTER 32

Kay shot up and drew her gun as Gina sped past. The guard had his back pressed to the car, trying to avoid being hit.

"Drive! Drive now or I'll shoot."

Julie let out a small squeal of panic as she put her foot down and felt the car surge forwards, for the first time since she'd bought it, making use of the car's powerful turbo engine. She too, got through the barrier, though it crunched the top rear of the car with a sickening scraping sound.

Both Sasha and Kay had shed their covers and were trying to get a clear view of the chaos they'd left behind at the border.

"Keep driving," Kay said with another thrust of the gun. "Don't stop till I say."

Julie could do nothing else but continue, immobile as she was, hunched over the steering wheel with her eyes fixed on the road, her foot already aching from the pressure she put against the pedal.

A short distance away, the car that had broken through the border just before them had come to a stop, straddling the centre line. Gina leaned out of the window, looking for Sasha and Kay.

"Pull over," Kay said and mercifully, Julie was able to break free from her frozen state and slow the car to a stop.

"Are you gonna let me out of here? Don't make me climb over," Sasha said, restless in the boot. Kay got out and hauled open the driver door.

"Get out," she said, still waving the gun. Julie almost fell to the ground, taking a few seconds to summon strength in her legs and run aimlessly away from them.

"Hurry the hell up," Gina called. "We need to meet them there before we get caught, let's go." Kay released the boot quickly and got settled in the driver's seat whilst Sasha made her way to the passenger side. Thank God it was an automatic. With so many bright lights and symbols on the digital dashboard, it felt like she was at the helm of a spaceship. She adjusted her seat as Sasha buckled her seatbelt with a huff.

"Follow me," Gina called and they were moving again.

A state of disarray gripped the border. For Rob, the old guard who'd only been vaguely curious about the reason for the female resident's hurry, the situation reached a new low at the sound of John's barking voice, calling for him in a rage.

"You idiot! Is it damaged?" The door of the security hut rebounded with a bang, an appropriate background sound to the large, lumbering figure, cutting through the scattered guards like a sluice as they rushed around the barrier. He set his sharp glare on Rob.

"You can explain to me how this happened once it's been dealt with."

"But," Rob said. "There are others too, they should have seen—"

"Silence," John said, stooping to look at the damage. He pulled out his phone and sighed. "I won't be the only one left with his neck on the block."

Rob turned away, looking out to the treeline as he thought of the scolding he now had to look forward to. He'd only taken this job to try and help out and get some space from his wife and her endless pilates group gossip. It was a brief reflection because what he saw approaching from the treeline, made his worries about John seem trivial.

"John?"

"Don't you dare speak to me," he snapped. But his attitude would soon change. From the road, two cars that had been driving curiously side by side, now split and left the road, one cutting left and the other to the right, leaving the smooth tarmac to drive across the weed strewn grass. In their wake, a mob of people came into focus, all that embodied Shaw Hill. The group, over fifty strong, was mainly women accompanied by some older men and even those looking to be in poor health. They were advancing to the border, some of them armed with wooden posts, tools and bats. Circling them were young adults on bikes, already shouting, looking for a fight.

"What in God's name is this about?" John said, his face beginning to pale. "Get your act together, men. Stop pandering about like lost puppies. You've been trained for this, remember? Prepare for the attack," he shouted. But the volume of his voice was a cover for his nerves. He called Ronan.

The engine kept ticking even after Jordan took the key out, trying to cool from its rough treatment after Jordan had taken the car from Ethan, making the most of what could be his last chance to drive. He'd parked a little way off from the wall, within throwing distance though. Everything was coming together.

"Open the boot," he said, squinting at the border like a general surveying the battlefield. The others got out of the car, laughing and jostling with excitement. His own focus was unerring, even as some of the girls steered their bikes onto the grass to come and meet them, circling the car. He eyed the glass bottles filling the boot; the cracked bucket filled with gathered rags. He reached into the rear footwell and took out the plastic fuel can.

"Enough messing about." He glared at the others, commanding their attention. The main group was about to come up against the gates, the noise of their commotion growing ever louder, and on the far right, he could see they were already putting stakes into the ground near the car, keeping low. It was time.

"What we doin' then, bro?" Kai said next to him. "Are we going to let loose?"

"Fill 'em up," Jordan replied, passing him the can. "Let's get this thing lit."

They met the border as one, shoulder to shoulder. Linda took the fore, choosing not to wield a weapon. Her imposing form was enough. The barrier was closed. The guards, their distinct opposites in terms of restraint and uniformity, faced them from beyond its protection. It did nothing to quell the anger or obstruct the target. The guard in charge, denoted by the detailed insignia on his uniform and the redness of his cheeks, used a loudspeaker to address them.

"Go home. If you continue to threaten our border in an aggressive manner, serious action will be taken, including but not limited to arrest and prosecution." There was a clatter as residents at the back began to throw rocks and shout obscenities in response.

"We're not going anywhere," Linda shouted, less than a metre from the stony faces of the guards. "Not this time." The concurring voices made her feel powerful. They all were now.

There was a high-pitched whistle as from the right the first of the fireworks were set off. Despite the stoicism of the uniformed men, their blank expressions morphed into uncertainty as they looked to their leader for cues.

"We're armed!" he shouted into the loudspeaker. "Don't

make us shoot."

Excited whooping from the youths on the bikes heralded the first smash of glass on the far left as they circled in close enough to throw petrol bombs over the wall towards the guard huts. The fire was finally spreading.

Chapter 33

Emily kept low and close to Raine, crouching by the perimeter of the conscript camp. They were in the thin strip of wasteland situated between the border wall and the chain-link fence, which marked its boundary. Through it, they could see the broad, blank wall of one of the warehouses with doors at intervals along its length.

"What if they're not here yet?" Emily said, trying to ignore the pain in her shoulder from the jump this time. Even though they'd come well prepared, the ground had been no softer and Ethan's catch had been clumsy.

He unzipped the dark holdall. "It doesn't matter. It won't take them long and we don't have to wait for them." He pulled out a pair of bolt cutters.

Raine had been quiet since they'd breached the wall. She'd been studying the visible area of the compound with a quiet focus.

"Move around to the corner," she said. If that's where they're being housed and I think they are, then we want to be behind those windows, there."

They moved towards the right and around the fencing, facing the back of the building.

CHAPTER 33

"Go on." She nodded at Ethan. He cut the fence, making precise incisions, enough to make a gap big enough for them to fit through. Emily's adrenaline was high enough that she hardly registered the scratching and tearing. She got down on her hands and knees and shuffled to crouch by the cold, metal facia of the building. Ethan joined her while Raine moved to look around the corner of the warehouse, trying to get a view of the entrance.

"What can you see?" Emily asked.

"Not a lot," Raine replied. She saw the metal glint of a knife and felt a cold shock run through her before she remembered what weighed down her jacket.

"Get it out," Ethan said behind her in a low voice. He was breathing hard, clutching a metal pipe.

"What? I—"

"Do it," he said. And the look in his eye told her he wasn't going to argue. She reached into her pocket and took out the handgun. It was cold and heavy in her hands. Strange to touch and alien to handle. She could sense his eyes on her, hear the hitch in his breathing.

"They're still not here," Raine called over her shoulder.

"I'm not hanging around here." Emily stood up. "Let's just try the first door. Are you coming?" She went ahead and put her hand on the metal handle but Ethan moved in to stop her.

"Let me go first." He opened the door before she had time to object. It opened into a dormitory room filled with beds and agitated young men.

"What's this about?" said one of them. Emily didn't recognise him. She couldn't help scanning through their surprised faces to look for Noel, even though she knew he couldn't be here.

"Did you get a message from Shaw Hill?" Emily said. "We need your help. The Council is attacking us now, there's no future for us unless we do something."

"We got the message," another, crop haired man at the back said, hovering by the door.

"Well, are you going to help us or not?" Ethan said. "It's happening as we talk."

Some of the conscripts nodded, getting ready to move.

"Take what you need and get everyone else. Let's go. Let's go."

This time more than a few conscripts sounded their agreement, energised and ready despite their grim expressions. He dropped the carrier holding the weapons to the floor and watched the men move in and take what they could. They surged for the door, their energy building.

"Go and join Raine," Ethan said to Emily. "I'll go with these guys."

"Hurry!" Emily urged him before returning to Raine. Emily heard the shouts before she saw the source. The calm vista of a sedate, inactive base had been shattered. She pressed closer to Raine as they watched a handful of uniformed guards and officers burst from the cabins and move purposefully towards the entrance.

The reason for their alarm soon became obvious. With a booming acceleration, the first of the two cars, commandeered by Gina, swerved towards the entrance and hit the barrier with a crash. The bonnet crumpled, its speed almost zeroed on impact. The barrier broke, splitting and bending away as the car smashed through it. The airbags were released, but they could see Gina moving.

The other car soon joined them. This one, a dark saloon

with Kay at the wheel, swerved a little more haphazardly, almost losing control and missing the entrance before she corrected it, navigating through the gap Gina had made. It kicked up a storm of dust as she parked it at an absurd angle and ducked at the sight of the raised guns.

"Where are the others?" Raine asked. Dark sweat patches were beginning to colour her loose tee. "We can't do any of this without them."

"They're coming." She lifted the handgun, sliding the safety switch off. Raine looked at the gun. "You know how to use that?"

But Emily was too focused to reply. The guards were closing in on the stationary cars, their occupants still hiding inside. It felt as though she would witness the end of her journey, the demise of all the day had promised. She brought her other hand to help grip the gun's handle and willed her index finger to embrace the metal curvature. She fired. The sound shocked her. The bullet had gone wild, far from hitting anyone, but it achieved her desired outcome.

The guards scattered, momentarily oblivious to the commands of their superiors. Their focus was split as they tried to work out where the shooter was.

Emily panicked. She pressed against the warehouse wall and tried to control her shaking hands.

"It's done. We're over."

"It's not," Raine said.

"But it is. We can't do this." Emily was drenched too now. She wanted to throw the gun; never look at its black shape again.

"Listen." Raine pulled at her arm. "I'm going to look."

"No, don't. You might get shot." But Emily could hear it

too.

"They're here, look."

Emily peered around the warehouse edge and saw the double doors of the main warehouse open wide as the conscripts streamed out. Shots fired in scattered bursts as the guards stationed closest to them got overwhelmed, attacked with fists and whatever else the conscripts had managed to bring. Some of the officers tried to run to safety but the path to their cabins had been blocked.

Fighting consumed the grounds of the base. But still, shots were being fired. The car doors opened and Kay, Sasha and Gina emerged, keen to help. Kay raised her gun, her attention fixed on the main group when an officer stumbled out of the left side cabin, clutching a gun. He took his shot before Kay saw him.

"No!" Raine turned to Emily, a frantic look in her eyes. "Shoot him, now!"

But she was too slow, her hands like a fumbling child's.

"Take it," she said. Glad to be rid of it. The thought of aiming it at another person was still an image she could not make peace with. They were both primed to run, but now Raine moved around the corner with more boldness than she'd had before. She fired a shot, but Emily could see it would miss without having to follow its direction. Raine's hands were unsteady, her eyes unfocused. The officer ducked and looked around for them, whilst behind him, Kay was on the ground, unmoving. A bullet peeled through the air in their direction, then another. Emily grabbed hold of Raine and pulled her back with all the strength she had, forsaking her balance so that they were left scrambling for purchase in the loose dirt.

"What now? Where's Ethan?" she said, panting. But Raine

didn't reply. Her hands became still and her face settled on a blank expression. She moved before Emily could stop her. The gun fired and a low moan resonated faintly in reply. They looked and saw the officer sprawled on the concrete, his stomach wet with blood. They had to go.

"Follow me," Raine said. Emily's heart raced with the sights and sounds of the fighting. She skirted wide around the motionless figure of the officer, the thought of seeing his face made her feel sick.

At the car, they crouched beside Kay. Her eyes were open, but her upper arm had been ripped open by the bullet, leaving her clothes torn and dark from her bleeding. Gina had already taken off her vest and fashioned it as an improvised tourniquet to try and stem the bleeding, just beneath the shoulder.

"Here, have my jacket," Emily said, shrugging it off and passing it to Gina.

"Press down, keep the pressure on," Raine said. "Kay? Can you try and get up?"

Emily looked past the car, feeling perilously close to the danger of heaving bodies. Fallen men lay on the ground; those in uniform were almost indistinguishable from the others, such was the concentration of those fighting. The car was a few feet away, the keys still in the ignition. This wasn't her fight. She pulled away, but Gina spoke, stopping her.

"She'll be alright. I can take care of her."

"But," Raine protested. "I can help." She moved to wipe the hair from Kay's forehead, but Gina's eyes were fixed on Emily. An understanding passed between them. In that moment, Emily could see the fight welling up within Gina, sense the longing to take up her weapon, and join the crowd to take her own kind of action, but she knew that Gina saw her own longing, a desire far greater than the transient lust for a fight. Her need.

"Go," Gina said. "Find your son."

"But, Ethan—" Emily started.

"Forget about him for now. Do what you need to do."

Emily stood for a moment thinking Raine would prefer to stay. But she too got to her feet. Emily looked at her with gratitude reflected on her face as they got in the car.

"Are you sure you're ok?" Emily said. "With leaving? I don't want you to feel like you owe me anything."

Raine looked over her shoulder as she reversed and left the compound through the narrow gap of the broken barrier. On the road, they picked up speed.

"What are you talking about?" Raine said. Some of her usual cheer came back into her voice as she finally relaxed a little. "Being with you has never felt like that. Where are we heading? To the council building?"

"Yeah. It must be in the main town somewhere. We should have enough time. I hope we can find the Commander there, or if not him, get a hold of something or someone who knows where Jack is."

"We will." Raine seemed certain and it was easy enough to find comfort in her calm confidence. But Emily knew that of all the Shaw Hill children, Jack was the least safe. She knew it probably couldn't be avoided. It would all come down to Ronan.

Chapter 34

They parked outside the formidable white stoned building after what had felt like a long and hazardous drive. They'd drawn an uncomfortable amount of attention driving the damaged car and had needed to stop twice to ask for directions. Both times, the women they'd asked looked as though they were considering calling for help.

But they had reached the hub of the Council, and thankfully, the doors were clear.

"No guards? Do you think they know?" Emily asked.

"They must. They've probably gone to help," Raine said.

They entered the foyer, Emily's eyes adjusting to the artificial light in the open, sterile space. There was a diminutive, mousy looking receptionist sitting behind the front desk.

"Where are we going to find him? I don't know where anything is in here," Emily said.

"Probably upstairs," Raine replied, glancing towards the staircase.

"Can I help?" the receptionist asked. Her gaze dropped from their faces to their clothes, Raine's still tarnished with dirt and blood.

"Where's the Commander's office?" Emily said.

The receptionist replied in a slow, cautious tone. "Access to his office is not permitted to the public. You'd need to contact the Council via letter or email if you have something to discuss. You can find our email online on our website." She returned to her files, clearly expecting them to leave. But whilst she'd been talking, Emily had seen her glance at the stairway. She nudged Raine in that direction and they made their way towards the steps.

"Wait! You can't go up there," the receptionist called behind them but they paid her no notice. They passed through the doorway before she could get up, but a guard had been coming down the stairs and now blocked them at the bottom.

"Stop where you are," he said, but Raine had already pulled out the gun, and pressed it towards him, motioning him to move aside.

"Don't shoot me." His back hit the wall, palms facing forward. "I'll leave you alone."

"Yeah, you will," Raine said. "Give me your cuffs."

Emily lingered on the steps, painfully aware of how little time they had. The Commander, or even Ronan, could be a matter of steps away.

"Raine?" She didn't want to wait.

"Hold on, I'll be right there." She jabbed the guard again. "Put them on and not a word, understand? Not until we're out of here."

The guard nodded, his concentration fixed on his shaking hands. From the foyer, the receptionist looked in and emitted a sort of squeak. She ran away.

Emily couldn't bear to wait any longer. She started up the stairs and turned the dogleg, already assessing the green-carpeted corridor. It was the third door on the left, with a gold-plated plaque that read 'Commander'. Raine caught up with her.

"I should go first," she said.

"This is between me and him. I'll go."

"I have the gun and I'm not going to let him hurt you."

Emily tested the door, letting Raine push close behind her.

"I'll be ok," she said softly and felt its handle release beneath her weight, opening into a dark, untidy office. The curtains were half-closed and the murky sky outside did little to shed some light on the gloomy, dark oak furniture. She held her breath, taking in the man that stooped behind the imposing desk, bent over one of its many drawers. He straightened. He was younger than the one she'd seen on the television news reports.

"Who are you?" he said, pushing the drawers shut with his knee. Emily recognised him as the person she'd spoken to at the estate and from the look on his face, she could tell he had the same realisation.

"Where's the Commander?" Emily moved to the desk.

"How did you get in here?" He looked towards the door, but Raine stood in front of it, giving him an expression that told him he was going nowhere.

"Never mind that," she said. "You need to answer her questions if you don't want to get hurt."

"Where is he? All I want is to find my son."

"I don't know. He asked me to meet him here but he hasn't shown up. I don't know what's going on right now."

"You remember me from before? From the estate." Emily lowered her voice and put her hands on the polished desk surface. "I don't care how it's done. But there must be some kind of database or list. I just want to know where he's being kept and where I can find him."

"You asked about Ronan before."

"Yes, I did."

"Does he know you're here?" His gaze once again wandered over Raine. Emily could see small droplets of sweat beginning to bead on his forehead.

"Don't try and stall us," Raine said from behind her and then directed her words to Emily. "We need to get the information and get out."

"Is your son's name Jack?" Kyle asked.

Emily felt like she'd been doused with a bucket of cold water. She wanted to grab him, hold him. Someone else who finally knew her son existed.

Yes! Jack! I have to find him. It's urgent, please. You need to tell me where he is."

"Ronan took him in," Kyle said, exhaling deep. "But that's all I can tell you. I'm not going to lose my job over this, or worse."

"You have to show us where his house is, give us directions." He took a step back. She saw his hand move towards his pocket. "There's no way the Commander will find out. You won't get in any trouble."

A look of confusion passed over his features. His grey eyes settled again on Emily's face, ignoring Raine's impatient tutting.

"You don't know? Ronan's the Commander now."

"And?" Raine interrupted. "What difference does that make."

But Emily knew. Her composure broke. "Please." But he was by the window now.

"He's used my son as a weapon. We know it was the Council

CHAPTER 34

who committed the plane attacks on the estate. I have photo evidence."

Kyle turned to face her. By the look on his face, she knew he'd had no idea. Raine joined her by the desk and pointed the gun at Kyle, making his lack of options clear.

"We're not giving you a choice," Raine said."

The car was still moving when Emily jumped out and ran up the neat stone path, stopping in front of the impressive double wooden doors, well-maintained baskets hung on either side. Her knuckles smarted as she rapped on the wood.

A shadow appeared beyond the slim glass pane and then the door eased open. The anxious face of a young, bewildered woman peered out, make-up free and flushed. Car doors slammed behind her. Emily knew that she didn't have long.

"Can I help?" the woman asked.

"Jack, I'm told he's here. He's my son." She tried to stay composed, willing the woman to not shut yet another door in her face.

"I—" the woman began. "I don't understand."

Kyle ran up the path to join them, but Raine stopped him from getting close enough to pull Emily away.

"Grace? I had to bring them here, I'm sorry." He looked at Emily. "Don't hurt her."

"I'm his mother, Jack's. Please, is he here?"

Grace looked at Kyle, her eyes wide with shock. "What's going on?" She turned back to Emily. The way she looked at her, Emily felt as though some deep, intense assessment was taking place. "You've been involved with my husband."

"Ronan?"

"Yes. I don't know what exactly, but I know something's been happening behind my back." She gripped the doorframe, looking suddenly unsteady on her feet. "Is he Jack's dad?"

"No, no it's nothing like that. He has been trying to be with me. He even succeeded for a while but it was only so I could get to Jack. He tried to keep me locked inside, but I got away. I never wanted that. All I want," she reached out to touch Grace, but her skin was clammy and unyielding. "All I want is Jack."

Grace glanced down at the phone she was holding in her other hand.

"He's gone. I'm so sorry. Ronan took him somewhere; he wouldn't tell me where and now he's not replying."

A phone rang. It was Kyle's. He took it from his pocket and answered, turning away. Emily's focus was on Grace and the house. She couldn't see behind her and the windows were too dark to get a look inside.

"Where is he," she said, but the words came out strained. "I've been through hell to get here, to be this close. I'm not going to give up now."

Grace jumped and checked her phone. "He's replied." Emily waited as she read, thinking of pushing past her, resisting the urge to grab the phone and do something, anything but wait. "He says he was only ever trying to do the right thing but his mistakes have caught up with him. He wants to know that I'll still stand by him."

"Where is he? Tell me. Where?"

"Grace?" Kyle had finished his phone call. He gave Emily a wary glance. "There's a situation at the border. The Council has directed all residents to stay indoors."

"Wait," Emily said. "If he was here then you looked after

him."

"I did. I love him very much, like a child of my own," Grace replied.

"Then you must be able to imagine how much pain I'm in. Ronan has no right to take him anywhere from me."

Grace looked at her phone again.

"I'll try calling once more but if he doesn't answer, I don't know how I can help."

She went to dial but before her fingers touched the screen, it lit up with a buzzing sound. Ronan was calling.

"Let me speak to him." She tried to move closer but Raine held her arm. Grace stepped back, covering her other ear with her hand. She spoke too quietly for them to hear.

"Are we getting anywhere like this?" Raine said.

"What else can we do?"

Raine sighed but Emily's feet were planted firmly where she stood.

"I'm not going anywhere. This is the only hope I have."

In the hallway, Grace turned around and faced her. Though her eyes were red from crying and her pale lips trembled, an expression of resolve had settled in her stare. She mumbled something unheard to Ronan and then held out the phone.

Emily pressed it to her ear.

"Hello?" There was a pause. In the silence, she could hear his heavy breathing and the seagulls calling. If she concentrated hard enough, every second whilst she waited, she could hear the soft crash of waves against rocks, of shoes that pressed on the shingle. He spoke. The closeness of him in her ear made her heart rate quicken.

"I should have known you'd go to Grace and lie to her too."

"I know you have Jack. Tell me where you are."

"As it was, I was about to head home. But seeing you're so keen and so insistent, you can come to me if you wish."

"Where?"

"Calder Bay. It's easy to find. I'll wait for you."

The line went dead. She handed back the phone and turned to Raine.

"He's at the beach. Let's go."

"Let me come." Grace tried to join them, but Kyle gently guided her back to the door.

"It's not safe. Stay with me."

Emily and Raine got into the car again.

"Put your belt on," Raine said as she made a turn on the gravel. "I want this over with."

Chapter 35

As they got closer to the coast, the road sloping downwards and sand beginning to streak the verges, signs bearing 'Calder Bay' appeared at every turn to direct them. Raine took a right turn away from the main seafront with its flowerbeds and wide, grassy verges onto a narrower, empty road with unkempt, grassy mounds on either side. To the right, the sea spread into a near indistinguishable blue horizon.

The car began to shudder. Raine let it slow.

"We're running out of gas."

"What?" Emily asked. "We're almost there."

"Somebody has been driving it all day, it was bound to happen," Raine said through gritted teeth. Her exhaustion was beginning to show. "If it stops, we can walk. It should be just down here."

Emily undid her seatbelt. She had to sit on her hand to keep it from hovering by the door handle.

The beach came into view. The tide was in, but there was still a broad stretch of rocks and pebbles. She spotted him standing not far from an old boatshed that looked like it had seen years of weather since its last use. The colour had seeped from its wooden boards and in contrast, the tin roof that topped it had darkened with degradation and rust. He stood on the rocks, his back to the incoming waves. She couldn't see Jack.

"He's there, speed up," she said, but the car shuddered for a final time and the engine gave out. Raine steered it onto the grass with the last momentum it had and turned it off.

Emily sprung out from the car and went running down the hill to meet him. The undulating ground made it difficult, but the grassy tufts were soft beneath her shoes. Ronan hadn't moved. As she reached the beach, he called out.

"I'll speak to you alone," he said. Emily looked back. Raine was trying to catch up as fast as the footing allowed. "If she comes any closer, this conversation won't happen." The wind made his voice faint but she got the message.

"You've got to wait there," she said to Raine, shouting to be heard.

"Will you be ok? By yourself?" She paused, frowning. The wind pulled at her t-shirt and blew her hair across her face. "What if he hurts you?"

"I've got to do this alone, for Jack. I'll be ok."

Raine stood still, her feet hidden by the Marram grass.

Ronan watched her come closer. He was motionless, expressionless. Still in a dark suit, as she'd always known him. Only the disarray of his usual smooth styled hair betrayed his situation. She stopped a couple of metres from him, determined to look him in the eye, hide her fear. He didn't deserve the satisfaction.

"I've come for Jack. Where is he?"

Ronan spread his arms and smiled but his eyes remained hard and impassive.

"Does it look like I have him? Are you sure you're not just

drawn to me? Forever kicking yourself over your stupid mistakes?"

"I want nothing to do with you. All I care about is my son."

"Really? Still? There are not many women who have good enough fortune to be able to turn away good men that offer love and security. You've found that fortune in Shaw Hill, have you?"

"You're not a good man. I met your wife at your real home. You'll probably lose your job too when people find out what you've done. I know it was Merredin planes that attacked the estate and others do too."

Ronan laughed, keeping his stare fixed on her.

"I'm the Commander now," he said, opening his palms. "It's you who'll lose everything. Not that you had much to begin with, no stable home, no family, no financial security or opportunities. Just a single mother, struggling in the slums by herself. Are you sure Jack's not better off without you?"

Emily's clammy fists were bunched by her side and her mind burned a constant question—where was Jack? But her words came without hesitation and despite the strong wind and the incessant calling of the gulls, her eye contact with him never wavered.

"There's no better person in the world for him than me. We need each other."

Ronan smirked, shifting his feet on the stones, but she continued. "I don't live in a fancy house or a wealthy neighbourhood like you, but I can love him as no-one else can. And I have support now, friends. I can make the best of our situation. I'm his mother."

"You think your people down there can make a difference. The arrogance that any of you have the ability to affect the

Council and change your situation through violence and intimidation—" He glanced towards Raine, where she stood, still, on the hill, watching. "They'll fail, they already have." His face softened; a mockery of care. "You've committed a serious crime; coming into Galven the way you did, turning up at my house. Don't think I'll spare you from the law. You forfeited that privilege through your own actions."

Something behind her caught his eye. Emily turned to look and saw a white car pull up at the peak where the road met the beach entrance. Grace got out and walked towards them, Kyle behind her. Ronan turned his attention back to Emily, but any previous tenderness in his expression, genuine or not, had now been replaced with tension. His hand moved to his pocket.

"You have no idea the kind of power I have here. You know nothing," he said.

"You have no power over me. Tell me where Jack is."

Grace shouted his name. She'd reached the beach edge now, but he didn't reply nor did he look away from Emily. The only reaction he gave to Grace's presence was a tremble in his body.

"Yet I'm the only person in the world right now who knows where Jack is. So really, I hold all the power where you're concerned."

Emily's lips twitched in an affectation of a smile, not with pleasure, but rather a moment of clarity.

"No." She shook her head. "Because I see you for who you really are."

She felt a kind of confidence wash over her as his expression faltered. For a brief second, all his bluster and sneering seemed to have been washed away with the sweep of the tide.

CHAPTER 35

He looked broken and fragile, all combined in one transient glimpse. And then he burst into movement, rushing towards her too quickly for her to see what he'd drawn from his pocket.

His body was against her. All at once, her view changed from the figure of him, the sea as a backdrop, to the sight and feel of his coarse facial hair, the oily pores of his skin. He was sandalwood and bergamot. Warmth and rage. His breath came hot and urgent by her ear.

"He's gone. Do you get it? He's gone."

Her hands had nowhere to go but against the yielding fabric of his suit. She realised with abject horror that his own hands were pressed to her body. His left hand curled around her lower ribcage, and his right hand was buried somewhere against her stomach. His fingers pressed an indent into the soft curve of her waist. But it was more. More than the feel of his skin, she felt an impossible hardness, an impossible pressure, then, creeping wetness. He had a knife.

"He's gone," he said again, softly, and somewhere behind her, Emily could hear Grace's shouts, blending into an indiscernible background. She exhaled against his neck and in the seconds since he'd closed the distance between them, breathing had become a strenuous, torturous affair. Pain spread like fire through her body. So much so that she could hardly distinguish his touch. Her whole awareness had morphed to pain.

He let her go, stumbling back as though drunk. She tried to lift her head to look at him but everything felt so heavy. She watched the rocks by her feet increasingly turning red. With great effort, she looked up enough to see the lower half of his body, somehow so still, so unaffected. How could his world be silent? How could anyone's reality be anything but the chaos and turmoil that engulfed her like a storm.

The rocks pounded. She heard the sickening crunch of feet crushing them together, quicker than the waves, more regular than the slowing of her pulse. And then an explosion. A shot, the sound of it tearing through the air like a bullwhip wielded by the Gods.

Ronan fell to the ground, writhing and moaning for a second before one more shot rang out silencing him forever. Grace's shouts became screams as Emily's legs gave way and she too found cold solace among the stones. Raine's arms wrapped around her.

"It's ok, let me look," she said. Emily moved her arm, uncovering her stomach where blood now saturated her clothing. Her fingers found the bare skin of Raine's shoulder as she bent over her, her skin felt burning hot compared to the cold that engulfed her senses. She realised Raine had taken off her top, that she had it pressed to the wound.

"Is he dead?" Emily asked.

"He's gone. He can't hurt you anymore."

"No!" She tried to sit up, but with the slightest pressure, Raine stopped her. Her eyes became wet with tears. "No, you don't understand."

"What? Emily, he's stabbed you. What else could I do?"

"He's the only person—" she trailed off. She let her head rock to the left. The movement made her dizzy and rocks cut into the soft flesh of her cheek but she had to see. Life had left him. He'd dropped the knife. It lay next to him, red from puncturing her. She tried to find Raine's face but the sky was so bright and the air felt like it was closing in on her, so confined, so torpid. "He was the only person who knew where Jack was."

CHAPTER 35

"I think you'll be ok," Raine said. "If I can slow the bleeding, get this stitched up, you should be ok. You'll need to come to the hospital though."

Emily let her eyes close and paid dim attention to the noises that seemed to swim far above her in the dark pool of her awareness, clouded by pain. Raine spoke to someone on the phone, her voice rushed and harried. Further away, she could hear Grace crying.

The memory of Jack's face came like a wave of agony rather than the hopeful optimism he'd summoned before. The realisation of her failure fell upon her like a shroud, thicker than any of her life's failings before now. She'd never find him.

Her eyes opened again and she fixed her gaze upon the gathering clouds; flying beneath them, the gulls rocked and swayed in the air like paper kites, ill-equipped for the fractious sea breeze. She thought she'd never get up. She didn't want to. The rocks she lay on would mould to her body, and in time, the pain would leave her be.

Grace's wailing came to a muffled stop, drowned out in a gust of wind. Emily couldn't see her; trying to would involve too much movement, but she made an effort to focus on the sound instead, what she said, what had happened.

"It's bunny, look," she was saying, or that's what she could make out. "He must have dropped him."

Her words made no sense. She pushed back against Raine and lifted herself off the ground just enough to be able to turn and look at Grace. She was by the old boathouse, looking at something on the ground. Kyle stood behind her, pacing with stress, hunched against the cold. What had she found?

Grace looked towards her as though she sensed the question

burning in her mind. She bent and picked up a small, grey thing, limp in her hands. She spoke a little louder, trying to make herself heard.

"Jack's bunny. Maybe Jack's here too." She looked up at the wooden structure of the boathouse, and all at once, Emily felt a spark of hope flooding her with enough energy to sit up fully.

"Don't get up," Raine said. "You need to rest while we wait for help."

"No," Emily replied. Pushing Raine's hand away from the sodden fabric that pressed against her waist. She replaced it with her own, using her other hand to push up from the ground and find her shaky footing.

"Emily? Wait."

"Jack," she said. Emily was unsteady on her feet and had to stop a few times as she walked to the boathouse, Raine following behind, her arms outstretched in case Emily fell. Grace stepped back at the sight of her, unable to mask her shock at her condition. Her wound was no more than a frustrating hindrance, the pain pushed away.

"You think Jack's in here?"

"I- I don't know," Grace said, stuttering. "This bunny is his, which means Jack was here." She held up the grey thing. Emily could see it properly now. A small soft toy rabbit, frayed at the ears from a child's excessive love. Grace looked across the beach to where Ronan lay on the rocks. She blanched, fresh tears wetting her cheek. "Is he?" she asked. She dropped her gaze to where Emily was bleeding. "He did that to you?"

Kyle moved to take her shoulders and usher her away, but she resisted.

"No. We need to look in there, maybe Jack is there, it's

CHAPTER 35

possible."

The double wooden doors were aged but solid. Each one had a cast iron pull handle and a plank of wood had been slotted through them both by way of securing it shut. She pulled the plank free.

"Jack?" Emily called, pressing her face to the mildewed boards. She heard nothing back.

Still, she pulled on the handles but they wouldn't give. She looked at them again, closer this time and noticed that a rope had been threaded through them too, tied tightly at the underside of the right handle. Her hands felt slow and clumsy. She couldn't untie it.

"Help me," she shouted. Raine was by her side.

"We don't know if he's in there," she said. "There's every chance he's not."

Emily fixed her with a cold glare.

"Help me, or leave me alone. Please."

Grace took a close look at the knot, her slender fingers prying at the cords, but it had been pulled tight with a strength that they couldn't undo.

"Kyle?" Emily turned and looked for him but he was pacing by the hill, talking on the phone with his other hand atop his head. She looked at Raine.

"This was all for nothing if I don't find him. I have to get inside."

Raine looked at her blood-soaked clothing again and put a hand on Emily's shoulder.

"As long as you promise me that after you've looked here, you're going to get treated before anything else. Can you do that? I'm not losing you."

Emily nodded. She watched Raine take a step back, making

a careful assessment of the doors and the wooden boards on either side of them. She swung forwards and began to kick at the wood, striking repeatedly at the bottom of the boards. They had blackened with damp and mould closer to the ground and had started to degrade. She kept kicking until the wood began to splinter and cave.

She paused to catch her breath. Emily bent forward and forced her fingers beneath the fractured boards, trying to pull them up.

"Let me help," Grace said, her eyes raw from crying. She wiped her tears with the back of her hand and she too began to pull and push in an effort to help break the boards. Raine had recovered and moved in between them. She was down to her vest, her top used to stem Emily's bleeding. She took over from Emily, who watched the taut muscles of Raine's toned arms as she strained to bend the wood.

"Stand back, it's almost gone," Raine said, and they watched as she levelled one more kick, right at the centre of the board's weakest point. It gave way.

Emily didn't wait for Raine's signal. She was back on the ground, pulling to make the gap bigger, wide enough so she could fit through. There was a loud splintering sound as another board gave way, splitting into jagged edges as years of weather and no varnish or upkeep proved their failing. She could just about fit but it would be tight. She got down to her hands and knees and felt a sharp pain shoot through her abdomen and towards her chest as her top, growing cold with its wetness, came away from her wound. It was a hot pain, burning and she knew the bleeding had not yet stopped.

"Be careful," Raine said.

"I will be," she replied, keeping her voice level to mask the

CHAPTER 35

pain.

She squeezed through, her knees meeting with concrete, scuffing against a thick layer of grime. As she moved forwards, the broken wood caught against her back. She kept pushing through, letting it scrape and tear at her top, fixed only on the dark space in front of her.

"Jack?" A murky gloom enveloped her. The space inside was dominated by an old, wooden boat in its centre, covered with tarpaulin. All around it, dark objects lay in scattered piles. Tools, buckets and discarded fishing gear had been strewn across the floor and left as clutter on the scant shelving and to the left, large pieces of wood and boat parts rested against the wall and on the floor. She had to strain to make out any details or moving figures in the low light. There were so many places a child could hide.

She acknowledged her fear like an old friend, wishing desperately to return to the open space, where light was abound and no murky corners faced her. But she had to see.

"Jack? It's mum. I'm here."

She felt her way around the boat, moving towards the left-hand side. She tried her hardest to listen, but the sound of her own shallow breathing filled her ears. She paused and held in her breath, listening for any slight sound, as faint as the beat of a bird's wing or the small puff of a child blowing bubbles or struggling to breathe. She crouched low to the ground, watching the space around the large, dark items that had been abandoned. She knew that to feel them, see behind them and to find nothing would kill her inside.

"Jack?" she spoke as softly as she could manage. "I know you're scared. I'm scared too. Will you help me find you?"

She picked up something. A faint, blip of noise, incongruent with her surroundings. A large piece of boat frame was in front of her, blocking her way. She rested one hand on it for support, her fingers slipping on the dust and cobwebs that had settled on its surface. With her other hand, she reached to its other side, groping blindly in the dark.

Her fingers found a soft, huddled shape laying low on the ground.

"Jack?"

Behind her, she heard more crashing and banging as Raine struck away at the gap to make it bigger, letting in more daylight. Emily could feel warmth, could see the edge of his slight body curled on the ground. She reached to him with both arms, wrapping herself around him. The sensation and smell of his fine, fair hair and the sight of his pale skin lifted her heart.

"Jack? It's me. I've found you, you're safe." She tried to turn him over, seeking his hands to hold. But he was stiff and still, his eyes squeezed shut and his mouth trembling with fear. She felt a binding across his wrists and saw that Ronan had tied him, too, with a cord.

"Emily? Is he in there? You need to come to hospital." Raine had made it inside and was pushing her way through to her. Emily couldn't speak. She burst into involuntary sobs at the wretched sight of him. She knew he wouldn't stay silent. He was locked up inside his mind, in a space that he often went, when he felt overwhelmed or anxious beyond retrieval.

"It's ok, it's ok," she repeated, smoothing his hair and lifting him into the cradle of her lap where she sat on the floor. She lifted his chin gently, laying her lips against every bare part of his face. His eyelids fluttered, then opened and in his gaze,

CHAPTER 35

everything she needed to know settled upon her heart. She'd found him. He was safe and he would come back in time. They were together again in an inseparable hold.

Raine crouched beside her, resting a hand on Emily's shoulder.

"We've done it," she said with a smile. "Now let's get out of here."

Chapter 36

Any nerves Emily had when returning to Linda's were dispelled in an instant once she entered the familiar kitchen. Linda put down the kettle and greeted her with a warm, soft hug. Emily winced at the pressure on her stomach and felt a passing panic as she was forced to let go of Jack's hand. Linda released her, her flushed cheeks shiny and round with the breadth of her smile.

"Be careful with her," Raine said coming out of the living room. "She's still recovering."

"Of course, you are," Linda said, stepping back to take a proper look at Jack.

"And you're Jack? I'm so happy to finally meet you."

Jack clutched his bunny tight to his chest and moved behind the cover of Emily's legs. Raine passed them to pick up her cup of tea.

"We're all recovering," she said. "But we'll get there."

"Hurry up," Ethan called from the living room. "It's starting."

Emily held Jack's hand and followed Raine and Linda into the small living room. Ethan smiled at her; his arm still wrapped in dressing from the gun wound he sustained. He moved up on the sofa to let Linda sit down.

CHAPTER 36

"You made it," Ethan said. "And Jack, too. At least some good came from it."

"Hold up and see what he has to say," Linda replied. "We don't know what's 'appening yet."

Emily could feel Jack's nervousness in the clammy quality of his hand. They'd spent two quiet, blissful days at home, soaking up each other's company. Emily was getting used to the idea that he was really here, and Ronan was gone. Jack had begun to act more like a child again, even if for a fleeting, joyful moment, bursting into laughter at her careful tickling the night before.

Now, she stayed by the door, crouching to his level to reassure him.

"Have you heard anything from the Council yet? I know they got Gina," she asked Ethan. He grimaced with pain as he shifted his injured arm.

"Nothing. Not from them or my dad. He still won't speak to me."

"Here we go," Linda said. And in front of them, the TV screen went black for a second before brightening with the familiar royal blue of the council emblem—in the centre, circled with yellow, the shield with its pronged star. Everyone fell silent as Kyle's face filled the screen, addressing the nation from the commander's office.

"Good morning, Merredin. This is a national broadcast. Two days ago, both the border and the conscript base were compromised by outside citizens—people who were armed and justifiably angry at the actions of the Council. I want to ask that every resident, wherever you are, remain calm and rest assured that the events in the last few days will not be repeated."

"Depends on what he says, dun't it," Linda said, shifting to the edge of her seat.

"Wait," Raine said, shushing her.

"As the new Commanding Officer, I have made detailed investigations into the cause of the events and the Council's own failings. In my new position, it is my responsibility to ensure things are done properly and compassionately. As has been reported, I witnessed Ronan's death. Whilst tragic, events of that day also led to the uncovering of several crimes and false fabrications that Ronan was complicit in to the extent of misrepresenting our nation's situation as a whole, both inland and overseas.

"As a result of the findings of a full and thorough inquiry, the chief of military, Couldry has also been charged with conspiracy. He will be put on trial. There have been communications with Nemico and an armistice has been reached. As such, plans will be made to return the conscripts to their own families and homes. We will be shortly releasing more details on when and how the evacuee children will be returned to Shaw Hill.

Positive change is coming. As the Commander, I aim to provide a sustainable community for all. Residents, both here and in Shaw Hill, should be able to access fair opportunities and have the ability to provide for themselves and their families. I believe this can be done, and by doing so, we will never again have to suffer violence from either side of the Galven border."

Emily hugged Jack close as Linda breathed a sigh of relief. Raine relaxed a little in her seat.

"Well, he says the right things," Ethan said. "Will he follow through with it, that's the question."

CHAPTER 36

"That being said," Kyle continued. "Lives were lost and crimes were committed. There are still perpetrators at large and the law enforcement will be working to investigate and bring those responsible to justice."

"That's me then," Ethan said. Linda shushed him.

"Please be reassured that full and proper procedures will be carried out and long-term policies will be announced in the near future, with the wellbeing and safety of every citizen at its heart. This new Galven will strive to improve the lives of everyone. Thank you."

Linda let out a breath as Ethan stood up and began to pace.

"It's about as good as we could hope for," Raine said. "We took a stand, enough to make some kind of impact. That's something."

"Yeah," Ethan replied. "But was it worth those we lost?"

Raine looked at Emily, her hands in her lap.

"I think so," she said quietly.

"All we can do is hope he'll follow through," Emily said. "We met him, me and Raine. I can't say if he'll be perfect but he can't be worse than- than the last one."

Ethan headed to the doorway. Emily stopped him as he passed with a touch on his arm.

"Thank you for everything you did, I won't forget it."

"I'm glad I was part of it. And my dad will come around." He smiled at Jack, reaching out to touch his bunny. Jack turned away to hide it, but eyed Ethan with a curious expression. "Don't be a stranger, will you."

"I won't," Emily said. He left with a wave, leaving the front door open as they all moved to the kitchen.

"Do you want to stay here for a bit with little Jack?" Linda asked. "I'm sure I can dig out some stuff for him, some snacks or books?"

Emily wanted to stay, but she looked down at Jack's round, anxious face. New people, new surroundings, she could see he was tired.

"Thank you, we'd love to another day. I want to get him home though and let him rest."

Linda nodded, wrapping Emily in a hug.

"You take care of yourself and drop by whenever you fancy it. I mean it, don't leave it too long."

"She'll be around," Raine said.

She stepped outside into the fresh, breezy air. Jack still clutched her hand as Raine followed them to the pavement.

"Will you be alright by yourself?" Raine asked. "You can always stay at mine. Consider it an open invitation."

"Thank you, really." It felt like so long since she'd stopped and really looked at Raine. She knew she was asking more, wanted more. But the tightly gripping fingers in her palm drew her attention elsewhere. "I have to look after Jack. He's still adjusting."

"I understand." Raine put her hands in her pockets.

"Maybe," Emily began. "Maybe you could spend the evening with me, once Jack's in bed? I'd like that."

Raine looked up, her face brightening. "Sure, I'd love to."

"Great," Emily looked at the sky. They still had some time before dusk settled. "I'll see you later then. I have something I want to do."

"What's that?"

Emily squeezed Jacks' hand to get his attention. She crouched down, gently moving his bunny away from his face. "Would you like to go to the park?"

Jack nodded. "Are the swings there still?"

CHAPTER 36

"Of course, sweetheart. We can play on the swings as long as you like."

Emily stood up and exhaled.

"Before the other children come back, and the sky gets dark, I'm going to take some pictures of Jack. Whether they're perfect or not, no flash. I don't care what they look like. Just that I have the chance to take them."

"Sounds perfect," Raine said. She gave Jack a little wave.

"Goodbye Jack, goodbye Mr. Rabbit." She let her gaze linger a little longer on Emily. "I'll see you later," she said. And they parted, for the time being, knowing they would forever be a part of each other's lives.

~

Author's Note

Thank you so much for purchasing and taking the time to read *The Galven Border*. This story means a lot to me, as it was my companion and outlet through quite a lonely and eventful period of my life. I hope you've enjoyed it.

As a self-published author, I'd like to ask a favour. If you enjoyed this book, please consider leaving a review on Amazon. Reviews are hugely helpful for authors such as myself, and it's a small gesture that is greatly appreciated.

If you're interested in learning more about me and keeping up to date with my works in progress and poetry, please take a look at my website, www.gemmaiversen.com, where you can find out more information including links to my social media pages.

You can also sign up to my reader's list, where my VIP readers can access exclusive insights and promotions, and get early notifications of any news or new releases.

Thank you again. Until next time,
Gemma Iversen

~

Special thanks to:

Cover design by Ken Dawson at Creative Covers.
 Editing by Read. Write. Relate with Aanchal Jain.